Krishna
The 7th Sense

*Comments on Debashis Chatterjee
based on previous works*

'The interweaving of stories into the narrative makes the ideas come alive. Thought provoking and most interesting.'
—**Kim Campbell**, First Woman Prime Minister of Canada

'As original as ever. A reservoir of creative thinking and truly inspirational for innumerable like me.'
—**Dr Kiran Bedi**, Former Lieutenant Governor of Puducherry

'The work you are doing is very important for the world.'
—**John P Kotter**, Konosuke Matsushita Professor of Leadership, Emeritus at the Harvard Business School

'I felt all that was said. There was so much power in the day and so much hope. The "coming back" of wisdom and integrity is realized through the work and words of Debashis Chatterjee.'
—**Ann Rickett**, Executive Director, Face to Face, Minnesota, USA

'The global appeal of his message is based on its humanity. He says, "People are saying, I want to go to a place where I'm fulfilled as a human being."'
—**Catherine Fox**, *Financial Review*, Australia

Krishna
The 7th Sense

DEBASHIS
CHATTERJEE

RUPA

First published by
Rupa Publications India Pvt. Ltd 2022
7/16, Ansari Road, Daryaganj
New Delhi 110002

Sales Centres:
Allahabad Bengaluru Chennai
Hyderabad Jaipur Kathmandu
Kolkata Mumbai

Copyright © Debashis Chatterjee 2022

This is a work of fiction. Names, characters, places and incidents are either the product of the author's imagination or are used fictitiously and any resemblance to any actual person, living or dead, events or locales is entirely coincidental.

All rights reserved.
No part of this publication may be reproduced, transmitted, or stored in a retrieval system, in any form or by any means, electronic, mechanical, photocopying, recording or otherwise, without the prior permission of the publisher.

ISBN: 978-93-5520-544-5

Fourth impression 2022

10 9 8 7 6 5 4

The moral right of the author has been asserted.

For sale in the Indian subcontinent only.

Printed in India

This book is sold subject to the condition that it shall not, by way of trade or otherwise, be lent, resold, hired out, or otherwise circulated, without the publisher's prior consent, in any form of binding or cover other than that in which it is published.

Contents

Author's Note	vii
1. Where Was Neel Going?	1
2. The Opening Question	4
3. The World's Oldest School	6
4. Looking Back	15
5. Affection	62
6. Desire	89
7. Ecstasy	114
8. Absence	134
9. Devotion	154
10. Parting	182
11. Freedom	223
Acknowledgements	235
Glossary	237
Bibliography	244

Author's Note

Strange happenings turn out to be real stories when they become familiar.

The story I am about to tell you seemed just as strange when I heard it for the first time. I was seated on a rocking chair, made of cane, in the stillness of my study. A ray of sunlight was sneaking its way through the folds of silver-blue curtains. I looked around—a small glass-panelled room with rows of books; a fluorescent laptop with a soothing indigo display on its screen; a rosewood writing desk; a finger-length marble statue of Krishna playing the flute; multi-coloured plastic folders containing details of various book projects; an N95 face mask to shelter my lungs from a stubborn virus that had brought about unprecedented changes in the world; and a ceiling fan whirring away overhead. Lulled by the cool air in the room I nodded off to sleep.

In that lucid state between dreaming and sleeping, I woke up to the world of an Indian business school professor. His luminous face reflected both passion and sorrow. The professor was struggling to rise above the gloom of an academic's life with no more than one question: *if livelihood is for life, what is life for?* This man sat hunched over the open pages of a book by the poolside. Around him a dull morning gave way to a sweltering summer afternoon somewhere in northern India. A reflective frown appeared on his forehead as he arched his palm to protect himself from the glare of the sun. The professor pondered over that one problem of his existence: what was the purpose of his life? What was this life locked inside his ageing body trying to tell him? Finding the answer to this question, he imagined, would solve the riddle of a life trapped between birth and death.

The day wore on and resolved into sunset. A few birds drew intricate patterns against the crimson afterglow of the evening. A stray dog appeared from nowhere, looked around and then lifted its hind leg and urinated on a signpost and ambled away. The professor sitting by the poolside heard a flute song that drifted from what felt like a timeless past. In my dream, I could visualize his face turning tranquil like the placid face of the water. All around the pool were stagnant trees and a worn-out-red-brick building on which darkness was creeping up. Everything in and around the pool belonged to the past. Only the stillness settling inside the professor's heart was fresh and alive. In that magical stillness made more enchanting by the strains of the flute, the professor found that his persistent question of a lifetime had resolved itself! While I was lucid dreaming, I saw the professor's entire life story unravelling in a jerky flashback and flash forward mode—as it usually happens in a dream.

Weeks later, two strangers who had come to attend a conference in Hawaii where I was one of the speakers sought an appointment with me. One of them was a vivacious American woman, Kaya Johnson, who worked in a multinational company as the Creative Director. Accompanying her was a much younger woman who did not introduce herself. Kaya was urging me to write an inspirational story based on the life of her former professor. I wondered why she wouldn't pen this story herself, especially since she had the creative writer's bug in her already. She said that it was because she thought I would write about her and her teacher more objectively than she herself could as the protagonist of the story. Who was her teacher? A man named Keshav Mitra, who took early retirement from business school, in search of answers to deeper questions of life! I had to pinch myself to believe what I had heard: *Keshav Mitra! Was he the same man I once saw in my lucid dream? How on earth could this happen?*

To tell you the truth, ever since my college days, I have been fascinated by the character of the iconic Krishna. I had written a couple of successful books based on Krishna's teachings in the Bhagavad Gita. They were classified as works of non-fiction written for managers around the world, or so I thought. I realized later that the art and practice of management were driven more by fiction than by facts. Organizations and nations were moved a lot more by stories than they were by theories. Facts impress people, but stories transform them. Whatever we are, scientists, managers or authors, dull or delightful, we are at the end of the day storytellers.

With all these queer ideas buzzing inside my head, reclining in a rocking chair, I decided to write this one love story of a lifetime. In fact, there are three narratives in this story that come together like the meeting point of three rivers. The first is the ancient story of the historical and mythological Krishna and his play on earth. The second is the story of Keshav Mitra, that charismatic business school professor whose life was wedded mysteriously to his love for Krishna. The third story involves Kaya, Neel and their peers and professors at the Indus Business School.

I spent a couple of thousand hours reading and researching the lives of ancient Krishna and his devotee, Keshav. I heard the story of the Indus school from the protagonist who, in a way, gave me the power of attorney to write the story. I wrote this entire script in bursts of inspiration while I was hunched over my laptop on the writing desk. There was no pressure of a deadline, no goals to be achieved or editorial targets to be met. I diligently checked the references of the characters, went through volumes of the *Srimad Bhagavatam*, the story of Krishna and other literary, historical and mythological literature. Then, I rolled out the ribbons from my imagination to fasten the many tendrils of the unfolding story, hopefully, into a comprehensible bunch.

Settling deeper inside my chair and looking through the windowpane, I saw a peacock feather wafting in the air before it fell on an empty can of Coke that had been tossed on the lawn. I could clearly identify the several shimmering colours of the feather, a play of pigments and photonic crystals. With my naked eye, I could count several shades in that one feather—blue, indigo, green, purple, yellow, copper, red and brown. To me, each shade seemed like the light of timeless love reflected in the palette of primal human emotions. The metal cola can on which the feather rested was red and white. The timeless totem of Krishna, the god of love, fused with the fizz of gaiety that a can of cola evoked.

It was as if the unseen hand of existence had choreographed the title of the story for me. This story is brought to life by both sentient and insentient characters. It embraces the ancient elements of this earth—the river and the mountains; exotic forest and flowers; sun and shade. Here you may discover a saga of love by an unlikely protagonist, a former business school professor, and his large circle of colleagues and students.

Writing this book has transformed the way I thought about love and how I understood it. It dawned on me that love was not something we fall in or rise to. Love is just the way we are. Love is the way the whole of existence is. Yet, this simple truth seems rather strange to us until we get familiar with the signature of love in our inner and outer nature.

Who would know about the secret love that the sky and the earth had for each other? Like most of us, I was also in the dark until a few drops of rain fell on my windowpane just as I started to write this book. With the rainfall, the sky and the earth mingled intimately. Invisible love became visible as a movement between two polarities—the brown earth and the blue sky.

The smell of wet earth awakened in me deeply held emotions. I sensed the rapture of a dance in the rain!

—Monsoon, 2021

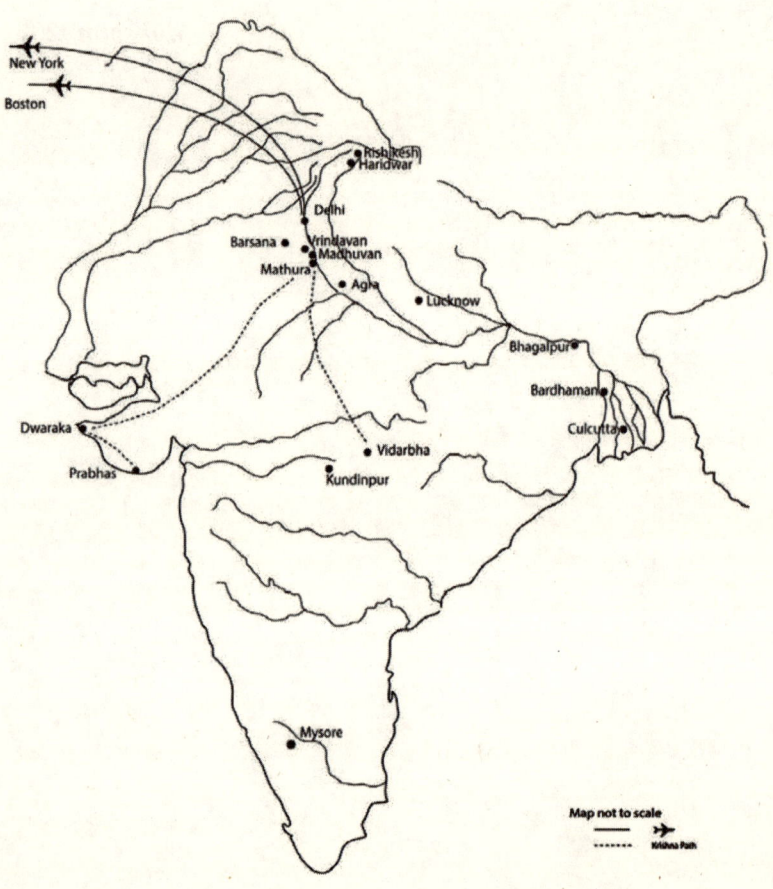

1
Where Was Neel Going?

'Where are you going?' Those words rang like the sound of a school bell in Neel's ears. Neel was standing dangerously close to the exit door of a moving train. A strong wind was numbing his face with bursts of cold air. He remembered those lines of the Bhagavad Gita from the retreat:

> *The mind is restless, O Krishna, turbulent, strong and unyielding;*
> *It is as difficult to control it as it is to control the wind.*

He was leaving Rishikesh on the last day of the retreat. Neel had almost made up his mind to take the next step. He seemed to have found the only answer that made sense at that moment. There was no purpose to this life. For him, it was simply a mass of bone, blood, flesh and a swirl of memories. Keshav's lectures on life echoed as a series of meaningless voices inside his head.

'This body is nothing but a story told by our limiting thoughts. The body is no more than ever-changing thought forms. Our body changes as our thoughts about it change. Fearful thoughts shrink the body. Joyful thoughts expand the body. All of our suffering comes from the drama created by thought.

'Awaken to the drama inside your head and you will surely break the chain of thought. That's what they call breaking the chain of karma.'

'Are you teaching us to be thoughtless?'

'No, I am teaching you how to be free.'

'What happens when you find freedom?'

'Only when you are free will you learn how to love. Love is about letting go!'

'Letting go of what?'

'Letting go of your false identity created by your five senses and your thoughts!'

Neel's entire life flashed before his eyes as he edged forward with one step on the footboard and the other in the air. He saw another train hurtling towards him from the opposite direction. He began counting.

'One. My mother had a permanent frown on her face...a fair, frail and whining woman... My father, a restless man forever suspicious of her motives...he was feared and rarely ever heard...almost smothered my life by his constant sermons...member of a disjointed joint family... My last words for my father were "I will not visit you ever again". I missed saying sorry to him before he passed away in the hospital... feel guilty for all my unkindness towards him...

'Two. Can I really take this jump?

'Three. An underachiever in love... My first crush in school...Alka...the girl with sweet lips and fugitive eyes who inspired me to read Pablo Neruda... I waited forever for the rains to drench her clothes...hated the hunk who finally married her...felt her absence in my solitude... The arc of her arm smooth as marble... Her face shone as clear as rain... Her throat awash in delicate shades of pink and white...

'Four. Two railway lines below seem to be meeting like mating snakes... Is there anything called afterlife?

'Five. Keshav seems to think that life is like an infinite circle and not a straight line... His words rang hollow like a message from outer space... There is no before nor after...whatever it is, it's here and now... This anger has been simmering inside me for a long time... What's the point of messing around with a wasted life...?

'Six. The train is speeding up...but the mind seems to be slowing down...breath is calming down...like those meditation classes...going nowhere...reaching without travelling...

'Seven. Manas...my soul...my dearest friend...the brother I never had...could never live up to your love for me...or your devotion to Keshav...

'Kaya. How I wish I could look at the brink of this life with your eyes... You are like a perfect night with many layers of starless eloquence... Your presence is as fleeting as the caress of a butterfly's wings...undeserved, unpossessed...remotely felt...

'Eight. My grandmother... The measure of your smile was in the comforting glow of your eyes... Your stories lent colour and enchantment to my drab afternoons... You and I had a common enemy in my father... You shielded me from his scorching discipline... You taught me the alphabet of love...

'Nine. Can you trade this life for nothingness at the other end...? Isn't it better to dig deeper into this very life, however muddy, rather than plunge into the rabbit hole of the unknown...? Feels a lot like a terrified swimmer on the edge of a diving board... How about a second life...another chance to return to love...

'Ten. No way...'

Neel held his breath, determined to act against the promptings of his own voice. He unclutched his hands and let himself fall forward freely.

2
The Opening Question

RISHIKESH, 2019, DAY 0

'Where are you going?' Keshav asked. He was raising his eyebrows, which looked like they were glued together to form a single unbroken stream of hair. His eyes were sharp and slanted like those of a deer. There was a spark of mischief in them.

'It does not matter how many times one asks this question. It does not matter whom you ask this question to. You cannot escape from yourself in the same manner that a fire cannot escape its heat and water its wetness. Isn't that so?'

Keshav drew a long and smooth breath.

'The ultimate destiny of a human being is to complete himself. It is the art of putting your whole life together—connecting yourself to your source! This is where you started. Your original nature is love. It brought your parents together.'

The murmur in the audience settled into the heart of deepening silence. In that silence, one could hear the hum of the ancient Ganga gushing through the smooth, white boulders of Rishikesh.

A restless young man, who was chewing his nails, asked, 'How does one reach this source called love?'

Keshav's lips twitched with a hint of a half-smile as he ran his long fingers tenderly through his hair. His eyes softened.

A dart of tenderness sprang from his face and reached his eager audience.

'Love is the lightness of our being. Our precious being accompanies us in all seasons: being successful, being clever, being haughty, being naughty, being sad, being glad, being euphoric or moronic; being this or that; being worried about abdominal fat!'

Keshav chuckled as he looked towards a hedge of purple-red flowers that were showing the promise of full blossom: 'That bougainvillea plant discovers the source of love by just being there. It does not have to go anywhere. Everything happens around it—the play of seasons, the birth of new leaves and the riot of flowers. The bougainvillea just sits there—beautiful, lively and defenceless.'

Then, turning to that restless man he said, 'Can you do just this? Can you simply bring your mind right now to exactly where your body is?' Keshav asked with his eyes narrowing in deep attention.

He flung this question to the class of students who had gathered like a buzzing hive for a week's special retreat. And with that question, the welcome speech was over.

3
The World's Oldest School

RISHIKESH ASHRAM, NORTH INDIA

The ashram stood wrapped in the mystery of the mountains. It had been there for thousands of years. The shrine of the deity was located on the bank of the Ganga that shimmered in the morning sun. The air around the stone-laid stairs leading to the main temple was thick with the fumes of camphor and marigold.

People came here from all over the world to offer flowers, fruits and incense. They petitioned the presiding deity—the centre of attraction—to grant them boons. The deity was a bronze replica of Krishna, a shepherd boy with an exquisite face, caressing a cow with one hand and holding a flute in the other. Here, they brought all kinds of desires and donation money that they thought would be appropriate. The donation amount varied based on the complexity of the challenges they faced. Sometimes it was the desire for a better job, or getting a visa to go abroad, or finding a devoted wife or a dependable husband. Someone prayed here for a cosmic cure for pimples on the face. Such was their faith.

The ashram priest was a key person in the administration of the flourishing temple. A short, stocky man with bulbous eyes like those of a frog. He was known as the purohit in the ashram.

The job of the purohit was to place the interests of the devotees before the deity and perform all the temple rituals. Amidst a steady drone of Krishna mantras, he would put clarified butter, sesame seeds, leaves and consecrated bananas into the fire and chant 'svaha' thrice in a sing-song way. With each svaha, he was shaking off excess sweat from the back of his hand into the sacrificial fire. Svaha meant 'so be it'. It was a form of divine promise towards fulfilment of human wants.

The purohit also doubled up as the storyteller during pravachans—daily talks delivered by the acharya, the head of the temple. A learned man well versed in all the scriptures, the purohit nursed a secret ambition to become the acharya of the temple some day.

Apart from being a wish-fulfilling institution, the temple and the adjoining ashram served another purpose. It was the oldest surviving school in the world. It was a mystery school that traced back its lineage to the descendants of Lord Krishna, an incarnation of Vishnu. Over the years, students and devotees had developed a rich tradition of spiritual folklore, alchemy and unique healing practices. The temple community had an unbroken tradition of learning through a succession of teachers.

The acharya of the temple was supposed to be an evolved human being who could see and foresee our world through what was known as the seventh sense. The ancient masters of the ashram discovered seven psychic centres of human consciousness. These centres were known as chakras or wheels of energy. They predicted that in rare cases a human being could activate the seventh chakra located in the crown of the head. The seventh chakra was the link between the human and the divine. The seventh sense was the plane wherein the physical world of humans was connected to the spiritual world.

The process of selection of acharyas was a well-kept secret. The acharya was chosen on the basis of one's character, and not personality. Prospective candidates had to pass several 'tests' and background checks by the trustees of the ashram before they were considered for the role of an acharya. An acharya would subsequently be chosen to reveal the deeper meaning of life and unveil the mysteries of Nature that baffled ordinary human beings. The head of the board of trustees of the ashram had declared in a short ceremony that a secret committee had ordained that Keshav Mitra was to serve as the acharya.

The acharya, a teacher and a guide, was considered higher than the priest. An acharya was expected to practise what was preached. Each acharya presided over the temple as its spiritual custodian. Each acharya passed on their experiential knowledge of truth to the next generation.

Neel, an old student of Keshav, was walking through the ashram's office door. He waded past a flurry of monks in saffron robes with clean-shaven heads except for a tuft of hair that hung on the back of the head like a lizard's tail. They wore white U-shaped tilaks on their foreheads. Their lips quivered as they carried on with their soundless chanting, and they had stringed beads in their hands that would be tucked inside cloth pouches once they were done. Neel was directed to the room of Acharya Keshav, his former professor at the Indus Business School.

Neel had been corresponding with Keshav on and off over several years to see if he could organize a special retreat in Keshav's ashram with seven of his close friends in the Indus Class of 2000. Neel wanted this retreat to be dedicated to the memory of Manas with whom Keshav, his American student Kaya Johnson and Neel himself shared a special bond. Keshav wrote back saying that he would be happy to organize a week-long retreat. However, he urged Neel to extend this invitation to several of his international students who took his course during his three years as a professor in the US. Most of his students were now veterans in their respective fields. Neel wrote back saying that there would be great enthusiasm among Keshav's past students to connect with their guru. He also added that he had been in touch with Kaya via e-mail and would ask her to coordinate with the international students.

Keshav disapproved of anyone calling him a 'guru' or 'master'. 'Those titles have to be earned and not given,' he often said. He urged the monks in the ashram to address him by his first name. In the last e-mail to Neel, he had light-heartedly described himself as the 'chief learning officer' of the temple community.

Keshav's new community was called Krishna Prem. A formidable business school professor to his countless students, Keshav had surrendered his heart to Krishna after an abrupt retirement.

Neel was so looking forward to meeting Keshav in a new avatar. As he stood before Keshav's room that had a swing door panelled with frosty glass, Neel was wondering how he should prepare. 'What face should I put on before greeting Keshav?' And it was not just the face. There were all these thoughts swarming inside his head. 'Don't forget that he can read minds. The last time we met at his Indus quarters Keshav told me that my organizing ability was better than my writing skills. He had complimented me so matter-of-factly, like giving a little treat to a dog that had fetched a ball. Nevertheless, I must not let my anger get the better of me here.'

WOW!

'Wow!' said Neel as he hugged Keshav without any formal greeting on entering the ashram headquarters. Then, almost pulled by a magnetic force he hugged again.

Keshav's new office was an airy room with large glass windows and a high ceiling. The leaves of an ancient banyan tree were dancing in the strong breeze outside the window.

Neel watched the patterns of light and shade they created on Keshav's face. He had changed very little in these twenty years, thought Neel. Except for his greying sideburns and now more salt and less pepper in his moustache, it would be difficult to tell that it was two decades since they last met in person.

'How have you been, Neel?' asked Keshav, pouring care and love into every syllable he uttered.

'I have been good, and you?' replied Neel.

Keshav looked Neel in the eye and said rather enigmatically, 'When the grass cools down and moist air blows over it, dewdrops show up without an invitation.'

Neel was all too familiar with Keshav's passion for the poetic. Yet, his eyes became round with fake astonishment. 'Kaya is also scheduled to arrive here in a few moments, and so will the entire gang of the Indus Class of 2000. Did you meet any of them?'

Neel was waiting to see Keshav's reaction on hearing Kaya's name. He wanted to figure out if they had been in touch with each other all these years.

'Not yet!' Keshav had barely finished his sentence when Kaya, Sardar, Swamy, Eva and Prasad tumbled in. To each other, they looked like a bloated, balding and more interesting incarnation of the Class of 2000.

They recalled how Keshav's classes used to have a mesmerizing effect on his students at Indus. They were like the rare rain on the dusty plains of north India. Kaya reminisced how students had been desperate to show up for Keshav's lectures even when they had not enrolled for his course. One of his most ardent admirers, Manas, who was also a class representative (CR), advertised his popularity with handwritten posters that read, 'Standing Room Only', signifying that all the seats were occupied.

In Rishikesh, time seemed to stand at ease. The temple stood there with its intricate arches and marble floors. The guest rooms were painted in pale yellow shades. International guests for the retreat—other than the Indus Class of 2000—had filled up the guest rooms. Neel had also formally invited Manas's parents to the retreat, but he had not heard back from them so far.

The walkway from the main gate to the temple office was lined with shrubs and marigolds. Crows perched on overhead electric wires were spraying their droppings liberally on the residents. The branches of the banyan tree leaning on the window ticked tirelessly against the glass pane.

'So, we are here again!' Kaya said with a smile that was somehow soothing. 'Thanks to Neel and his tireless efforts to bring us all together!' she cooed with delight.

A warm flush rose on Neel's face. 'We ought to know why we are here—to rekindle old sparks and to remember Manas and our time together with Keshav.' His voice was throaty and raw with emotion.

Swamy said, 'Frankly, candidly, honestly, I am here to see if I can still find my match here.'

Eva and Kaya giggled and nudged each other hard with their elbows.

'Keshav will share with us rare insights...knowing which, every human problem of the universe can be resolved—that is what we hope to learn here!' Prasad parroted an old script rather pompously.

'Would you like something to eat?' Keshav asked rather gently, changing the course of the conversation. He did not want to draw too much attention to himself or his teaching.

Prasad was now completely bald. The semblance of hair growing over his ears on the sides seemed to compensate for the stark emptiness of his crown in vain.

'Solving all the problems except one,' chipped in Sardar, 'the problem of irreversible baldness, Prasad.'

Prasad finger-combed whatever hair was left on his head. They all shared a hearty laugh.

Swamy, not to be outwitted, blurted out, 'Coincidentally, curiously, conscientiously and covetously, we have collected here to know our true selves even as we are bending towards our graves.' Swamy had not lost touch with his tongue twisters in twenty years.

It did not seem like twenty years had rolled by as the Indus Class of 2000 caught up with each other. They animatedly recalled those rapid fire text messages they shared with each other to keep themselves updated about their lives.

Keshav went about organizing a meal for them.

'Knowing which,' the words began to churn inside Neel's head, 'every human problem can be resolved!' Those words of Keshav seemed quite flaky to Neel!

Keshav spoke like a mystic to these budding managers in a B-school. 'He was such a gorgeous and welcome misfit in a management school,' recalled Kaya. Neel noticed that Kaya's face was tinged with a hint of pink as she spoke those words.

The other international visitors were giddy with excitement as they looked at the temple surrounded by hills on three sides. One end was flanked by the Ganga that had been flowing for centuries without a break. The rocks around the temple were all more than a thousand years old. If rocks could speak, they would have had so many stories to tell about the living and dying of civilizations. About human desires and their fulfilment; and the deepest mysteries of nature that would baffle the most intelligent human brains. A human lifetime would seem like less than a moment compared to the millions of years of a rock's life. Generations of teachers carried with them the code of life that was perhaps as ancient as these rocks. Those teachers who preceded Keshav whispered timeless truths about life that survived their death.

'What happens to the teachings when a great teacher in the order of the ashram passes away?' One of them was curious to learn.

The purohit was explaining to them, 'Death changes nothing here. In death, those teachers do not go up there somewhere in heaven like the smoke spiralling over their cremated bodies. Teachers here just grow up as learners in another realm, in another classroom. In this school, unlike in a business school, we do not strive to leave everyone else behind in a race. Here we grow up together as a community of learners.'

Kaya was heard telling an American visitor that unlike a twenty-first-century school of law or business, these ancient schools did not teach students to just make a livelihood. They urged the students to live the mystery of life itself.

THE CLASSROOM

The classroom of the ashram was a natural amphitheatre. It had a semicircular seating gallery that was cut off from the hilly landscape. A flat rock surface served as Keshav's chair. He light-heartedly called it his rocking chair. The students sat on marble slabs and tufts of grass growing on fertile soil. 'The audio-visual effect was provided by the gurgling Ganga and the high-rise Himalayas that would dwarf the Manhattan skyscrapers,' Kaya thought.

The Ganga streaming down from the Himalayas to Rishikesh assumes different colours depending on the contents of the riverbed and the slant of the sun—blue, green, muddy and mystical. The Ganga is a sacred body of water stretching from the Himalayas to the Bay of Bengal, a journey of over 2,500 kilometres. The river trickles, meanders, flushes and flows. It is not in a hurry to reach anywhere. It is just content to be a river, nurturing the land it flows through—nothing more, nothing less.

Meanwhile, the retreat's participants were hovering around like fruit flies knowing that this would be their teacher Keshav's very special retreat in a long time. Attendance was by invitation only. Kaya, Neel, Prasad, Sardar, Swamy, Eva and the latest arrival, Anju—the group of seven or G-7 as they liked to call themselves—just had a reunion of sorts organized by Neel in the local tea shop, slurping ginger tea and bread pakodas.

'You look the same, Neel,' remarked Eva.

That was not the truth.

Neel noticed that in Kaya's eyes he wasn't the same any more.

Eva was in a live-in relationship with Sardar. Prasad had married Anju. It was a marriage of utter inconvenience propelled by caste and lust. Swamy was a bachelor and he was still searching for 'The One' on assorted dating sites. For both Neel and Kaya, the relationship status was, as things stood, a fair bit complicated.

The classroom was close to the German café overlooking a suspension bridge, the Lakshman Jhula. The café was abuzz with a motley crowd of international visitors whom Kaya had invited to be a part of Keshav's retreat. The group of seven led by Neel soon joined them. There were liberal hugs, high fives, and camaraderie. It was a 'been there, seen that' moment for Neel. 'You missed my last text message.' 'Oh! I am so looking forward to hearing Keshav again.' Remarks like these continued to move back and forth among them.

Neel drew Kaya aside and said how much he had missed her and that long distance calls and messages would never make up for seeing her in person. Kaya was sipping from a cup of ginger tea with a circle of lemon floating on it. She acknowledged Neel simply by raising her crescent eyebrows.

4

Looking Back

Neel and Kaya were destined to meet again, after a long time in Keshav's ashram. The last time they had seen each other was three years back at Neel's bidding. They had met at an Indian restaurant in New York during one of Neel's official visits there. There was barely any spark between them in that meeting. Kaya kept asking Neel if he had had a chance to meet Keshav and that she would love to visit India again, if only to meet him.

This was a much anticipated get-together of Keshav's extended circle of students, friends and admirers. After his voluntary retirement from the Indus School, Keshav chose to live a contemplative life in this ashram located on the outskirts of the town of Rishikesh. He vigorously wrote books based on his life in Rishikesh and responded to a huge volume of correspondence with his students and admirers. His work was translated into many languages. Neel kept track of Keshav and bought all his books diligently, although he barely read any of them.

Most of Keshav's students remembered his classes as vividly as their first love affair. His appearance was very different from any conventional business school professor. Old students did not recall if he ever wore a suit or a tie except once—the day he arrived at the interview to be hired as a professor. He usually put on a turtleneck shirt with a sleeveless jacket on top. His rectangular, rimless glasses merging seamlessly with his eyes were barely visible from a distance.

Keshav always walked with a slight stoop that came from his addiction to reading. He was a deliberate walker. You would see him, even when he was quite young, trudging unhurriedly towards the classroom as though he had the whole world and infinite time to himself.

Keshav's resignation from the Indus Business School several years ago surprised many. It was then seen by his colleagues as an abrupt decision as he was peaking in his research and teaching career. 'Why is he leaving school?' his students asked with considerable heartache. Keshav had announced in a short unsentimental speech that he wanted to move on. It was around the time when he had just published a book called *The Call of the Flute* based on his spiritual journey. He delivered the last formal lecture of his optional course in the school cafeteria, and not his usual classroom. That was twenty years back. Yet, most students would still remember most of what he said about his decision to quit business school teaching.

That day he spoke in his calm, clear voice: 'This is not the end of my journey. Like all of you in the Indus School looking for jobs or romance or fame, I too am on a pursuit. This is going to be slightly different from all the other journeys I have had in life. For now, I have decided to travel farther up north and live near Rishikesh. You will get to know my whereabouts through my published books.'

Keshav then gently waded through a stream of students who had assembled at the school auditorium for his farewell.

Kaya vividly remembered the words she spoke during Keshav's farewell speech. She quoted from his own writing: 'When all else is broken, love remains. Love is invincible.'

What followed was a long standing ovation from all the attendees in the auditorium. Keshav closed his eyes trying to recall something. 'That is what I learnt from my mother,' he said.

It was a promising Wednesday in the year 1963. In a small town in West Bengal, the sun crept out of the white oval dome of a temple like the yolk of an egg easing out of its shell. The mother looked out from her hospital bed through the foggy glass window. In the wee hours of the morning, with the throaty wake-up call of pigeons, a new life was breathing next to her.

A pale beam from a street light crept from a small crack in the glass, and settled on the edge of the baby's lips. A faint smile flickered on those lips. The mother inhaled the fragrance of the wild, flowery baby smell wafting in the autumnal air.

Her voice was soothing and husky as she spoke to him: 'You are my firstborn. Through you, I am now born as a mother. Your heart will beat with mine. When you smile, my world will light up. When you cry, tears will run down from my eyes. You are the one I will love the most in this life. When I am no longer here on earth, remember your ma will live inside you forever. Your ma loves you beyond the reaches of the five senses.'

The baby rolled over. His unblinking eyes, dark and wondrous as the deep sea, were fixed on his mother's face. It was as though he had come prepared with all the lessons of love from her womb. His tiny wax fingers were curling over his mother's breasts.

'Impatient brat! Just like your father,' the mother cooed at the baby, rolling her eyes in feigned anger.

'You have visitors from home,' said the attending nurse with a deadpan expression.

The boy's grandparents, almost bursting with pride, conjectured that his birth was a result of an unworldly conspiracy. His grandmother was especially convinced of a divine connection. The night before he was born, she dreamt that the face of the household deity turned into a wispy smoke and morphed into a baby's face. 'Maer dibbi,' she swore by the newborn's great-grandmother. She thought of her dream as an auspicious sign that the baby was being delivered as a result of divine will. His grandfather, in between checking his dentures and his hairless head before the mirror, called him Keshav—a name celebrating a graceful lock of curly hair that he was born with. It may not have occurred to him then that Keshav was yet another name from the hundreds of names of Krishna.

His father, flushed with parental pride, began to cough vacuously to hide his emotions. He scanned the astrological charts in the local newspaper to fathom the destiny of the newborn.

'Ore baba! Your firstborn is destined to be a rich businessman or a spiritual guide,' he said to the boy's mother.

None of this pleased the mother, of course! She always disapproved of everything that the boy's father said or even planned to say. You know those odd couples.

She earnestly desired that her son should be a government servant with an artillery of cars and waiters and a fat income both over and under the table—known as upri in local parlance. His father was a small-time government clerk in the Indian Railways. All her married life, the mother quietly suffered the genuflections she had to offer to his father's superior officers and their puffed-up wives by bending her head and back considerably. The modest dreams of a clerk's wife could only be fulfilled if her son could become a Chief Assistant Engineer, a Class I officer, that would help reverse the flow of back-bending namastes towards her.

The two sons, Keshav and his brother Utsav, born to the Mitras were lucky enough to go to the only English medium school in town, St Xavier's. Their enterprising father had played on the headmaster's weakness for horoscopes and fortune seeking to fast-track his children's admission to Xavier's.

In school, Keshav was addicted to reading. He would sit next to a pile of books and magazines, rest his back on the wall and read. Sometimes when he got tired of reading, he would drool over the different volumes of Encyclopaedia Britannica. His mother worried that he would often forget to take his meals. An introvert, unlike his brother, Keshav shied away from girls in his neighbourhood. He was attractive without being particularly handsome. Due to his sharp and bony appearance, he earned several nicknames in school. His cousins would poke him in the ribs and call him Hercules—a back-handed compliment referring to his frail figure and several visible bones of his ribcage. The dream-like quality of his eyes was, however, a saving grace. His aunt noticed that he had a thick unibrow. His two eyebrows met tantalizingly above the bridge of the nose. She said it was the sign of a lucky man!

KESHAV MITRA IN LOVE

Keshav defied the admonition of his father and the aspiration of his mother, making sure that he would not become the Chief Assistant Engineer any more. It was now his brother Utsav's turn to be smothered by his mother's unfulfilled ambitions.

While Utsav began to lose his hair over joint entrance examinations, Keshav developed a passion for studying literature. He got into the best liberal arts college in town that was nicknamed Vrindavan for admitting a disproportionately large number of girl students. Keshav would ride on his creaking Atlas bicycle with a basket full of books to college every day. Ringing a bell with a sharp metallic sound 'tring... trong', he swerved dexterously past his classmates, and the dogs sleeping on the street, in hip-hugging jeans.

Keshav was committed to the rigorous Bengali middle-class pursuit of knowledge and omitted the equally demanding mastery of mystery wrapped in saris and salwars. Every once in a while, his eyes would stray towards a classmate with a rectangular face and short pigtails. And if their eyes met accidentally, Keshav would quiver nervously from tonsils to toe. Unlike most members of his school gang, he was clumsy at whistling. His lips would manage to let out only a faint 'foooosh' through his teeth!

In the Mitra household, maintaining an unblemished record in examinations was as sacred as preserving one's virginity. It was not surprising that Keshav graduated with a first class in college, won a gold medal, and was soon headed to a graduate school in the US. His brother, Utsav, emerged successfully from the concentration camp of the coaching centre with a semi-bald head and an admission to IIT. He was a proud member of the human herd that let themselves be engineered by parental aspiration.

In his twenty-one years of life, Keshav had not permitted himself to lose his mind to meet the desires of his heart. He would keep his eyes firmly on the ground while listening to after-class advice from a heavily perfumed research scholar of English. He would stand stiff when she leaned in towards him to drive home the hidden insight in a John Donne poem:

I am two fools, I know,
For loving, and for saying so.

However, in the small town, he was unwittingly warming up the matrimonial market. After three years of college, his thin adolescent features had fleshed out considerably. After dodging several snares and well-oiled matrimonial traps, he was ready for his flight to the land of freedom, oomph and opportunity. His mother tried hard to hold back her tears when he hugged her goodbye. While seeing him off at the international terminal at Kolkata airport, his father, usually a man of few words, parted with teary eyes and a solemn and cautionary advice, 'Sabdhane theko, conquer hearts and keep your parts safe!'

∽

KESHAV'S KRISHNA

Keshav had his share of heartbreaks as a PhD student in the US. The pangs of parting were less severe than what he had imagined. However, he was still left with a bittersweet aftertaste of not being loved and accepted unconditionally. He avoided alcohol and stayed away from nightclubs, a deferred obedience to his mother's last two requests, and largely lived in solitude. The messenger of love had called on him with great earnestness, but each time it had turned out to be a missed call.

While leaving India, Keshav was given a copy of the annotated version of the Bhagavad Gita by his grandfather. He had said that the Gita was Krishna's song of hope for a dejected and demoralized Arjuna. Just open any page in the book when you are in distress and it will have a message that is just the right one for you. 'I sort of doubt that,' said Keshav tucking the book reluctantly inside his suitcase. 'If you doubt what I said about the Gita, then go ahead and doubt one hundred per cent. But if you do have faith in my words, have cent per cent faith as well. You know, Keshav, even Mahatma Gandhi turned to Krishna's words in the Gita to sort out all his problems!' Those words seemed rather enigmatic to Keshav. He decided to randomly open a page in the book. His eyes froze as he read a few lines from the book:

> As a fire is covered by smoke, as a mirror by dust,
> As an embryo is enveloped by the womb, so the soul is veiled in desire.

He then flipped a few pages and came across the following words of Krishna:

> *I give the knowledge of my presence to one who seeks me with love!*

The solace for a sick heart was a Krishna temple that many first-generation American Indians used to visit. It was a small temple built inside an erstwhile church building that was sold off to a Gujarati entrepreneur. Non-resident Indians, who are good at acquiring and reviving failed American businesses, turned around a decaying church building into a flourishing temple. Devotees crammed into the premises that were loaded with gladioli and chrysanthemums shooting out of ornate Chinese vases. There were plastic pineapples, luscious bananas and apples made of glazed clay as offerings to a blue replica of Krishna.

This temple offered a cool retreat from the frenzied, cerebral life of a PhD scholar. It quenched Keshav's increasing thirst for something more comforting than cracking the code of numbers and alphabets. By then, Keshav had finished the defence of his PhD thesis. In fact, he had begun his teaching career, and was contemplating the road ahead.

He was increasingly disenchanted with his own life in the US. He saw himself morphing into a slot machine: getting, spending and getting spent at the end of the day. His heart's longing was only sharpened by the hollowness of his accomplishments.

One evening he was sitting and gazing intently at the luminous Krishna statue inside the temple, thinking of what to do next. It was then that it happened.

His slouching back clicked into a ramrod straight posture. An unseen force was straightening his spine and fixing his body into a perfect yoga movement. He felt as if he had become aware of an existence beyond the body. His physical body now felt like an empty shell of skin, like a hollow drum that was sitting there motionless as a statue. Keshav was blown away by the immensity of what he had experienced. It was bizarre! He couldn't believe that he had an identity that had nothing to do with his body or even his restless mind. An indescribable burst of energy filled his being. Keshav had never experienced anything quite like this before.

For the next three days, he lived under a spell of joyous anticipation. Then, the memory of that experience began to fade like a distant dream.

∽

A few days later, while rushing to catch a flight from Boston to Minnesota, he met an Italian taxi driver who was wearing a baseball cap and a bead necklace. While taking him to the airport, the driver asked him, out of the blue, whether he had heard of Krishna.

'Of course, I have,' Keshav said, unable to conceal his bewilderment. In turn, he asked the cabbie, 'If I may ask, what is your connection with Krishna?'

'Ciao, professoressa! I haven't gone to graduate school like you have,' the cab driver mumbled, 'yet I have read a lot about Krishna. I think he lived thousands of years ahead of our time,' the cabbie gushed. 'What are you doing here in this crazy world, amico? Life sucks here!' He had spoken those words as though he was spitting bits and pieces of a rotten almond from his mouth.

'You should head back to your land where Krishna breathed, lived and walked once.'

He then proceeded to take out Keshav's suitcases from the trunk of the car and arranged them neatly on a luggage cart. Keshav turned around and reached for his wallet to pay the cab fare, but the cabbie had melted away from his view like snowflakes withering away on the asphalt road.

He left without taking his payment! Keshav could not believe what he saw! How could he have vanished like that without leaving a trace?

He was thinking of those words he had heard in the temple discourse on the Bhagavad Gita:

I manifest my powers in all without prejudice
In whatever form they invoke me, I accept and serve them.

☙

On reaching St Paul in Minnesota, Keshav saw a mail dispatched from the Indus Business School in Lucknow, India. He tore open the rough brown paper envelope that had a distinct smell—that of Indian soil. The school was looking for faculty in Human Resource Management. They urged Keshav to apply for the position with his latest curriculum vitae. This was a decisive moment in Keshav Mitra's life and career in the US. He felt like soft clay in the hands of destiny. His head swam in hope and disbelief.

Within a few days, Keshav received a letter of appointment that stated that he was to join the institute as an assistant professor and would soon be promoted to the rank of an associate professor, provided he relocated to India as soon as possible. The bright gaze of the Italian cabbie with the baseball cap, bead necklace and the words he uttered floated inside Keshav's head.

'Ciao, professoressa...'

FAREWELL

After obtaining a PhD in Organization Behaviour and Leadership, Keshav was invited to teach undergraduate classes at a university in Upper West Side in Manhattan, New York. He detested being part of the publish or perish world that was a survival requirement in the university. During his three years of university teaching, Keshav's greatest joy came from the after-class conversations and the frequent one-on-ones with his students in the cafeteria. He did not hit his research targets but surely touched the deeper chords in the hearts of his students who often brought their personal and professional problems to him. He was generous with his time and money and often allowed his students to drop by in his modest apartment close to the university. By the third year of his teaching, he even made it to the dean's list for his teaching performance. When he told Kaya, a student he had known for over two years, that he had decided to leave the US for India, the news spread like wildfire. Keshav was worried about Kaya's life and what it had in store for her. She often clung to him for support as her life was turning on its head.

His farewell at the university was something for him to remember. Keshav had quite a fan following among the undergrads. He was teaching a hugely attended course called Self-Mastery: Learning from the Greats. His students swooned over him as he imbued his classes with an extraordinary life-like energy, as though he was indeed living the characters he was talking about. Gandhi, Confucius, Lao Tsu, Mandela, Rumi and Florence Nightingale rubbed shoulders with the Buddha, Christ and Krishna.

His last lecture—of the course on Krishna—ended with a flute song that students were asked to listen to with their eyes closed. It was a hymn to Lord Krishna composed by an Indian maestro intermingled with lines translated from a great thirteenth-century Persian poet, Rumi:

A craftsman pulled a reed from the reed bed,
cut holes in it, and called it a human being.
Since then, it's been wailing a tender agony

*of parting, never mentioning the skill
that gave it life as a flute.*

Only when the song was over did the entire class open their eyes, as instructed. They looked around to see what Keshav had to say in conclusion. Strangely, Keshav was not there! There was nothing more to be said. Their star teacher, Keshav, had quietly left the classroom even as the music was playing. It was like Ronaldo abandoning a football match before the final whistle.

For a while, the students kept sitting in stunned silence. Then, the usual buzz of surprise, shock, appreciation and a flurry of exclamations spread among the students. It was an uncanny end to a great course for most of the class.

After a formal departmental farewell that evening, Keshav was clearing his desk at the university academic block. He saw a small manila envelope with a message stuck inside. He read the note scribbled in flowing letters on a yellow stick pad. It was from a student.

Dear Keshav,

The Master's classes have transformed me forever. Knowing you for the last couple of years, I have come to understand what it means to be truly human. My small family will forever remain grateful to you for your generosity. For me, India was a land of mysterious enchantment. After meeting you, that enchantment has deepened into love.

I hope to spend this weekend on a retreat in the Catskill Mountains in New York State.

I will hear your voice in the babble of breeze breaking the vast solitude of a forest. I cannot describe what shape love takes. You inspired a song that was long lost in my heart. The flute of reed will never know who created the song. However, if life wills it, I would some day reach the other end of the world to see and hear you again.

Stay blessed,
Kaya

Keshav neatly folded the note and tucked it inside his wallet. It was among the few keepsakes he took from the university on his last day.

RISHIKESH ASHRAM, DAY 1, MORNING
ACCEPTANCE: THE FIRST SHADE OF LOVE

Professor Keshav Mitra assumed the role of Acharya Keshav in the ashram with the ease of a flowing river filling up a new terrain. However, some of his old habits did not change. He was always a stickler for punctuality. He arrived for his first formal day of the retreat on the dot at 8.55 a.m. Every step he took towards his seat seemed conscious, as though he was stepping on another planet for the first time.

Neel soon recognized that Keshav no longer had that old stoop of his Indus days. He appeared more radiant and alive than how his students remembered.

Kaya was gazing into Keshav's still, soulful eyes. He sat straight on an orange velvet mattress spread over a rock. His face was soft and unmasked without a ripple of exertion.

The morning sunlight slanted to the left of Keshav's face. When he smiled, Kaya's heart lit up in the surge of that magnificent moment. She whispered to a Western woman sitting cross-legged beside her, 'He now appears like a man living between a dream and reality.'

Neel's gaze drifted to Kaya. She looked so gullible and starry-eyed. Kaya wrapped herself in a blue pashmina silk shawl. Blessed with a face with high cheekbones, she looked luminously beautiful. A large golden earring caressed a question mark of hair falling on her cheek. Neel sensed a jab of envy somewhere inside his gut when he saw Kaya arch her graceful neck and look intently at Keshav. Her attention was wholly focused on what Keshav would say now.

Neel wondered where that pang of envy came from. He had had Kaya in mind when he set about organizing the retreat. She was sitting so close to him now and yet seemed so far away!

A Middle Eastern woman in the audience, sitting next to Neel, said, 'Tell us where love begins.'

Keshav's voice, crisp and clear, pierced the ears of his listeners. He began by thanking Neel and Kaya for putting this retreat together. His words fell on their ears like the rapture of wind rustling through bamboo leaves. 'The first shade of love is acceptance. Without learning how to fully accept either yourself or someone else in your life, you will never learn to love. Acceptance is about breaking the barriers of your ego that will take you some place else rather than where you are right now. Acceptance brings you to the very heart of your being, where love is.

'We all worry about being something and being somewhere. The worrying ego puts you on a collision course with the life of a pure being. Do not let your ego step ahead of you. To stay in your being is to embrace the is-ness of life rather than the busy-ness of the ego. The morning is. The river is. I just am. You simply are.

'Before your ego gets into judging this is-ness as good or bad, strange or boring, experience your spontaneous being without judgement this morning. Don't jump to your first conclusion about everything. Relax and soak in the first impressions of being alive. Love blossoms the moment you learn to relax your being.' He took a deep breath and spoke again.

The river finds fulfilment in its flow,
The jasmine in its blooming,
The swallow in its flight,
And gold in its glow.

His words sounded like a lyric.

'A human is fulfilled when she breaks the resistance of the ego and dissolves into a pure being.'

Many heads, blonde, bald and black, nodded as though they were in synchronized movement. Some were simply nodding to keep up an appearance of understanding even if they had only understood very little of what Keshav had said.

Neel wanted to say something but since Keshav had already started to speak, he checked himself.

'Krishna, whom we celebrate and worship in this ashram, is a complete being. He embraces the whole of life. My life as well as yours. His mind is not stuck in judgements and his consciousness is not wrinkled by conventions. Krishna removes the physical and mental illusions brought about by our five senses and the sixth sense that we describe as our mind. He sees the spiritual unity of all of life through the seventh sense. When these illusions of our ego-based separateness are gone we become one with the is-ness of life. Such a life becomes a benediction. Through the seventh sense, the human being receives the grace of the divine.'

THE HUNCHBACK OF MATHURA
SEVERAL THOUSAND YEARS BEFORE CHRIST WAS BORN

A soft breeze wafted the purohit's voice to his audience, making it loud and clear. He began with an ancient incantation:

Om nama bhagavate vasudevaya!

In the ashram, every day began with the purohit reading out a story about the life and legend of Krishna.

> On their way from Vrindavan to Mathura, Krishna and Balarama sat with their backs touching. The two brothers were as different in appearance as one could imagine. Balarama was fair, strong and stout with a sharp temper. Krishna was dusky blue, elegant, with a soft smile that hid a whole cartload of mischief. There was great bonhomie between them. Balarama teased Krishna about their dalliance with the maidens of Gokul.
>
> 'How do you so easily cast your charm on those village belles?' asked one of the cowherd boys accompanying them. 'How do they get so drunk in their love for you? What is your secret?' The boy was curious.
>
> Balarama was wondering what profound stuff Krishna would come up with.
>
> Krishna said, 'My great secret is just this: acceptance.'
>
> Balarama had no pretence of being a philosopher like his younger brother. He poked Krishna in his ribs and said, 'What acceptance, huh?'
>
> Krishna arched his back and shoulders to avoid Balarama's knuckles aimed at his ribcage. 'Acceptance of life is the doorway to true love!' he said.
>
> Balarama couldn't make head or tail of Krishna's words as he stuffed another luscious yellow jackfruit in his mouth.
>
> They were hanging out in the city of Mathura awaiting an encounter with their dreaded uncle Kamsa. For the two rustics from the dusty village of Gokul, the city of Mathura was a treasure trove of new experiences. With mouths wide open and jaws dropping, they savoured the sights and sounds of city life. The splendid city gate had elaborate arches strung with festoons and flowers.

The residents of Mathura had already heard about the two legendary brothers who were capable of mind-blowing feats of courage and power. Their reputation as giant killers preceded them like rumblings before a thunderstorm. Men climbed on to rooftops and women left their household work to stare at the spectacle of the two wonder boys strutting about in their city.

The brothers got some beautiful clothes from a tailor and garlands made of marigold from a local florist as gifts. Krishna looked stunning in those sizzling silk clothes. He soon noticed someone with a huge hump inching along the road. The human being soon revealed herself to be a woman who was carrying a perfumed sandal paste for Kamsa, the dreaded king. She was a royal beautician whose original name was Malini. The hump on her back was why she was nicknamed, Kubja. She was often the object of laughter and the butt of jokes for the city dwellers. In their eyes that reflected pity and scorn, she was frequently reminded of her ungainly physical appearance!

'Pretty woman, where are you headed?' Krishna asked while surveying this self-conscious woman rolling past him.

Balarama and the other boys hanging around were taken aback by Krishna's words. 'What a strange pick-up line for a woman who didn't appear all that pretty,' some of them thought.

Kubja felt that Krishna's words were adding insult to injury. She lifted her eyes towards this astonishingly attractive young boy and was instantly in tears. 'I can see that you are mocking me. Why should I bear this taunt from you without a murmur?'

'You are indeed a pretty woman, as far as I can see,' continued Krishna, without even a hint of regret on his face.

The residents of Mathura had by then assembled in a crowd to have their share of fun out of this encounter.

'How can you be so cruel?' pleaded Kubja. 'I know, in fact, everyone in the city knows that I am ugly to look at. They just bear with me because they are scared of Kamsa. They know I report to him as his personal beautician.'

Unruffled, Krishna continued, 'My fair lady, I do not see your body parts. I just see a woman of extraordinary beauty in you. Why don't you beautify me with some of your sandal paste?'

Kubja's anger began to cool a little. In fact, she was so carried away by Krishna's compliment that she hastened to apply some sandalwood paste on his hands and the rest of his body. 'How graceful and sensuous his hands are,' thought Kubja.

A thrill of pleasure shot through Krishna too as Kubja rubbed his forearm with the practised tenderness of a royal masseuse. Kubja didn't realize that Krishna had drawn very close to her. She felt the warmth of his breath on her face. In one swift motion, he pressed her feet with his toes, lifted her face towards him and looked at her intently. Time stood still for both of them as his infinite gaze seemed to penetrate her eyes like a bolt of lightning. Her soul was stirred and she felt an intense burst of energy. Krishna literally pulled her up with a jerk. Everyone around saw the miracle that was unfolding before them with unblinking eyes. The hump was gone and Kubja's back was straight like an arrow. She stood erect, tall and appeared exquisitely beautiful!

Kubja could not believe what had transpired. Tears of gratitude rolled down her cheeks. Her face had turned red. Her straight and shapely body was now shaking with delight. She felt an irresistible sensual attraction towards the handsome boy.

As Krishna was turning away, she dragged him by his clothes in full view of the astounded onlookers. Shedding all her modesty, she looked flirtatiously at her liberator and said, 'Why don't we go home so that I can please you with all my art?'

Balarama anticipated what was coming and loudly cleared his throat. He was signalling his younger brother to get away before this magically transformed woman turned delirious in her lust for his younger brother.

Krishna held her by the hand and said, 'Oh yes, beautiful lady! I shall visit your parlour some day to accept your tender and loving services. For now, I have some serious business at hand.' He nudged Balarama to move ahead.

Kubja looked at Krishna with a longing she had not experienced in a lifetime. She murmured to herself. 'Yes, my Lord. I shall wait for you to visit my home. Even a lifetime's wait is worth it.'

A former judge, his face evidently cold and devoid of emotions, raised his hand. He, who had spent a lifetime judging others, asked, 'Without judgement, how can we discriminate between good and evil?'

Keshav seemed unperturbed by the question. His gaze was intense. He responded, 'Being able to judge is a crucial function of the mind, but becoming judgemental is a disease. It is only a stuck-up mind that becomes judgemental. The mind's true nature is to flow. Being judgemental chokes this flow. This mind thus becomes sick like a streaming brook arrested in a sewage dump.'

The judge pressed his lips in a hard line as he listened to Keshav. 'Sewage water stagnates within the limitations of the dump. A mind trapped in judgements cannot look beyond the limitations of shape, comparison of forms and narrow world views. A judgemental mind loses touch with the spontaneity of life. Observe how life eases past a judgemental mind as a river does—streaming, rubbing, dissolving and drilling its way through the resistance of the land.'

The grim look on the judge's face intensified further.

Keshav carried on. 'Krishna accepts life as it is. His vision stretches beyond the limitations of names and forms. When he looks at that hunchback Kubja, he does not see a deformed body. His vision of Kubja is not stuck in her body parts. In fact, Krishna sees the beautiful light of her being. His clear sight penetrates all appearances to the core of life that is indeed beautiful.

'Don't they say beauty lies in the eyes of the beholder? But so does deformity. His clear vision brings about an inner transformation in both Krishna and Kubja. The holder and the beholder of beauty are awash in the unifying ocean of love. This is nature's alchemy. Krishna's consciousness conjures up love in everything he sees.'

'Krishna may have had the power of alchemy. But how does Kubja redeem herself from her deformity?' a physician asked in a tone that was clipped, cold and clinical.

'Listen carefully,' Keshav said, arching a brow.

'Our pain and deformities are physical. They may have to be endured if they cannot be cured. But all of humankind's suffering is psychological. Suffering comes from a psychological state defined by the absence of love. In the absence of love, our deformities and pain begin to define our lives. The more we judge ourselves by our negative states, the more guilt we accumulate within. The greater the guilt, the greater is the suffering.'

The face of the physician softened slightly as the insight that distinguished deformity from suffering dawned on him. Yet he was unable to grasp the story of a hunchback woman being cured so miraculously.

Keshav went on. 'When Krishna accepts Kubja as she is, notwithstanding her physical appearance, he touches the very heart of Kubja's being. Krishna's ultimate nature is love, which is just another name for an undivided being. Unlike Krishna, however, our minds are fragmented by our faulty emotional GPS: guilt, pride and shame!' There was a ripple of laughter in the audience. 'Then, add to it the million mutinies of our ego positions. They cause conflict and suffering. When Krishna turns his deep gaze towards Kubja, that one look resolves all the conflicts within her. The love that he embodies showers its bounties on her. The greater intelligence of love enters her through the path of total acceptance. The frail walls of reason are broken by this gush of love. Love becomes the ultimate reason! When Kubja experiences this love, she is healed for she truly becomes whole.'

Just then the ashram bell rang and the morning session of the first class was over.

POST-TEA BREAK

The temple bell rang again, signalling the resumption of the first day's class. The invitees to the retreat began to occupy their chosen seats, demarcated by chips of stones, sunglasses, hair clips, cardboard files, writing pads and crumpled handkerchiefs, among other things.

Keshav adjusted the red scarf on his dark turtleneck jacket. He put on his glasses, and looked intently at Sardar and Eva as though time had rolled back twenty years and he was still in the Indus classroom with them. Eva had noticed that he hadn't changed his manner of wearing those rimless glasses.

During the tea break, Keshav's old students were discussing how his fame as a teacher spread through word of mouth generated by his students in the LOVE (Leadership of Voluntary Enterprises) course. Keshav had become sort of a legend among business school students. His second book, *Awaken Your Heart*, based on his course teachings, turned out to be a national bestseller. A large number of students, including foreign students as well as visitors in the exchange programme, would talk about the course long after they had graduated. For one, the LOVE classes were a refreshing break from the typical business school courses.

Indus cramped bright minds with pie charts and numbers and reduced a human being into theories of demand, constraints and behaviour. Keshav was often sought after by the business media for his outrageous views on management education. Neel remembered how a quote by Keshav had created quite a buzz in the media. A business magazine had quoted him as saying:

Nature designs and manages perfect organizations. Trained managers merely create patterns of interference.

His professional colleagues howled at him for his anti-establishment and subversive ideas.

Now in Rishikesh, Keshav was speaking to an earnest audience who were seekers and his admirers from all around the world. They had read his books and heard about his esoteric teaching. Here, he seemed to be speaking to near converts who were almost aligned with his way of thinking.

Keshav began the session with a simple, yet crucial, tenet. 'To learn acceptance, you have to know how to wait. If you wait long enough, you will see that everything about a human being, including their darker sides, will begin to appear lighter and more interesting. And why just a human being? Even a cactus looks beautiful when you accept it as your own. A human being is a whole universe of possibilities. Light and shade both live inside us in equal measure. Those we like and those we dislike are just reflections of the same being.'

He paused and asked, 'By the way, do you recognize what

all of you are actually searching for in the name of wealth, pleasure or fame?'

Keshav would ask these provocative questions to get his audience out of their comfort zones. This was his unique style of teaching. His classes often ended with a question, and sometimes with some kind of instrumental music.

Neel recalled those days in Indus, the word 'globe' was fast becoming a part of students' lingo. Globe loosely meant 'too abstract' or 'fuzzy', or 'beating around the bush'. The word originated from going around the globe in circles. Keshav's lectures would be considered globe by those hardened operations and finance wizards of the B-school, especially his arch-rival Professor Malhotra.

Malhotra's wife Mridula, however, looked up to Keshav for something that she had noticed about him as his neighbour in the Faculty Residential Block. She once shared in the faculty wives' meet that a pack of stray dogs that barked furiously at every passer-by fell silent when Keshav walked by them. She also reported seeing squirrels and monkeys coming down from trees to Keshav's lawns to move about fearlessly around him. Some faculty spouses attributed her stories to a 'soft corner' she was supposed to have for Keshav.

Most campus residents began to notice that strangers tended to just pop up from nowhere looking for Keshav. When Malhotra asked Keshav light-heartedly if he knew some kind of 'black magic', he simply laughed it away saying, 'I know nothing about black or white magic.'

INDUS DAYS, LUCKNOW
THE TEACHER BECOMES A SEEKER

Armed with a PhD in Management from the US, Keshav landed in India to serve as an assistant professor at the Indus Business School. That was his day job. By night, he became a seeker. He read voraciously and meditated for long hours on his breath. He began to discover dimensions about his life that he did not know existed.

Keshav learnt to experiment with conscious breathing practices. He realized that his breathing became long, harmonious and deep whenever he paid close attention to it. He discovered that there was a calming midpoint between the inner and outer breath—in his awareness—when his breath became completely still. In that stillness, a pure being shone like a starlit sky reflected on a still pool of water. As he began to identify himself with that being of light, he could sense a reality that connected him to his surroundings and made him a part of a living, throbbing organism. His chair, table, the floor below his feet, his entire body and the open sky above him were all part of an ocean tide of one self-aware entity.

Keshav began to experience a spontaneous surge of energy that radiated through his body from the crown of his head. When that energy reached his chest, he felt an expansive space inside the cave of his heart. There was a welling up of deep gratitude and all-embracing compassion. It was as though a genie of love that had been bottled up and mired in lifelong ignorance was finally let loose from his heart.

Students flocked to his residence in the Faculty Residential Block like bees swarming around a blooming tube rose. Several corporate executives showed up for his classes from India and across continents. A handful of them came without prior notice or an appointment. On some days, he taught classes in the wee hours of the morning, in the bitter cold of North India. He held open air classes when the first rains arrived. He travelled widely in Europe and North America. In one of his lectures at Oxford University, he talked to a large number of students about the Fifth Dimension of the human personality.

'All of us know that we have a three-dimensional body. The body is linear. It can move from the past to the future. It cannot reverse its journey. The mind is the Fourth Dimension. The mind can go backward and forward, unlike the body. It moves between the memory of the past and the hope for the future. Yet the mind too is mechanical. It cannot achieve anything beyond what it is programmed to do. All humans have the capacity to live in the Fifth Dimension. This is the dimension of awareness. Unlike the mind, awareness is not programmed. Awareness is an intelligence that is free from the divisive and binary movement of the mind. With awareness, we can grasp reality much faster.'

Then, pointing towards one student in his class he said, 'If you look up at a clear night sky studded with stars, you are likely to experience what I just shared with you. Your awareness will take you to the entire constellation of stars in the blink of an eye—much before the mind can come to grips with what it sees with a telescope.'

The student was awestruck. He had something more to ask, but was unable to find the right words like a theatre artist who had forgotten his lines. Keshav seemed to have read his mind. 'Isn't awareness an extension of our senses?'

'Yes, yes! That was exactly my question,' said the student.

Keshav smiled. 'We all know about our five senses responding to the five elements of our universe. The eyes respond to fire and give us the sense of sight and light. The skin responds to air and gives us the sense of touch. The ears respond to space and give us the sense of sound. The tongue responds to water and gives us the sense of taste. The nose responds to earth and gives us the sense of smell.'

'Eventually, all the five senses report their data to the mind. Isn't it?' the student was quick to add.

'Correct,' said Keshav before adding, 'the mind is, therefore, called the sixth sense. It is subtler than the five senses. But you can sense the mind through the working of your thoughts, emotions and memories! You can verify the reality of the five senses as well as the sixth sense that you call the mind. But awareness cannot be sensed or verified in the same way.'

'You are right. Isn't awareness something like an illusion, then?' said the student.

'No, this world of matter and mind is the illusion. Awareness is the only reality. It is like a magician working his magic through the six senses. The magician stays even when the magic is over. The magician can trick your five senses, and also your mind, into believing something that is not real. He can make a train apparently vanish into nothingness and pull a rabbit out of nowhere. When you are aware of the presence and the play of the magician behind the magic, then you realize that the tricks of the six senses are just overpowering illusions—nothing else.

'I have discovered that Krishna is the magician behind the magic. He is the Seventh Sense who willingly takes part in the magic of the six senses. His birth in Mathura, as you will soon see, is nothing but an enchanting, magical event.'

RISHIKESH ASHRAM, DAY 1
THE UNBORN IS BORN
MATHURA, INDIA, 351 BCE

This is the story of Krishna's birth. The storyteller had begun his narration that afternoon. The story of a love without a beginning or an end started to unfold.

> Several thousand years ago, an indescribable darkness developed in Mathura, north of Bharatvarsha. It was the kind of darkness that soothed lovers and excited murderers. Who would know that the eighth-day moon in the month of Shravan would witness the birth of the

lord of love in the killer Kamsa's prison? Devaki, the wife of the imprisoned Vasudeva, was tossing around inside her prison cell. She was expecting her eighth child. Kamsa, the child's uncle, did not want the prophecy to come true. How could he? The stars foretold that Vishnu's avatar, the divinely gifted child named Krishna, would snuff out that tyrant Kamsa's life and end his reign of murder and terror.

Kamsa's guards stood vigilant so that they could kill the eighth child as soon as he came out of the womb of his sister, Devaki. For the past nine years, Kamsa had been killing every child that was born to Devaki and Vasudeva. This time there was an air of expectancy in Mathura and the surrounding villages of Vrajabhumi. The villagers started marking the time since the last child of Devaki, her seventh, was killed by Kamsa. They wondered how the eighth child of Devaki would survive Kamsa's sword. They were eager to know when their prophesied saviour Krishna would be delivered through Devaki's womb.

Under strict orders from Kamsa, the prison security guards were changed every day. Putana, Kamsa's devil sister, kept vigil over Devaki and routinely reported the pregnant woman's health condition. In order to abort any uprising and protest arising from killing the eighth child of Devaki, Kamsa posted his spies in key locations in Mathura.

It had rained throughout the day. The dark half of the month of Shravan seemed darker as clouds hung on the horizon like ink-soaked cotton wool. Long before the sunset hour, darkness fell over the town. Putana had left for her home in the morning. She could not return to Kamsa's prison to keep a check on Devaki as the streets outside were flooded. The palace guards, unable to bear the chill of gusty winds, huddled inside their rooms, leaving the door open in case Putana decided to show up.

The palace was pitch dark except for the flickering of the evening lamps that created ghostly patterns on the stone walls. Thick sheets of rain were drumming ominous rhythms on the roof of the prison. A bolt of lightning flashed, followed by a loud thunderclap. Devaki clutched on to her husband Vasudeva's hand. With eyes brimming with tears she announced, 'The lord of love is on his way out.' Vasudeva held her in a tender embrace. Soon, a dazzling blue baby boy, their eighth child, was born. At that midnight hour, the prophecy of the birth of Krishna, the incarnation of Vishnu, had indeed come true!

Vasudeva was too dazed to remember the message that the family priest, Gargacharya, had whispered into his ears when he came to perform the mandatory rituals inside the prison. The blue boy had to be carried in a basket to Gokul where he would be exchanged for the newly born daughter of Nanda and Yashoda. This was a strategy worked out to escape Kamsa's wrath. Everyone knew that Kamsa would never spare the eighth child of Devaki who would bring an end to his reign of terror.

Vasudeva woke up to the reality of the imminent threat to the newborn's life. He gave the baby a bath, put a drop of honey in his mouth and gently laid him down in a straw basket. Devaki gave a long look. Her eyes lingered on the child who lit up the jail with its presence.

It was raining incessantly. The residents of Mathura were in deep sleep. The monsoon rains poured in with spasms of thunder and howling winds. The Yamuna had swollen up and water began to overflow the banks. Devaki and Vasudeva were drowning in a whirlpool of emotions. To their surprise, they discovered that the doors of the prison were flung open by a gust of wind. Putana had not returned yet and the guards lay asleep as though they were under a hypnotic spell. The prospects of a miraculous escape thrilled Vasudeva and Devaki. Vasudeva lifted the straw basket and made his way to Gokul across the river. With the basket perched on his head, the anxious father waded through neck-deep water. Surprisingly, the rains slowed down. The waves of the river curved like the head of a cobra, protecting the prodigious child on its way to his new home. Vasudeva navigated the journey to Gokul with some help from the five elements.

On the opposite bank of the Yamuna, Rishi Gargacharya and Nanda, the head of the Yadavas in Gokul, waited breathlessly under a tree. As soon as Vasudeva arrived, they went to Nanda's home. Gargacharya took the basket carrying Devaki's newborn son from Vasudeva and handed him another one that had a beautiful girl child. That girl was named Yogamaya, meaning the illusory power of Vishnu. She was conceived to trick Kamsa.

'Yashoda gave birth to her daughter early in the morning,' mumbled the misty-eyed Nanda. The exchange of the two newborn kids took place just as destiny had willed it.

Suppressing the pangs of separation from that wondrous blue baby, Vasudeva gushed in gratitude. 'How can I ever repay your debt, Nanda?' he said.

Nanda looked at the pristine child in wonder. The kid had dark skin and a blue-black sheen on it like a rain cloud. There was a deep mystery in his little eyes that kept gazing intently at his foster father. A wave of affection swept the heart of Nanda. The pain of letting go of his newborn daughter was somewhat lessened by the compassion he now felt for the dark-skinned kid whose life was threatened by his uncle.

For the time being, it seemed that the lord of love had outshone the forces of darkness in Kamsa's world. In the cloak of that auspicious night Krishna, the unborn, was born.

AFTERCLASS DISCUSSION

The incredible story of Krishna's birth held the retreat audience in a spell. Prasad with a nervous twitch on his lips asked, 'Tell us more about the mystery of Krishna's birth, Keshav.'

'Listen,' Keshav said, 'what I am about to say to you is as ancient as the hills. Every child born is a living proof that nature is still striving for the perfection of its species. A human birth is nature's work in progress. The birth of any living being is the result of the urge of existence to complete its unfinished business.'

'So where was Krishna before he was born?' quizzed Prasad whose face began to twitch in many directions. There was an intense pause.

'Or, you could ask, was he born at all?' quipped Keshav. 'Isn't birth merely an appearance of a time-bound body on the infinite canvas of timeless life?'

Keshav had stumped his audience with that question. After a while, he continued, 'The story goes that Krishna was conceived inside a prison on a dark, new moon night. The disappearance of the moon does not mean that the moon was gone. It simply means that the moon disappeared from our view only to appear again another day. The moon was very much there. Only our view of the moon was blocked by the clouds. Likewise, think of the birth of Krishna as merely an appearance. He was always there as an existential potential waiting to appear.'

Keshav paused again. The temple bells had stopped

ringing. The day was beginning to fold itself into the comforting lap of the evening. 'Have you ever wondered why creation often takes shape in darkness? The seed of a flower incubates in the darkness of the soil. A soulful song wells up from the depth of a despondent heart. A child is conceived inside the dark folds of a mother's womb. Don't you see this everywhere?'

'Where does this creative impulse of life come from?' said an artist from Mexico City who found himself engrossed in the talk.

Keshav explained. 'The creative impulse of life is inherent in life. The source of this impulse is so subtle that our mechanical mind cannot grasp it. To understand the mystery of birth, you first have to accept the fact that the creative source of life is a place where the human mind or the five senses cannot reach. The magician can grasp the magic but the magic cannot get hold of the magician.' The analogy made him laugh. 'Birth is a place of darkness for the non-illumined mind. Krishna simply appeared in a prison. Tell me, for that matter, who isn't born in a prison? The first prison sentence is served in the mother's womb. After we are born, our conditioned minds become our new prison. It is just that we do not know we are in a prison of our own making.'

'But, Krishna would have to appear from some place. Where was he before he was born?' the muddled Mexican artist probed further.

'Are you really asking where he was before he appeared? He was inherent in the infinitude of life. All human birth is nothing but the imprisonment of infinite life in the finite form of a body. Life is eternal. Life is neither born nor annihilated. Only life forms come and go like ocean waves. You are asking where were the waves before they appeared on the ocean bed. Why? They were part of the ocean itself.'

With a delicate manoeuvre of his hand, his palm

upturned, Keshav said, 'When a sparrow lives, the sparrow eats the ant!'

Then turning his hand around with his palm pointing to the ground, he said: 'When the sparrow dies, the ants eat the sparrow! Life just appears in one life form and disappears in another! If you look closely, you will discover this for yourself.'

Looking at the distance, he said, 'That which propels the movement of life from one form to another is the invisible stream of love.' Then, he went into raptures saying:

> *Love is a man in quest for the child within;*
> *Love is a woman longing for the fountain of life;*
> *It is a saint's search for the immortal Self;*
> *And a traveller's lust for the world.*

With closed eyes, Keshav continued his lesson. 'Love expresses itself as a movement. It is the unseen mystery of the great magician Krishna that makes sure that people move on their paths, and planets in their orbits. To accept Krishna as your guide is to accept love and its innumerable movements. Thus, love begins with acceptance.'

After a while, he said, 'You see, Krishna's life is a see-saw of magic and misfortunes. He is threatened by Kamsa and a slew of demons. He works those miracles of wondrous manifestation and defends himself and his people against great odds. In all of this, love manifests through light and shade. Love finds its way inside the labyrinths of an arduous life!

'Whatever life throws at him by way of a challenge, Krishna accepts with a smile. He does not murmur. He does not react. He simply loves.

'Look at the paradoxes that he negotiates in his life. He is the liberator of his people, but he begins his own life in prison; he hails from a royal family, yet he accepts the life of a common cowherd boy; his body is conceived in the womb of Devaki, but he embraces Yashoda as his mother. Acceptance of all is the thread that runs through all of these.'

MATHURA, INDIA, 351 BCE

With Krishna's appearance on earth, Maharishi Garga was invited by his foster father, Nanda Baba, to conduct his naming ceremony. Garga urged Nanda to keep the ritual as secretive as possible. He did not want the cruel Kamsa to get the slightest hint of the whereabouts of the child. So, Krishna's naming was performed along with that of his brother Balarama in a hushed-up manner in a cowshed.

Garga whispered to the foster parents, Nanda and Yashoda. 'Your elder son will wield great strength (bala) and delight (rama) the hearts of his people. So, we will name him Balarama. Your younger son, dark blue in complexion, will attract everything in the universe. He will be called Krishna. His dark complexion is the symbol of the unfolding mystery of love. The blue tinge around the dark skin stands for the infinite. Krishna will be a premayogi, the embodiment of love that is infinite.'

Maharishi Garga could almost foresee the appearance of a purna purusha, the complete human, as he glanced at the beatific face of Krishna. He said, 'Krishna will live as an ordinary human being among all of us. He will be aware of his identity as an infinite being. His love will be unconditional for all of you. Yet, he will be attached to no person or place. He will know everyone as intimately as the reflection of his own being. He will be an impersonal dispenser of dharma—the law that maintains balance in the universe. He will be the custodian and supporter of a royal family that would be unfairly banished from their legitimate kingdom. He will be a guide and a counsellor in the mother of all wars, yet he will never be a warmonger.'

The gopas and gopis, the guileless men and women of Vrindavan, listened to Garga rishi's prophecy with their jaws dropping in wonder. Garga then continued. 'Krishna will live in this village for a short while. His physical charm will be irresistible. He will attract the attention of the world with the ethereal melody of his flute. He will be a master of all the sixty-four art forms known to humankind. Women and men will be simply transfixed while looking at him. The elements will dance to his tune. He will be enigmatic and exemplary—a multi-dimensional human being.'

'Friends of Gokul, do not judge your Krishna by the miracles that he performs or by his inexplicable actions. He will not be static or consistent in his actions. His character is that of a jalapurusha—someone who would flow like the water of a river, accepting everything, taking in his stride obstacles as well as opportunities. He will be an eternal traveller and the world's greatest yogi. His last days will be spent alone in silence and solitude. At the end of it all, he will breathe his last in the shadow of a tree, as unpredictably as he had appeared on earth—the divine will finally leave behind its mortal coil.'

Garga's body began to glow in the fire of inspiration even as he was finishing his reading of Krishna's horoscope. With that, Maharishi Garga's prophecy of Krishna's life came to an end.

The mystery of Krishna's birth was thus unveiled.

CONVERSATIONS AFTER DINNER

The ashram dinner was an austere meal of chapattis and boiled rice with a mixed vegetable curry and some milk. The eating in silence was accompanied by the clanking of stainless steel thalis and spoons, the slurping of buttermilk, and the occasional burping of elderly members of the ashram.

After dinner, the visitors ambled along the banks of the Ganga, reflecting, chatting, some even texting messages to their families back home. A few adventurous ones were puffing away at a chillum, savouring some exotic weed that was smuggled by the cleaning staff from the local grocery store.

Walking with the group, Keshav reflected on Krishna's life. '*Krsna* means someone who attracts. He is the deep and dark blue god that attracts everything in the universe.'

'Is Krishna like a black hole that draws every particle to itself? Is he the universal soul to which every human body belongs?' Neel wondered.

Kaya, who was walking behind Neel and eavesdropping on the conversation, soon caught up with him. A television screen flickered in the ashram office where a cricket match was being streamed. Kaya was talking to Eva and Anju about the enigma of Krishna. The three women stepped ahead of the men, Sardar, Prasad and Swamy, who were sharing a chillum. Kaya was in a reflective mood. 'Krishna could accept everything because his love was so vast. It could contain and reconcile all differences,' she thought. Kaya found it strange that hardened gossip lovers and soap opera watchers in the city were now glued to bedtime stories from the unfathomable past of human civilization.

Keshav seemed to have read Kaya's mind. He said, 'Listen to this story before you retire for the night.'

'A young boy studied in a village school a few miles away

from his home. Every day he had to go through a thick forest to reach his school. His mother was a simple woman and a devotee of Krishna. She would not begin her day without chanting the name of Madhusudhan, one of Krishna's many names. Among his many heroic feats in his lifetime, Krishna slayed a demon called Madhu who tormented his people. That is why he was called Madhusudhan. Then, she would diligently drop her son to school and bring him back every day.

'One day, the mother fell sick and was unable to accompany the boy to school. With her eyes filled with tears, she urged her young son to go to school by himself that day. Before seeing her son off at the door, she said, "Remember to shout the name of Madhusudhan dada in case you are scared. He will be there to help you."

'The mother knew that Madhusudhan was not a person but a name that she had repeated a million times in prayer. It was just a proxy name to give the child some confidence as he would be on a long and lonely journey to the school. The boy set off on his journey through the forest. As the woods became thicker and darker, his heart began to throb with fear. He heard a shuffle of feet in the dense foliage.

'"Was that a tiger crouching somewhere near me?" The boy was scared. His pulse was racing like that of a deer being hounded by a hunter. He ran and cried out, "Madhusudhan dada!" as he remembered his mother's instruction.

'The innocent child did not know that Madhusudhan was just another name for Krishna. He thought Madhusudhan was an acquaintance of his mother living in the jungle. In his sheer innocence, he believed that Madhusudhan would soon appear. He was relieved to see that a tall and dark body emerged from behind a thick aswattha tree and smiled at him. He then patted the young boy's back, held his hand and dropped him to the school. The boy bid him goodbye as he safely reached the classroom.

'That day when he returned home, the boy's mother asked him if he was scared while travelling alone. "Yes, I was for a while. So I called Madhusudhan dada as you had instructed and he appeared as I had expected."

'"What!" The mother couldn't believe what she had heard. She did not know anybody called Madhusudhan. She just mentioned Krishna's name so that her son would be comforted. A thrill ran through her spine. Her son had accepted Krishna in reality. It was his faith in Madhusudhan dada that made Krishna appear in the forest!'

'Does Krishna really still appear in person thousands of years after his death?' Kaya asked, still unable to come to grips with the mystery.

Keshav peered into the dark of the night and said, 'If he was never born, what makes you think that he had ever died?'

'Just as he appeared then, he appears now whenever he is called with love. Krishna accepts everything in his infinite embrace of love.'

Keshav recalled those lines of Krishna that he had read in the Gita: 'In all your thoughts and actions, just accept me. I shall protect you. In such devotional love, you will be fully conscious of me! You will pass over all the obstacles of conditional life by my grace.'

They walked silently on the pebbled pathway of the ashram, meandering through the indistinct shapes formed by the trees, watching the moonlight rippling on a waterbed at the edge of the river.

INDUS CAMPUS, LUCKNOW, 1999
A BUSINESS SCHOOL COURSE CALLED LOVE

The distance between the teacher and the student is bridged when they learn to accept each other as whole persons. Teaching then becomes a joyful act of love rather than a chore or duty.

Walking in the rain with him, his students in Indus would let Keshav's radical ideas sink in. When his class got over, they would drop by at his home for snacks and coffee which they would brew in his generously stuffed kitchen. However, Keshav's living room-cum-study was actually the place to see. It was more like a couch, table and bed attached to a bookstore. The books were arranged on the basis of the shape and colour of the book covers, and not according to the titles.

'I remember a book by its colour more than I remember it by its title,' he said with self-deprecating laughter when a student quizzed him about his quirky way of organizing books.

There would be books tucked away in his kitchen and neatly arranged above his toilet seat. A copy of *The Practice of Management* would be rubbing shoulders with *Man's Search for Meaning* and *A Brief History of Time*. He would ponder over the mystery of the black hole. With the intricate interplay of his index finger and his thumb, he would explain the concepts of space and time. Small groups of students in his study would hold animated, quicksilver conversations over a cup of tea served in earthenware cups.

Students, to the best of their knowledge, were of the opinion that Keshav was not married. He deferred questions about his marital status saying his life was a series of experiments. He alluded to the difficulty of finding a partner who would voluntarily suffer the idiosyncrasies of his creative and somewhat unpredictable life. He would mostly avoid questions about his personal life.

Those who had known him for a long time closely testified that Keshav had mellowed considerably over the years. In the fervour of his youth, he was insensitive in the way he spoke of women and had a sharp tongue. He was vocal about his dislike for buck teeth, an obtuse nose, or puffy cheeks. Now, he was less hostile to girls with dopey eyes or even those munching potato chips very audibly in his class. He remarked to a girl in class, rather cordially, 'You can eat those chips gently without those crackling sounds, please.' He would accept women as they were. As he entered his thirties, things that would have earlier made him mad, such as veganism or feminism, were met with a tenderness that reflected a broad mind and an open heart. In short, Keshav had transformed like an Alphonso mango, which is sour in its early phases but becomes sweet and delicious once it's ripe.

One day, while the enrolment for the postgraduate programme courses was going on, Keshav received a note from the Programme Office. A record 120 students had enrolled for his elective course, 'Leadership of Voluntary Enterprises' (LOVE). Surprisingly, among those enrolled was an American business school student, Kaya Johnson!

Keshav's mind whirled back to his days in Boston and New York and froze in one of his undergraduate classes. 'That was another life.' He smiled as he looked at the backyard through the window.

The wicket gate leading to the vast wheat field behind his house was thrown open by a gust of wind. A bolt of lightning quivered in silver streaks! A mass of swollen clouds was aching to pour their hearts out in silver lines of rain.

KAYA JOHNSON VISITS INDIA

Kaya Johnson was preparing to board a flight at Logan Airport in Boston. She was wearing a blue cardigan and a pair of faded jeans. Her blonde hair was drawn back and there was a spark in her eyes. There was a sharp edge to her looks that drew instant attention. She called for a porter, smiling, revealing her gleaming white teeth. Her heart was pounding with a delicious tension. This was her first journey to India, a place she had always dreamt of visiting at least once in her lifetime.

Kaya was not a light traveller. Her two hugely stuffed pieces of soft luggage were bursting at the seams. She hoped that the contents of those purple suitcases would see her through the few months she would spend in India.

The talkative porter, a dark man in his fifties with a crop of curly hair, came forward with his cart. She hired him to help her with the luggage.

'Jeeesus Christ!' he cried as he lifted her baggage on to his cart. 'These are like a tonne of bricks! What are you carrying to India?' He was blinking in utter disbelief behind his horn-rimmed glasses.

'Largely books.' She smiled.

The porter accepted the tip graciously after he uploaded the bags again on the check-in desk. He did not fail to notice a copy of *The Autobiography of a Yogi* that was peeping out of her green leather carry-on bag. Furrowing his forehead he said, 'Interesting book. I read that one during our happy, hippie days. You can also read the biography of Srila Prabhupada. Amazing stuff!'

Kaya was looking out of the window of the plane that was now cruising over the Atlantic. A shaft of sunlight shining through the half-blinded window cast a soft light on her eyebrows, her slender neck, her sloping shoulders and her high cheekbones. She was watching the patterns of clouds below. She raised her eyelids slowly and noticed the smoky outlines of the clouds shifting shape across the sky. An unnamed yearning was burning like an incandescent fire in her heart. The weather was clear. A few high clouds like fluffy cotton balls with delicate golden edges floated by. With *The Autobiography of a Yogi* on her lap, Kaya dozed off and dreamt of the unknown land she was about to visit.

The two stopover flights that connected Kaya from Logan Airport to Lucknow in India only helped her bridge a physical space. Mentally she was already roaming around in Keshav's country.

THE INDUCTION

The director of Indus, Jaswant Lal Bal, stepped into the auditorium with his trademark swagger. Before his arrival on the stage, the programme announcer, a short, stout lady wearing pencil heels, warmed up the air with an eloquent description of the director's many accomplishments.

The director was the chief executive officer of Indus. He was the man who had the power to instantly irritate anyone on the campus. His inner circle comprised one of the two deans, a handful of faculty members, and some employees from the administrative department. His outer circle had a large circumference of critics consisting of staff, students and faculty. In general, the faculty were considered his natural enemies.

Most of the faculty at Indus were hard-pressed to put up with the director's insufferable airs and monotonous speeches. Director Bal's twisted way of communicating a point earned him the unofficial title of 'Jalebi'. This was a juicy nickname culled out of the first three letters of his official name, JLB. The two deans, Professor Nataraj Nandy and Professor Dimple Damle, were seated on the dais flanking the director's chair on each side. They stared at him with their necks slanted at appropriate angles towards his left and right demonstrating fake obedience and pretentious listening skills. Jalebi got up from the centre chair with a sharp click of his ageing knees and dragged his legs towards the podium. His speech, as usual, began with, 'When I was in London...' The deans opened their mouths in slow motion as though they had a lollypop in their mouth. Suggestive nods and elbow jabs of recognition swept the large auditorium that was full of freshers at the induction programme.

'Director Bal was planning to cut down on the consumption of complimentary food and beverages given to the staff and faculty of Indus!' Professor Malhotra blurted out.

What!' Professor Chakru squeaked in surprise.

'Oh yes!' whispered Malhotra. 'Jalebi had calculated that the faculty had consumed cashew nuts worth ₹11,059 and 1,131 cups of tea at the cost of the institute in the faculty tea club. That's too much consumption of tea and snacks given the faculty's cost compared to performance for the month. This is what Jalebi had remarked pointedly to the chief accounts officer. I noticed that the accounts guy was struggling to decide what face he should put on before the director. He did not know whether to express sorrow or surprise at the faculty's conspicuous consumption rate. Finally, the director had decided, in his own wisdom, that the institute will only subsidize one cup of tea per faculty per day. The rest they would have to pay out of their own pockets. And cashews would be downgraded to peanuts!'

'How mean!' cried out Sangma, the librarian, who was eavesdropping on the conversation from behind.

'Not only that,' Malhotra lowered his voice to a conspiratorial undertone, 'Jalebi was ordering closed circuit televisions to be installed in all strategic locations, including the tea club. He wanted to spy on all the campus gossip that was supposed to be brewing around the tea club.'

Professor Chakru reminded Keshav about those lines of the Bhagavad Gita:

The demonic hold distorted views on everything...

Director Jalebi was shuffling the pages of his speech and thumping the podium with his clenched fist. He was urging the new students to behave like managers of their own future: 'Discipline, decorum and die-hard competitiveness. Those three Ds are the foundation for achievers. That's the culture of Indus we wish to preserve!'

Dean Nataraj was shifting his buttocks from the edge of the chair to the back. Keshav was looking at a lizard policing the ceiling of the auditorium. It was inching in a jerky motion towards an insect that held the prospect of a nice dinner.

Jalebi turned the tenth page of his speech. His eyes glazed over as he shuffled the pages. He looked at the dimly lit auditorium. Unable to make eye contact with his audience, he was speaking alternately to the two heads of the microphones raised on the podium. 'What you cannot measure, you cannot manage. Get the measure of everything you see around you. Leave nothing to chance...'

It was then that the lizard in its greed to gobble its prey slipped and fell with a plop from the ceiling on to the programme announcer's shoulder. The scared announcer, standing precariously on her pencil heels, thrust herself forward and held on to Director Jalebi's shirt to balance herself. The director pulled away from the podium with a shriek, his notes scattering in all directions. The announcer fell forward in what looked like a sliding football tackle towards the director.

Dean Dimple Damle was seen chewing the edge of her handkerchief trying to suppress her laughter. The students sensing mischief burst into an uproar. Dean Nataraj got busy doing damage control, gesturing to the students to be quiet. In between, he was stooping to help Director Jalebi pick up the notes.

Appearing rather unsettled, Director Jalebi cut short his speech. His concluding words, spoken incoherently, were an assertion of no-nonsense professionalism. It was also about holding on to the tradition of Indus against all odds. The two deans then spoke, one after the other. They were rambling about rules, rituals and campus protocols. This was followed by a question-and-answer session with the post-graduate programme chairperson and Dean Dimple Damle.

Professor Malhotra was heard saying sarcastically to a colleague, 'Dimple had destroyed the morale of the entire PGP class last year single-handedly by insisting on 90 per cent compulsory attendance!'

The induction programme ended with the playing of the national anthem.

The PGP students spilled out of the auditorium. Their foreheads were greasy with perspiration. They were eyeing the pyramids of samosa and potato chaat masala simmering over hissing gas burners in the snack counters outside the auditorium. While the students stuffed samosas into their mouths, the faculty went into a huddle trying to decipher the meaning of Director Jalebi's concluding comments on 'professionalism'.

Indus was designed to be a faculty-led institute with all the previous directors playing second fiddle to the professors whose academic credentials and achievements were so strong that they were viewed as connoisseurs of their field. The faculty was supreme in deciding on course curriculum, school discipline and students' affairs. However, Jalebi, the control freak and efficiency maniac that he was known to be, was inventing ways to destroy the liberal culture of Indus. The faculty seemed more worried about Dean Nataraj Nandy than they were about Dean Dimple. Dimple was flippant and predictable in her manners. Nandy was the silent operator who spied on the faculty in their unguarded moments and leaked their intimate secrets to the director.

The faculty exited the auditorium. Turning back, Professor Chakru observed Nataraj Nandy cosying up to the director in his sly, foxy way. The director was leaning against the chair and whispering something into his ear with his smug, all-knowing smile, as though he had just defused a live bomb.

∽

The Indus classrooms had swivel chairs. The desks had name tags attached to them to confine each learner's soul to a single seat for the entire year.

Professor Erol T. Sequerra, better known in the business school as Professor Et Cetera, had just finished his Business Strategy class. He was slightly built and had hairy arms and a sharp metallic voice. Sequerra could talk vacuously on any subject under the sun. At times, he made frightening attempts to tell a poorly rehearsed joke.

At the end of an excruciatingly boring ninety minutes, Manas said, 'A sleeping pill can put a man to sleep, a good mother can put a couple of kids to sleep but a professor of strategy like that can put a whole nation to sleep.'

Manas always came up with a cynical comment bordering on the funny. Swamy backed him up with a flurry of breathless expressions. 'You are right, Manas...without a speck of doubt, an iota of disbelief, a morsel of suspicion or even a fraction of falsehood!'

Swamy had a way with words and spoke in an effeminate voice. He rolled his eyes, leaned forward and embellished each word he spoke with elaborate hand gestures.

On the very first day of class, Sequerra would parade his academic degrees like a peacock stretching all its feathers—B.Tech, MA (Oxon) DIOP, DDG, DIP IN PPM, PhD ending with the word 'etc.' Those last few letters became his identity—a tribute to his numerous fuzzy qualifications.

Professor Chakru taught a popular course called Philosophy of Management. Something he said in class made a lot of sense to Neel: 'If you assume that your students are inherently lazy, stubborn and unmotivated, you are likely to see more of them. On the contrary, if you hold a view that they are hard-working, diligent and enthusiastic, they will turn out to be so. The same holds true for manager-employee relationships.'

Manas could not agree more on this. So, he made it a point to compliment Professor Chakru at the end of his class.

After class, there was always some gossip brewing in Kamal Dhaba, adjacent to the shopping centre in the campus. Near the coffee machine installed in the dhaba you would get free, freshly brewed stories about what happened in the classroom. This was a place to let your hair down, to crib about rotten mess food and to figure out who was making out with whom.

Sardar, an unapologetic foodie, said, 'The food in the main mess obeys the law of marginal utility that you study in Economics: the more you have, the less you want to have.' Sardar had just touched a raw nerve that opened up a floodgate of complaints.

Neel, who was busy tossing away a burnt brinjal off his plate, said, 'The mess cooks don't know the difference between stir-fried vegetables and vegetables that are butchered and cremated.' Eva giggled graciously as her eyelashes fluttered rhythmically in assent.

'Yeah, yeah. Hundred upon hundred!' grunted Prasad rubbing off coffee cream from his half-inch-long moustache. Prasad was desperate to improve his conversational English that had a rather false foundation in a municipal school in his village.

Sardar and Prasad were the perfect examples of contrast. Sardar was six feet, two inches tall. He had a wrought-iron body and an oblong face of which 65 per cent was covered by a forest of facial hair. The guy would always look over his shoulder, to the left and then to the right, worried that someone might overtake him. Sardar suffered from a perennial fear of being overtaken.

Prasad on the other hand was round—barely five feet, a rolling ball of flesh. He never had a beard or hair on his chest. Neel referred to him as maku, a term imported from Bengal, to describe a boy with no facial hair.

Eva Reddy was an attractive Andhra beauty—dusky, long-haired, full lips with a prominent pout. Eva's face had the liquid mobility of a trained Bharatanatyam dancer. She laughed economically even as she flung a sidelong glance at Neel. They were all guarded in their behaviour. Most of these business school students were trained like that. Their steps were measured, emotions held in check, they spoke in low husky voices and fussed over placement packages. Neel was thinking how this business school was sowing the seeds of competitive success. A success that was like a bottle of sparkling cola—frothy and instantly stimulating, with a bittersweet aftertaste.

He reckoned that a mind caught in this competitive frenzy could not appreciate the present moment with all its intensity and beauty. A mind caught in the vortex of ruthless careerism had forgotten to care. Such a mind sought relief from its conflicts, boredom and stress in the pursuit of trivia, one-upmanship and alcohol. The school taught you that statistics, however cold, swayed minds. And that speed and greed won the day.

What the business school generally did not teach, however, was that unrequited love was the basis of all human perversions—love twisted, tortured and mangled to fit into one's ego space. It was the same love that exalted the human being, enabled him to rise above the mundane, and helped to humanize an animal. Now, that love was used as an instrument of production: transforming a man into a slot machine.

Neel kept thinking how the whole class was struggling to fit into a mould of sorts. We have to change and strive constantly just to be where we are—like monkeys moving up and down a grease pole.

He thought of one more thing, but forgot what that was—until he saw Kaya Johnson walking alone to her hostel.

5
Affection

RISHIKESH, TUESDAY, MORNING
DAY 2 OF THE RETREAT

A column of sunshine was breaking through the vast banyan tree in searching, sensuous spirals.

Keshav's voice rang like a bell: 'Love creates an alchemy of attention and affection. It attracts everything to itself: capturing attention and evoking affection. Both intellect and emotion come under its sway.

'When a teacher tells a student "Learn by heart", he is simply trying to say "Find the centre of your attention in your heart". Similarly, when a lover says "I want to hold your hand" to her beloved for the first time, her heart is conveying the affectionate ferment of the first crush.'

Eva nodded vigorously as the talk went on. She was inhaling the sweet fragrance of sandalwood wafting out of an agarbatti.

'Love pulls the delicate strings of the heart. Affection carries the pulse of a throbbing heart through our veins and arteries. It is like the sap flow system that nurtures the many branches of a banyan tree. Some seeds of the banyan tree, carried by winged creatures, land on its tender parts. These tender parts develop roots descending to the ground. These prop roots can develop to be as large as the original trunk, which makes it hard to recognize the main trunk from the new one.

'If this banyan tree of love loses a delicate branch to a storm, it feels the loss. But the tree of love soon recovers and channels its sap of affection through another living branch that can make up for the absence of the missing one.

'Such was Yashoda's love for her foster son Krishna. She lost her own daughter Yogamaya to Devaki to hide Krishna and protect him from Kamsa's wrath. Little Krishna was now the sole centre of her affection.'

Keshav then urged the storyteller to share the tale of mother Yashoda's affection for her foster child. While the stories were being told, Keshav listened with his eyes shut. He became deeply immersed in the characters, as though it was his own story that was being told.

> Krishna remembered his growing up years in Gokul in the lap of his mother, Yashoda. A mother's love is like your own breath—it can neither be remembered nor forgotten. It sits there, subtle and untraceable, like your own being. The absence of her own child made Yashoda pour all her affection on Kanha—that was her pet name for Krishna.
>
> Her Kanha was a consummate prankster whether he was crawling, standing or walking about. He would slip into the homes of the gopis and create chaos in the lives of those unsuspecting milkmaids. When the gopis scolded him for his mischief, he would disarm and charm them with his innocent smile. He would go one step further and steal whole pots of butter from their homes. He would give some butter to his cronies and also feed some wild monkeys with it. If it caught his fancy, he would untie the cows tethered in the cowsheds and set them free.

That day, Yashoda was looking for Kanha, who she knew was up to some new mischief. She called out in a voice that trailed off into the distance. 'Kanha...where are you, Kanhaaaa?'

Hearing this, a bunch of boys ran towards Yashoda and complained that Kanha was not only rolling in the dust but had also put some mud in his mouth. Anxious, Yashoda ran to see what had happened. She asked, 'Kanha, what am I hearing? Did you eat mud?'

Krishna pressed his lips tightly together as though sealing a deep secret.

Yashoda raised her voice and asked again, 'Did you eat mud or not?'

Kanha shook his head sideways as if he was saying 'no'.

Yashoda turned to Balarama and asked if Kanha was telling the truth.

'No!' Balarama swore. 'Kanha had actually eaten mud. I saw it with my own eyes.'

Exasperated, Yashoda asked Kanha, 'Open your mouth and show me what is inside!'

Reluctant to obey, Kanha firmly pressed his lips and made a noise. 'Mmmmmmm.' Finally, he relented and opened his mouth. Yashoda could not have imagined in the wildest of her dreams what she saw...

'What did she see there?' asked Kaya, unable to contain her curiosity any more. She was clutching on to Anju's dupatta in anticipation.

The audience waited eagerly for the storyteller to break the suspense and continue with his narration.

Yashoda peeped in and she saw the entire universe going around in a swirl inside that tiny little mouth. She saw the stretch of infinite space, the five elements, the sun, moon, planets, stars and galaxies. Strangely, she also saw the entire village of Vraja and she saw herself standing there peering into the mouth of Kanha. There were many worlds unfolding simultaneously inside his mouth. She saw all the living beings on the planet, all the gross and subtle qualities of material and spiritual nature. She perceived the ego and its manifestation, the five senses and the object of the senses. In short, she saw the entire cosmos in manifestation. All of it inside that child's mouth!

'O Kanha,' Yashoda cried out, 'have I lost my mind? Why is this happening to me?' Her head was spinning like a whirling top. She began to speculate on the divine nature of her child and the power of his play to create an illusory universe. She was confused and confounded.

'Is this real or am I just deluded?' she said.

Seeing his mother on the brink of despair, Kanha shut his mouth. In a few moments when Yashoda came back to her normal state, this bizarre vision was erased from her memory. She felt like someone who lost a dream after waking up.

'What have you been stuffing into your mouth, you terrible brat?' Yashoda said. It seemed that she had forgotten all that she had just seen. She hugged and caressed her Kanha, pouring all her maternal affection as she took him indoors.

Balarama and the boys, expecting to watch Krishna get a thorough spanking for his mischief, were now surprised to see his mother doting on him.

At the end of the story, the mystery surrounding the world's oldest classroom became even more mysterious.

Kaya, who had been transported to another world, asked, 'What did Yashoda actually see? Or did she lose her mind completely? Why was she fearful of what she saw?'

'Can I have my dupatta as well as my own hand back, Kaya?' Anju urged as she saw Kaya had pulled away her dupatta and was now clutching her hand as she was totally lost in the story.

Keshav took a few more seconds to weigh the question before he responded. 'Krishna reveals the face of reality that we mortals often fail to see. Our existence is woven in an infinite web of cosmic order. Our little lives are just a point of view—a narrow perspective of one infinitude that seamlessly stretches through us, inside us and outside us. What we see with our ordinary senses is a fraction of that infinite order. We are but tiny little sparks of a great bonfire.'

Keshav drew Kaya's attention to the point he was about to make. She felt his intense and searching eyes on her.

'Kaya, think of a man climbing this hill town of Rishikesh. He cannot see the whole town as well as the river and the valley below from his narrow perspective. However, if he were to stand on the hilltop, the whole vista would appear before his eyes in a flash. Isn't it? Yashoda had a momentary glimpse of this hilltop view of the universe.' Keshav chuckled.

'But, why did Yashoda experience fear when she saw the cosmic vision?' Kaya asked.

Keshav said, 'We are attached to our past experiences of the known world. We fear letting go of the known images when the unknown and the unseen visit us.

'Our fears are not caused by the world as it is. What causes fear is living inside our heads. This mental world with its egotistic walls creates the division between "you" and "I"; between the past and the future; between the part and the whole.

'Yashoda had a glimpse of the universe beyond the partitions of the ego. She saw the face of infinite reality inside Kanha's mouth. For Kanha, in all his innocence, mud eating is not bad behaviour but earthly play. His little mouth is not just an orifice of the body but an integral part of a dimensionless space. In this endless space, asteroids and atoms swim around. This space is where the infinite and the infinitesimal spin in their orbits. It is here that the endless chain of karma, the laws of cause and effect play out.'

He laughed loudly and added, 'In business school, they would call it the big picture.'

Kaya was bemused. She was about to say something to Anju but ended up giving her a high five instead.

Keshav said, 'If you wish to see the big picture, just be aware of your cup of tea during today's tea break. What you drink as tea is nothing but photons of light and heat falling on green tea leaves turning them brown. When boiled with water and fire, the brown tea leaves produce a dark brown liquid concoction. You mix a white fluid with that concoction. That white fluid was produced by a black cow eating green grass. We call it milk.' Someone in the audience burst into laughter. 'The dark brown liquid tea now turns light brown with the addition of milk. Then, you draw the sap of the earth through a natural pump called sugarcane. The crystallized sap now becomes a sugar cube. When you stir the sugar in your cup of tea, do you realize what you are doing? You are stirring the five elements—air, water, fire, earth and space—into a cosmic conspiracy called "chai" or "tea". That's what the big picture of a cup of tea is all about.'

Keshav was a born teacher. He unmasked the deepest mysteries of life ever so effortlessly.

Then, referring to Yashoda, he said, 'After that extraordinary vision that affected her whole being, Yashoda returned to the rut of humdrum life. The living universe inside Kanha's mouth turned out to be just what ordinary senses would see as filthy mud. When Kanha denied having put mud inside his mouth, he wasn't exactly lying. The child of divinity was experiencing the mystery of the universe, not mud. Like the English poet William Blake put it so beautifully:

> *To see a world in a grain of sand*
> *And a heaven in a wild flower*
> *Hold infinity in the palm of your hand*
> *And eternity in an hour...*

'In Kanha's universe, there was no inside or outside, no mind-made divisions of inner or outer. He was living in a universe of non-duality. The ancient teachers of India had a beautiful expression for it: Ekam eva advitiyam Brahma—the one undivided awareness of the creator without a second.'

With these words, Keshav signalled that it was time for a tea break.

Walking towards the canteen, Kaya chuckled as she muttered to herself, 'This time a cup of tea will feel like the kiss of the cosmos.'

INDUS CAMPUS, LUCKNOW, YOGA ROOM
WHEN NEEL MEETS KAYA IN THE COBRA POSTURE

Neel looked at his face in the mirror and thought, 'Is this the face Kaya was looking at when we faced each other bent in the cobra posture?'

It was not so impressive a face. The eyelids were puffed up; the left cheek was unshaven in patches. A face that may have become more twisted by the exertions in that reptilian pose in the yoga class. It was a face that would at best evoke amusement, not romance.

He remembered Kaya's laughter ringing behind him as he turned to assume his yoga posture. Neel's train of thought worried him. He stood on his toes and put on a lost look so that he would appear taller and more vulnerable in Kaya's eyes.

'Vulnerability brings out a woman's maternal instincts and

evokes empathy,' he thought.

Neel somehow put on a sad half-smile that would make him appear as the underdog. He then gazed at his own image in the mirror. At five feet seven inches, he suspected he would be considered short by American standards. His faint smile barely reached his eyes. Yet, he felt this thrill of experiencing a shared strangeness with a woman so utterly beautiful.

Everyone knew that Kaya Johnson from the US was visiting the school in India mid-year as a foreign exchange student in the two-year MBA programme. She took the campus by storm. Her arrival upset the pecking order of the desirability of female students in Indus. Her complexion, a sonorous voice and blonde hair threatened to derange almost the entire male population in her class. Twirling their handkerchiefs on their fingers, the girls in class spied on her to look for the not-so-obvious manufacturing defects in her tall frame so that some sanity would be restored in their lives. They found none except a little mole on her face and the dance of arrogance in her eyes. Kaya Johnson never had to ask any male member to accompany her anywhere in the campus. There was always someone in the mess plotting to find an excuse to sit next to her. Even the most unchivalrous second year boys were opening the door for her in the library and the otherwise indifferent campus staff were flinging hi's and hello's with awkward gestures and postures.

Neel liked everything about Kaya. Well, nearly everything! He liked her hair, neatly tied in a ponytail; her beetroot-red lips and perfect oval face; the Cindy Crawford mole on the edge of her upper lip; and a smile that was as sharp as a 7 o'clock shaving blade.

In a poetic frame of mind, Neel wrote a confession in his diary. 'She crept into my heart like the sunrise.'

Neel was lucky to meet Kaya in the optional yoga class that they both took as part of the business school's wellness programme for stressed students. They first made eye contact in that cobra posture—head up, torso stretched. He had never seen green eyes so closely until that day. With those eyes flashing, she checked him out visually.

This yoga class was a required activity in the programme for all international students. The Indian students who voluntarily attended said that this worked well for them too. What was not so obvious was that the Indians were beginning to rediscover the subtler art of yoga through blue, green and brown Western eyes!

The enthusiastic students were in the process of settling down. Yoga master Usman shot out his instructions like bullet points. 'No talking, only stretching. Embrace the pain in your joints—the pain is nothing but your knee joints saying hello to you!'

A collective groan swept the yoga room.

'Pin-drop silence, please!' Usman warned. 'Observe how this posture stretches your abdomen—good for digestion!'

Everyone in the class was grim-faced in forced attention. That was when it happened. Sardar, with his abdomen stretched like that of a fat ox, puffed up with a heavy snack, pierced the silence with a prolonged burp lasting almost a quarter of a minute: 'aggggrrrrrrrrrrrrrrrrrrrrrrr!'

Giggles! Frowns! Uproar!

Usman tried in vain to restore control in the classroom. 'This is one of the unintended benefits of this posture— elimination of excess air through all available passages.'

A couple of international students rolled over on their mats unable to contain their laughter. Prasad and Eva nearly collapsed against each other laughing.

Neel surveyed Kaya's face to see what effect that dramatic event would have had on her. He saw her smile. Just a half-smile that took a full toll on his heart. He noticed her slightly uneven teeth and a faint wrinkle at the edge of her lips as she struggled to keep up an appearance. Neel's eyes froze on her timelessly.

It dawned on Neel that love is the electricity that sparks off the moment one moves beyond the first impressions of forms and shapes. Love is the elemental union that is achieved when one accepts the other completely, warts and all.

That evening Neel added a few more lines in his diary:

The sensuous asymmetry of her teeth
The unexplored mystery of gold, blonde hair

By some strange alchemy, a tedious yoga class turned out to be more acceptable for Neel—a thing to savour in the future.

AFFECTION GROWS WITH THE FIRST RAIN OF THE SEASON

It rained that morning. There is something about the rain that makes the heart leap out like a grasshopper. When it pours down, the sky mates with the earth. Frogs frolic, insects chirp, and wild mushrooms spring to life. The simmering sound of wet earth is the stuff that love and longing are made of.

Kaya asked Neel to hold her hand as they negotiated the slush on the slippery mud road beside the Godavari Hostel. Drops of water trickled down like rivulets over her face. Her hair was dishevelled. Kaya noticed that Neel's white shirt was wet from the rain and it was clinging to his body. The space between them was charged with anticipation. Neel felt her warm breath on his face as she turned to thank him. He could distinctly smell her sensuous perfume infused with the aroma of exotic spices. She planted a soft kiss on his unshaven cheek, leaving a faint lip mark. It was his unexpected reward.

Kaya's feather-light peck on the cheek had Neel's face flaming. That gentle kiss felt like an electric current. A thrill crept down his spine. Neel wanted to sing, but his passion seemed to have choked his vocal cords. He was awash with pleasure and he felt Kaya everywhere—seeping through the raindrops; sprouting inside a new leaf; in the chorus of insects.

Love infuses everything in nature with a golden haze. At that moment, even if Neel had seen a dead gecko in his mess food, he would have forgiven the cook with a benign smile.

They had walked from the hostel to the library under a single umbrella. Neel's hand occasionally brushed Kaya's arm and her shoulder. When two human beings begin to affect each other, nature too strives to close the distance between them. Love's magic was turning two rain-soaked bodies into magnets of attraction.

The walk from the hostel to the library, a few hundred metres, seemed a little too short for Neel. 'What was Kaya thinking?'

She was thinking of the yoga class precisely when Neel was fantasizing about her. Kaya confessed later that she woke up in the middle of the night, remembering the yoga class incident of Neel watching her in the cobra posture and Sardar's explosive burping. She doubled up and laughed until her stomach ached!

Neel recalled their first conversation, the way Kaya had introduced herself without a trace of self-consciousness.

'My name is Kaya Johnson, and yours?'

'I'm Neel Kamal Ray. You can call me Neel if you like.'

She wore a playful floral fragrance that carried subtle notes of jasmine, strawberry and sandalwood. Neel thought that his nose and the million olfactory cells inside him were designed precisely to savour that exotic perfume.

'That name, Neel Kamal, rocks!' she said, rolling the 'r' ever so tantalizingly on her tongue like a true-blue American. She stole a glance at his features from beneath the veil of her lightly fluttering eyelashes. How eager he was to win the admiration of those eyes!

Kaya remarked that the one-day stubble on his cheeks made his face look more attractive than he thought it did. Neel detected faint sparks of affection. Their initial encounter held the promise of a full-blown campus romance.

RISHIKESH ASHRAM, DAY 2
POST-TEA BREAK

The storyteller was narrating another story of Yashoda and Kanha, continuing from where he had left off in the morning.

> An angry Yashoda was hell-bent on punishing Kanha. His acts of mischief had become too much for her. One day, she was breastfeeding him and savouring her motherly love for her child. As luck would have it, at the same time, a pot of milk was boiling over on a stove in her kitchen. Yashoda put baby Kanha aside and ran to prevent the boiling milk from spilling over. Left unattended and unfed, Krishna was angry. He clenched his lips tightly. He gave vent to his anger by picking up a piece of stone and hurling it at an earthen pot of yogurt that was hanging on a rope.
>
> When Yashoda came back, she saw that there were broken pieces of the pot and some yogurt spilt on the floor. She was beside herself with anger. Her nostrils flared up and beads of perspiration appeared on her soft, comely face. She picked up a stick to scare Kanha before he could think of unleashing his next prank.
>
> To her horror, she now saw Kanha seated on an inverted wooden mortar. He was quietly extracting butter from a pot that was hanging from a swing on the ceiling. Yashoda crept towards the child from behind to catch hold of him. Sensing capture, Kanha ran ahead dashing his mother's hope of capturing him red-handed.

Yashoda went around in circles to get a grip on the brat. But Kanha was too fleet-footed and far too agile for his mother whose ageing knees were not up to the chase.

Yashoda sat down, panting heavily. The decorative flowers on her head had fallen. Streams of sweat ran down her forehead. Unable to inflict any more distress on his mother, Kanha finally let her catch hold of him. Seeing him restless to escape again, she decided to tie him up with a rope as that was the only way she could arrest his next naughty move. She found a rope to tie him up, but the rope fell short by two fingers while she was tying the final knot. Yashoda looked for an additional piece of rope. To her surprise, this rope too fell short by two fingers. Even after she had connected all the ropes available in the house, the final knot was still short by two fingers!

She couldn't believe what she was experiencing.

Yashoda was tired and frustrated beyond endurance. The gopis, watching the mother and child's cat-and-mouse chase, were engrossed in the rollicking fun. Yashoda looked at her son and went down on her knees, almost begging him to agree to be tied. The lord of love, seeing his mother's plight through the innocent eyes of a child, finally relented. He offered himself to be bound by his mother's love.

The storytelling was over. Keshav had already arrived wearing a flowing maroon kurta and it was time for the customary question-and-answer or Q&A session. Keshav preferred to call it the question-and-question (Q&Q) session. He believed that all learning was about generating and asking better questions.

'Why does a mother's love become a bondage for the child?' asked Anju, who was thinking of her own growing-up years at home.

Keshav looked at the charcoal-dark clouds that were slowly swelling in the shape of a huge black elephant. They held the prospect of imminent rain. He said, 'Love does not bind. What binds us are affection and attachments. They are the physical and mental boundaries that confine love, as though it was exclusive. You can try to part the water in this flowing stream of the Ganga in front of you with a long stick in the middle of the stream. Yet the water trickling past both sides of the stick cannot be separated. They will soon merge with one another and lose their exclusivity. The nature of love is like that flowing stream.'

'Are the boundaries of love real or are they illusory?' asked Kaya.

Keshav said, 'Look, all the boundaries around love change over time. Even the water in the sap of a tree is not permanently bound. Soon the tree will dry up in the heat of summer and the water inside it will evaporate. The water in the sap is connected to the water vapour in the environment by the law of love. Love connects diverse appearances of form and phenomenon into the unity of existence.

'Affection creates transient boundaries around love. The difference between being free and being bound, between love and affection, is merely a matter of perception. These are boundaries we create inside our heads. So, how does one get rid of this illusory boundary then?

'The best way to break the illusion of boundaries inside your head is to spend some time in nature. Our rishis, the lineage of teachers of this ashram, did all their research in the lap of nature. They discovered that in nature everything was connected to everything else by a boundary-less intelligence. They found, on deeper investigation, that this intelligence was nothing but love. They discovered the presence of this intelligence in what they described as the cave of the human heart. Just as crystalline water comes from the cave of a mountain, a pure heart is the source of unconditional love.'

'What was significant about Yashoda's struggle with the rope that was always falling short?' Anju asked.

An aircraft was passing overhead making a swooping noise. Keshav fell silent allowing the plane to pass. Kaya wondered how this gathering in Rishikesh would look like if seen through the window seat of a plane. Seen from that window up in the sky, most of the human interaction and those petty voices of separate individuals would lose their definitions.

Keshav's voice was audible now. 'Yashoda's wish was to bind Krishna with the ropes of affection. Ironically, she fell short of Krishna's boundless love by the measure of two fingers. Two symbolizes duality. It is a binary measure. An either-or universe. You are either bound or free. You either like or dislike. Yashoda was a prisoner of her own perception of duality. For her, Kanha was just a naughty, cuddly kid who could be physically and emotionally bound. Yet, in reality, how can the boundless love of Krishna be bound by a rope? This is like trying to part the water of a river with a stick.

'The essence of Krishna is non-dual love. Such a love thrives on the oneness or is-ness of life... Love is an expression of the is-ness of our whole and undivided existence. You describe every phenomenon in the language of is-ness. You say things like this is and that is. It is raining. It is not raining any more. Everything in the universe is connected to this is-ness, which is a constant. The universe simply is, without exception. Everything that you can see in and around the ashram: the trees, the temple, the sky and the river exist in this all-embracing is-ness. You have to sense this is-ness behind every experience.

'Finally, when her Kanha volunteers to be physically bound by mother Yashoda, he still remains free in his awareness—his unbounded is-ness. You know what? Prison bars and prison doors do not make us prisoners. When we are unaware of our free nature, we become prisoners unto ourselves. Haven't you heard the story of the two people who were stuck in the same prison? One who was blind to his original nature saw the prison bars. The one who was aware had a glimpse of the distant twinkling stars!

'Krishna plays out the act of bondage like a character plays a role in a drama. The man playing the role of the imprisoned human in a theatre knows that it is just a role and he is a free man outside the boundary of his role. Krishna's perception is clear and non-dual. He is in the role of a bound kid, who is at the same time unbound in his awareness.'

When Keshav finished speaking, Eva had this flash of fear in her eyes. She asked earnestly, 'What is the process by which someone who is forever free gets bound in a body and mind as Krishna did. Isn't that suffocating?'

Keshav stroked his hair, revealing a smooth forehead without a wrinkle.

He said, 'The one who is always free only appears to be bound by three dimensions. It is like a cage with three walls: time, space and causation. Our usual life is a never-ending race with time. Eventually, time wins. A human being, the traveller of the infinite, becomes a prisoner of his mind's conception of time as past and future. Bound in time, he divides his life into many anxious moments. He thus steps out of the uninhibited grace of life and becomes a prisoner of his memory of the past and his desire for the future.

'The one born unbound appears to be bound in space too. In space, he is confined within a withering form of skin and bone. Guarded by the senses and enslaved by the five elements, he is bound in a prison of his own making. His essence, the love inside him, flutters like a caged bird. Ironically, he forgets temporarily that he is both the prisoner as well as the prison guard.

He forgets that he can set himself free in a jiffy if he truly recognizes that his body is merely his temporary address. He understands that his life does not come from a house of bones but from the infinite life itself. He can realize it only if his awareness is free from the ignorance of his true nature as a boundless life.

'Krishna teaches us that you are free from the bondage of time and space when your awareness, your seventh sense, dawns on you. You can be imprisoned in time and space only when you see yourself enslaved by the five senses, and the sixth sense of the mind.'

Kaya imagined that such wisdom could only come from an ancient world where there was once just land, water and open sky. This was a world ruled by the elements rather than passports.

There were just people rather than nationals. The space and time of the world were not determined by technology but by human imagination. People's vision was not restricted to tiny computer screens, but they would marvel in amazement at the vast, open spaces where time stood still. Wasn't that more like the world that Keshav was describing?

Keshav concluded, 'Finally, the boundless one becomes a prisoner of causation. The limitless mind gets stuck to the succession of cause and effect, the cycle of karma. Deceived by the illusory forces of maya, he begins to see himself as a lifelong chain of experiences and events. Causation is nothing but the never-ending procession of mind and matter. He forgets that matter is just a shape and mind merely a name he gives to his nameless and formless essence, that is, love. He sees his being as temporary waves of events rather than one infinite and timeless tide. When love becomes affected by time, space and causation, this is what happens: 'One who is born free, sadly, finds himself bound by the chains of his self-created illusions.'

EVENING SESSION

The storyteller in Rishikesh was reading out how Krishna stole the clothes of gopis.

Krishna closed his eyes, took a deep breath and lightly touched his bamboo flute with his lips. The flute was one with his breath. Krishna did not play the flute, he simply lived it. It was an intimate instrument for communicating his soul's delight to the universe. The trilling notes wafting from his flute spread miles from his forest hideout, Madhuvan. The gopis could not bring their minds to do anything else except imagine his face as they heard those soul-stirring sounds. The cows, caught in a trance, stopped grazing. Tufts of grass remained half-chewed in their mouths. The flowing river too seemed to have fallen in love with the flute song. The ripples crashing on the banks of the Yamuna quietened to a hypnotic lull. Even the breeze quivered and became still, as though enraptured by the music.

In Krishna's presence, the flute was like a magician's wand. The waves of sound it produced were the whispers of his soul. They penetrated the inner world of every element. Nothing in creation could resist its rhapsody.

The lovelorn gopis, in particular, were captivated by it. Spellbound, they would forget their everyday chores and tune into the sound that captivated the soul. They visualized Krishna's form, resplendent in his yellow silk dhoti, slowly fading away into the distance. Their physical senses, like the limbs of a tortoise, drew inwards and they entered into samadhi—a communion with their ecstatic innermost being.

The unmarried gopis of Vrindavan who were all besotted with Krishna, merely a seven-year-old boy, as their playmate were preparing to take a ritual bath in the Yamuna. They performed the austerity of bathing naked in the cold river to please Goddess Katyayani, who would give them the boon of the husbands they desired. The gopis huddled around the riverbank with garlands, incense, grains, lamps, twigs of plants and all other accessories. Holding one another's hands they sang, laying bare the closest secrets of their hearts. After removing all their clothes, they placed them on a heap at the turn of the river. Then, they dipped themselves in the flowing water to purify themselves. The clothes lay on the sand in a riot of colours—peacock green, turquoise blue and red like the beak of a parrot.

Tired of the gopis complaining about him stealing butter, Krishna was waiting for this opportunity to get even with them. He had graduated from stealing butter to stealing clothes. He collected all their garments in a bundle and climbed up high on the top branch of a kadamba tree. His cronies, the other boys of his gang, took up strategic positions on the lower branches to observe what was happening.

After taking their bath, when they came looking for their clothes, the gopis were at a loss to see them missing. Their eyes darted everywhere, but the clothes were nowhere to be found. It was then that a young gopi spotted Krishna perched on a treetop.

She pleaded, 'Krishna, we are your devotees. We will do whatever you say, but please do give our clothes back.'

'No problem,' Krishna said, 'you can come here one by one and I will hand over your clothes.'

His boys hiding in those branches giggled endlessly anticipating some more fun. The gopis were upset. They threatened Krishna that if he did not return their clothes, they would have to complain to his father

Nanda Maharaj against him.

Krishna retorted, 'Did you not promise that you will do as I say?' Cold and shivering, the gopis just looked at each other in visible embarrassment. When they realized that they had no other option but to collect their clothes personally, they came out of the water, hiding their bare bodies with their slender hands.

Not to be deterred, Krishna said, 'How do you complete your worship of the goddess without raising both your hands in prayer.'

Time was running out for the young girls. They couldn't dither any longer as the early morning bathers of Gokul would soon be on the riverbank and be aware of their plight. Like puppets pulled by a string, the gopis raised their palms over their heads and tiptoed towards the foot of the kadamba tree where Krishna gave them their clothes. One by one, the gopis collected their clothes while Krishna curiously explored the enchantment of feminine forms.

Once the clothes were recovered, the gopis got out of a magic spell. They felt that they were in some kind of a trance. To their utter surprise, they discovered that their clothes were exactly where they had left them.

In the distance, they could hear Krishna's voice trail away, 'I know your minds. Now that you have conquered shame, your deepest prayers will not go unanswered.'

'Was that real or just the stuff of dreams?' they wondered while rubbing their eyes in disbelief.

THE WALK AFTER DINNER

'Isn't it bizarre that the lord of love would be such an eve-teaser, deceiving and shaming those young girls the way he did?' said Eva, unable to contain her bewilderment.

'Look,' Neel said, 'this Krishna we are talking about was a seven-year-old kid—someone who accepts life without much of the inhibitions of civilization. Clothes are not just worn for our comfort and conventions—they are also expressions of our social and personal identities. Clothes conceal as much as they reveal about our true nature. That seven-year-old child is not affected by the sight of a naked woman as a normal civilized human being would be. He sees a human body as a spontaneous expression of nature without those assumptions of culture.'

Prasad, glassy-eyed, butted in, 'Consider the cows in the ashram. Will they judge you by your jeans, Eva?' Eva twitched her face in disgust. Prasad, as always, had the ability to reduce a serious conversation into total trivia. He was slapping his thighs in celebration of his sense of humour.

Keshav was listening to this conversation in silence. A cool breeze was blowing across the river. His voice rose above the rustle of the ashwattha tree. The motley group of former students walking with him were all ears. 'As I said earlier, our being is the source of love. Just to be is to be in love. Yet, this source is covered by layers and layers of skin that serve as the outer clothing for our being. The physical skin is the outermost layer of clothing. Human contact, a skin touching another, creates a sensory experience. A hand brushing against a hand; a knee refusing to move away when touched by another knee. This outer layer affects us as we experience the first promptings of love.'

Prasad, leaning close to Anju, became self-conscious and promptly pulled himself back on hearing this.

Keshav went deeper. 'The next layer of skin is our vital breath. Our breathing changes as we encounter the deeper stimulus of love. Breath synchronizes with breath creating a shield of security and comfort.

'The third layer is that of the mind. The mind is like an inner skin. You can touch this skin with words and gestures. A gentle word soothes the mind and a lovelorn look tingles it.

'The fourth layer of the skin is the layer of intellect. The skin of intellect sorts out and decodes the multiple stimuli around us. This intellectual layer divides the world of duality as outer and inner, good and bad. The mind doubts but the intellect decides.

'Finally, there is the skin of bliss. This skin is very close to the source of love. The skin of bliss savours the warmth of love in a quiet, uninhibited way. In deep sleep when we are oblivious of multiple layers of clothing, all of us experience the skin of bliss. That is why deep sleep, like love, is so refreshing.'

Keshav continued, 'Krishna's innocent prank had the gopis unwittingly exposed to luminous love. The light of love saw through the defences of their multilayered skin. When Krishna returned their clothes one by one, the gopis were no longer the same human beings who slipped into the river. They were transfigured beyond the shame of the body and the guilt of the mind. They became embodiments of guileless love like little children. They had shed their layers of outer skins like snakes shedding their scales. Those gopis experienced the very source of love that knows no defence and therefore needs no clothing to cover itself up.'

The group now sat huddled close to each other around Keshav. There was a faint drizzle. The hum of temple bells was echoing in the surrounding hills.

Ahmed, a practising physician with prominent eyes, who had come to the retreat all the way from Egypt, said, 'Tell us more about how you see a human body.'

Keshav spoke. 'The body is a melody of five elements—air, water, fire, earth and space. It is an instrument with five strings on which the music of the spirit is struck.' He paused. His voice was low and soothing as the silken breeze of the night scattered the drizzle away.

'Your body, Ahmed, is like a house of shadows hiding the light of your spirit. You may also say that it is like a lantern of knowledge that is covered by five layers of dust. When we clean the dusty glass cover of the lantern, the light of love is revealed within us.'

Ahmed asked, 'Does all that happen inside this single body?'

'There are many bodies within a single body. All our emotions too acquire their own bodies. Sometimes our multiple emotional bodies go to war with each other. Two bodies in conflict can become a battlefield of passion and dispassion. Sometimes, the body of anger sizzles like a flame and the body of understanding cools it. The body of fear recedes before the body of determination. All these bodies are temporary formations of the five elements in different proportions.'

Ahmed pondered. 'If the body is not a permanent thing, why should one bother so much about it?' he asked.

Keshav responded, 'However fragile and impermanent, this body is the only temple we ought to visit. For while it lives, the body is the only shrine in which we can see the shadow of the fleeting eternity in us. A river of blood and a bank of bones, the body bears witness to the ever-present current of life. Just think of your body as a prayer. The passions that arise inside it mark the beginning of an aspiration of becoming a greater being. Only true lovers know that the life stirring in their bodies—their fugitive eyes, arrested lips, drunken limbs and flaming hearts—are the only ways to quicken their journey to an immortal love. Lovers stretch their entwined limbs to catch a silken thread of love hanging loose from that one cosmic body of being.'

Kaya, listening with undivided attention, asked, 'Were the gopis experiencing that spontaneous love in the company of Krishna?'

Keshav said, 'The gopis of Gokul had a taste of that natural being as they shed their multiple skins of shame, guilt, pride, anger, lust and finally that of the ego. Through the innocent pranks of a seven-year-old kid, they discovered the very source of love.'

PERIYAR HOSTEL, INDUS CAMPUS, LUCKNOW
RESTLESS RENDEZVOUS

The smell of fresh filter coffee filled Room No. 101 of Periyar Hostel.

Swamy was one heck of a coffee devotee. He would meditate for a good fifteen minutes before brewing a special coffee powder that he had brought from his home town, Mysore. The prospects of a divinely dispensed cup of coffee were more effective than an alarm clock as a wake-up call for his roommate, Neel.

Neel soaked in the aroma of coffee and the simmer of the electric kettle with his eyes still closed. He was in that languorous time zone between waking up and getting up.

Buzz! Beep! Ring! Tring! Crash! Thud—five alarms that he had set up went off.

As the alarms rang, Neel turned and with a practised flick of his wrist managed to put the clock in the snooze mode. How he did this with both his eyes closed, he would never know.

In Neel's mind, the association between coffee and Kaya was obvious. He visualized Kaya walking to class. He adored the way she moved—lyrical, breezy and full of bounce. Her windswept blonde hair curled rather poetically over snow-white earlobes. He loved the way she often pronounced the word, 'perfect'—her lips fluttering sensuously like a butterfly's wings as she delivered the word with a whiff of coffee-rich air escaping her mouth—purrrfect!

Neel took two rapid sips of Swamy's cup of coffee and

rushed to the hostel bathroom. Time passed by like a speeding bullet train and he felt that everything here in Indus happened at a mind-numbing pace. Whatever happened just fifteen minutes ago seemed like a previous birth.

Neel had to set his own pace and make critical decisions about time management. Life in the morning was about answering several multiple-choice questions such as:

A. Have a bath and breakfast (and show up late for class).
B. Have a bath but no breakfast.
C. Have breakfast but no bath.
D. Have half a bath (chest downward) and half a banana for breakfast.

Every day, Neel took solace from the fact that some people arrived in class in far worse shape than him; others fought a losing battle with sleep, became glassy-eyed and then dozed off, often in full view of the class. Prasad sat in the front row with a smear of hastily drunk Mother Dairy milk still visible on his moustache. Sardar sat bloated with the effect of trying to digest eight boiled eggs that had barely commenced their descent through his food pipe. Swamy sat next to him with a liberal dust of talcum powder unevenly sprinkled on his face and the back of his neck. You could mistake him for a mason emerging from the debris of a construction site.

Neel lumbered off towards the last row and on his way looked at the class noticeboard that had this announcement:

Quiz at 10.30 a.m.

The news spread faster than a killer virus through staircases, the students' mess and the library. This meant another hour of frenetic page turning followed by head reeling and sitting emptily through mindless quiz questions.

For Neel, the morning yoga class before the quiz was such a welcome diversion.

Usman, walking around scattered yoga mats, spoke in his practised monotone. 'Focus on the space between your nostrils and your upper lip and feel your breath there—for the next five minutes.'

Neel focused with clenched teeth and stiff jaws but he was distracted by wild thoughts—his mind was minding itself without reference to the instructor.

'That is the difference between a monk and a monkey. The monkey mind is never in one place, while the monk's mind is...' Usman's voice trailed off.

Neel tried in vain to stop the flow of his imagination that was now affected by Kaya's presence in his life: Kaya, in a swimsuit, walking towards a river to bathe; her back swerving like a dinghy boat tossed about by a gentle breeze. Coming back to his senses, he saw Sardar whose deep breaths kept bifurcating his moustache, reminding Neel of the Biblical episode of Moses parting the sea. They were now bent in the crocodile posture, which meant that the participants had to lie on their belly and raise their head. All of them looked like a float of crocodiles performing a drill in stretch pants.

Neel's eyes met Kaya's neck. It was as slender and soft a neck as he had ever seen. She wore a silver necklace with a blue pendant that settled on a well-formed cleavage. His heartbeat went up slightly and his cheeks warmed up. Kaya was unapologetically herself. Neel looked at her from as many different angles as possible, priming his own neck for an attack of spondylitis. Then he closed his eyes and imagined her in as many ways as he could. The muscles in the pit of his stomach hardened suddenly. Neel was saying to himself. 'I hunger for your lips, the glitter of your teeth, your plucked eyebrows and the glitter of the sun in your smile. That slender neck needs to be kissed, stroked and worshipped. That beautiful head needs to rest against mine, I am telling you! I wish you could spread yourself over me like white butter on brown toasted bread;

I long to hold my skin close to your skin. The ends of your blonde hair caress my cheek. I am inflamed. My heartbeats lock themselves with yours in one rhythm like two chiming clocks.'

Did Kaya have the faintest clue about those queer thoughts going on in Neel's mind? Neel came back to a stark realization of the nature of how love could affect human life. Twenty years later, he began to reflect: 'I had gone some distance in my understanding of the physical and mental aspects of affection. But I had no clue that Kaya would be affected by a yet undiscovered seventh sense to be close to Keshav. I had no understanding of that.'

6
Desire

RISHIKESH ASHRAM, WEDNESDAY, MORNING DAY 3 OF THE RETREAT

The theme for the third day's retreat was desire. The storyteller transported the listeners to Vrindavan in ancient India.

They were childhood playmates, Radha and Krishna. She saw him growing up in Nanda's courtyard, a crawling, prattling kid. Years had passed. Baby Kanha was now a handsome boy whom all the village girls fancied. Time rolled on. Radha was married off to Ayan, who now served in Kamsa's army. Yet, her soul was still wedded to Krishna. Radha remembered his flute songs. They bore the rhythms of Krishna's own voice. She remembered how, as the sound of his flute trilled forth, her heartstrings were pulled by an invisible hand. The music had sunk deep inside her along with the heady fragrance of naag champa.

Radha wondered, 'After so many moons had passed, will Krishna still remember me?'

'I am Radha from Barsana. My father is Vrishbhanu and my mother, Virabali,' she said.

'I am Krishna, son of Nanda and Yashoda. However, I chose my own parents, you see. How else could I have decided where to be born?'

Radha was shocked at his temerity. She was older than him in years, yet he spoke as though he was her grandfather.

They walked along the sandbanks of the Yamuna. Spring was in the air. The forest of Vrindavan was redolent, the river zig-zagged through the woods, and the soothing fragrance of the newly blossomed jasmine wafted in the breeze. Tender buds bloomed, and cuckoos let out their mating cries from their hideouts in the mango trees.

'It is very dark here,' Radha said, her steps faltering inside the dense forest.

'Only when the darkness is deep enough can you glimpse the moon in its full glory,' whispered Krishna. He led her through the labyrinth.

Krishna was dressed in rich yellow silk. A wild flower garland caressed his shimmering dark skin. His forehead and arms were smeared in sandalwood paste. A circle of peacock plumes crowned his thick curly hair.

Radha, her eyes adapted to the darkness, now moved rhythmically alongside Krishna, graceful as a goose. Her anklets rang around her feet. Her fair complexion glowed in the silver moonlight. When she fixed her gaze on Krishna, her lips quivered nervously. Krishna noticed her slender waist, wide flaring hips and deep navel glistening with sweat.

Krishna's voice fell on her ears softly. Radha knew he was skilful in rousing passion in any woman with his words just as he did with his flute. She smiled as she pushed him back in mock anger. Soon, her resistance became as limp as a vine. Her desire for him was too overpowering. She remembered somewhat vaguely that he drew her towards himself with his long sinewy arms. Her eyelashes fluttered languidly as he traced the contours of her cheeks with his flute. Then he tilted her face upward towards him and his eyes drank from her lips. Krishna's gaze was at once intimate and overwhelming for Radha. She swooned over him and was lost in a trance.

In a daze, Radha felt the warmth of his arms around her waist, and her cummerbund loosened like a falling leaf. Her fingers were competing with each other for caressing his chiselled back. Her hair was in a tangle and her body bore his nail marks. Radha's eyes transgressed the bounds of modesty as she looked at him. Waves of quivering flesh were awash in each other's sweat.

'Drop your noisy armlets and anklets, Radha. They interfere with our silent communion,' he said. His voice was hushed like dew falling on leaves. He was so near her yet so far away like a distant observer pervading the entire night sky.

Radha was still in her reverie. Her lips opened like a fragrant lotus. Her necklace slid off her neck. She was like a bare reed of flute through which Krishna blew the elixir of life.

'Come closer, Krishna.' Radha yearned for him with her eyes half closed.

'I am nearer to you than your own skin,' he whispered.

'Where is that?' said Radha.

'In the space deeper than your breath,' he teased her.

'Really? But, where?' she persisted.

'In that state that is subtler than your own mind. Your Krishna is your seventh sense.'

Radha felt waves of bliss creeping up her spine as the trail of his last few words pierced her heart. 'I am here, as intimate as the life coursing through you.'

She lay there transfixed, swept by an awareness that was infinite and all-encompassing. All her senses were now magnified! When her passions were spent, Radha murmured, 'Krishna, restore the rows of bangles on my hand and fix the anklets on my feet. Paint the colour of my cheeks and fix the girdle on my waist. Twine my braid of hair with flowers.'

Krishna obeyed like a youngster deferring to an elder's entreaties.

'Was this the Krishna who held her in a timeless embrace or was it just her fertile imagination at work?' Radha wondered. As the night deepened and inched closer to the breaking of dawn, the blazing desire inside Radha's heart mellowed into the luminous light of love.

Neel noticed that Kaya sat on the edge of a boulder that was right in front of Keshav's rock. Her hair was a scattered golden flame blown by a strong breeze. Kaya looked astonishingly beautiful in her Indian attire. She wore a sleeveless orange kurti with a bright embroidered design on the neckline and deep green leggings. The wind caressed her billowing dupatta that she was struggling to hold down. Her cheeks, now fuller with age, shone like oyster shells.

Neel recalled that the years of separation had not weakened his longing for Kaya. He remembered her sea-green eyes twinkling, her pouting in feigned displeasure, her lips twitching with a half-smile. An infinite longing crept inside him with the rising of his breath.

An Australian, a seller of antiques, seated to the far right of Keshav, asked, 'Tell us now about desire.'

Keshav said, 'Desire is the darkest of all the shades of love. A dusky, invisible seed buried deep in the soil, desire holds the promise of the flowering of love.'

The sun winked its presence through a swirl of clouds. Keshav's eyes were transfixed on the green-grey hilltop peeping through the morning mist. The learners found themselves in an enchanted space. His eyes swept through the large gathering and then he spoke: 'The root of all desires is the desire for life. All other desires spread like branches from that one desire to live. The world is a web created from one seed of desire. Imagine how a flickering flame from a single lamp can set a whole city on fire. A little seed of desire can fill the whole world with a trillion shapes and forms. All that is brought to life is nothing but the fruit of desire.'

'Is desire not blind like an animal's instinct or the raging passion of a human?' someone from the audience asked.

Keshav said, 'To be able to desire whatever he can imagine or think of is a human's special privilege. No other species on earth can desire as much as a human being does. Human desire embraces the entire spectrum from kama to prema—from lust to love. Our desires sweep the whole vista of existence from the ephemeral to the eternal. We are the only species that can evolve our desires in the direction of the desirable.'

'Why does desire work that way?' asked a scholar of philosophy.

'Let me explain further,' Keshav said. 'Desire contains the script of our growth and evolution. Life's desire expresses itself in multiple evolving shapes and forms. When life desires to fly high, it creates an eagle. When the same life desires to swim, it creates fishes and aquatic animals. When life wants to both swim and crawl, it creates a turtle. This thirst for defying the rigidities of a particular form, mating one form with another and producing a third form that is distinct from its parents—all this is possible because of desire. When a human being experiences the first inkling of love, his life cracks open the shell of the ego in search of a bigger identity.

'Lust is desire's gross propelling power that pushes a man and a woman to look for a mate. However, lust cannot sustain itself for too long. Courtship matures into mateship. With the birth of a child, there is the flowering of compassion. Strange but true. The lotus of compassion blooms in the dark soil of lust. So you see, it is ultimately love that baptizes carnal desire into a greater and ampler unity of life.'

'Doesn't Krishna's love for Radha cross the boundaries drawn by human civilization?' asked a former nun.

'When boundaries come in the way of powers of desire, it is desire that triumphs. The higher the wall, the greater the will to climb it. You can cut down all the fragrant flowers and drive away all the insects and birds, but can you stop the spring season from showing up?' Keshav tossed the question to the questioner.

Then, after almost a minute's pause, he continued as though he was talking to himself, 'Krishna lives and loves as another ordinary human being. Yet, he is able to transcend the barriers of his ego. The ego is the only hurdle between the human and the divine. When you transcend the ego, you go beyond the wall that separates you from your divinity. In the same breath that he accepts Radha as his paramour, Krishna can go back to being her servant in helping her with her clothes. His ego is not bloated by desire. Lust leaves no residue as an egoistic experience on Krishna's mind.'

'Placid as a mirror, his consciousness just reflects the various colours of life without attachment. This consciousness is unaffected by what it reflects. He wades through the crosscurrents of desire, untainted and untethered. Therefore, Krishna can transcend his own nature at will by anchoring himself in the seventh sense. He can graduate with utmost ease from kama to prema—from the delirium of lust to the devotion of love.'

Keshav became aware of his self-absorbed monologue. He turned his back to the class and said, 'Let me share with you a question that the gopis of Vrindavan asked Krishna... The cowherd girls of Gokul looked at Krishna with earnest desire.

Their faces were a choreography of passion. Bees clustered around fragrant water lilies and hummed their courtship call. One of the gopis asked, "We know that love has many shades like the colours of a rainbow. There is the possessive lust of the senses and the purity of the devotional love. Which of these is the greatest form of love?"'

There was a brief pause and then Keshav continued. 'Now let me explain to you, as best I can in my own words, what Krishna had tried to convey to those guileless gopis.

'There is no visible difference in the source of lust and love—kama and prema. Both have desire at their root. Desire is sankalpa shakti—the power of primordial will within us. Sankalpa unites our body and mind to pursue a goal until it is achieved. You can call desire an intention propelled by sankalpa shakti.

'When desire becomes a pleasure trip between two people, it becomes a trade. Love is reduced to carnal lust, a mutual exchange of emotion and sensation, inflamed passion and the friction of skins. When desire becomes a little more unselfish, love turns to nurturing kindness, such as the love of a mother for her son. Finally, when desire is completely fulfilled to the point of self-contentment within a person, he learns to love for just love's sake and for no other reason.

'The trajectory of desire now moves from an object outside oneself towards inner self-knowledge. The desire of a saint for the divine is nothing but the desire to know his own original nature. When this refined form of desire achieves its goal, the saint senses that his true nature is nothing but love—pure and unconditional.'

'How does one achieve this exalted state of love?' Kaya asked.

Keshav said, 'By simply turning the trajectory of desire in the direction of the desirable. When we are in the grip of the lowest form of desire, we love only to expect love in return. This is kama. In kama, we are bound by the laws of expectation. When our love is not reciprocated, we feel miserable. When our desires are a little more refined, we learn not to expect anything out of love. Love for love's sake quenches our deepest thirst for fulfilment. Fulfilment comes from giving all and taking nothing. And who could express this better than the poet-lover Rumi:

> *When light returns to its source*
> *It takes nothing*
> *Of what it has illumined.*

'We revel in and are fulfilled by our true nature, which is the inexhaustible light of love itself. The source of love is the heart; the full heart transforms the lover into love itself. In this transformational moment, desires dissolve into desirelessness. Do you now see where all our desires find fulfilment? The craving for water ceases the moment our thirst is quenched. All hunger and desire end at the point of satiation. This satiation point is nothing but a state of desirelessness. To be rendered desireless is then the ultimate goal of all desires. Isn't that so?'

With this, the morning session on desire was over.

INDUS CAMPUS, LUCKNOW

The mid-semester exams loomed large before the first-year students. The conversation ranged from discounted cash flow, critical path analysis, the bullwhip effect of operations management, econometrics, and the intricacies of behaviour in organizations. The examination time of two hours was a ritual of collective mourning in a big hall with rows and rows of chairs attached to foldable desks. An uneasy silence was broken by the occasional swish of a page turning, or the scribble of a pen.

Sardar scratched his back with his sharp pencil while struggling for an answer to a tough econometrics question. It was as though his intelligence was stuck on his shoulder blade.

∽

The campus was pitch-dark outside. It had just stopped raining. The mud road from the library to the girls' hostel turned slushy. A single dysfunctional street light winked intermittently like a kitten's eye. Kaya's hand lightly brushed Neel's. His right hand seemed to have grown eyes that could see way beyond the tactile world.

By then, every student in the business school knew her name well. Kaya Johnson filled a lot of post-dinner conversations at Indus school. For one, the school always had an adverse sex ratio. This meant that within the campus, there were few girls, and among them there were fewer who were considered strikingly beautiful by the law of contrast. For the discerning girls, the number of handsome, unattached boys per square kilometre was less than what could be counted on the fingers. This is what prompted Neel's wingmate, Prasad, to describe Kaya's beauty in the only way B-school students described their grade point averages in class.

Prasad, chewing his lips, said, 'Kaya is a nine point seven on a scale of one to ten.' Even the most conservative faculty at Indus would halt in their tracks and fling fleeting glances at her. They did not audibly sing or sigh. But it would be fair to say that most male faculty members did a bit of mental singing and exhaled deeply as they passed by her. Neel overheard Sardar entertaining his classmates about how a guy in Periyar Hostel was trying to make eye contact early in the morning with Kaya. In desperation, the fellow even put an alarm for 5.30 a.m., synchronizing with her movement within the campus so that he would accidentally meet her on the jogging track. Others would position themselves strategically in their balconies, ostensibly hanging their towels and clothes out to dry. Yet, their eyes would be frozen firmly on the entrance of the girls' hostel.

When Neel asked Kaya how she was dealing with all the attention she was getting, she simply said she never frowned, twitched her face, or displayed any intent. In short, she never displayed any sign of being available. Neel was happy knowing that. Yet, that loudmouth Sardar's observation left a bit of an unpleasant taste in Neel's mouth. He sensed a surge of anger within. His fist closed involuntarily and his jaws tightened. A violent thought entered his head. 'Those lechers should be made to stand stark naked in the balconies and bullwhipped until they fall dead!' he growled.

Swamy, adding a dash of milk to his coffee, quickly chipped in: 'Yes, I agree—whipped comprehensively, upside down, top to toe, black and blue!'

Neel tried to mumble some rehearsed lines before seeing Kaya off for the night. Sensing that she had put on a stern face while coming to terms with all the gossip around her, his passion ebbed a little. Kaya walked away unenthusiastically inside Godavari Hostel, flinging her blue scarf over her hair, apparently not paying attention to Neel's rambling voice.

On her way in, she absent-mindedly dropped her pen that she had tucked inside her notebook. Neel bent forward to pick it up. One end of the pen bore Kaya's teeth marks. Neel had observed that she had the habit of chewing pens in class. His cheeks warmed as he visualized her flashing, large teeth. He had half a mind to refrain from handing the pen back to her. Eventually, he slipped it into his pocket as a well-deserved memento.

When he trudged back to the hostel through the football field, Neel could feel a halo around his head—his steps had an unusual spring in them. His heart had swelled to the size of the football ground. He noticed that the grass on the field had acquired a deeper tint of green with the first rains of the monsoon.

Back in Periyar Hostel, Neel was walking towards Manas's room to collect the class schedule. Manas was allotted Room 102, which was next to Neel's. Manas was like those philosopher types and had no real interest in management education. He adored Neel for his intellect and for being a good listener. Neel would patiently listen as Manas would share all about his bizarre experiments in life. Neel remembered how he shared a story about his surviving one full month drinking nothing else but tea.

'Life is lived first hand through experiments not by second-hand experiences of others,' Manas said. Neel acknowledged that it was an amazing way to think about life.

Among other things, Manas and Neel shared a common passion: Sharon Stone. Both of them freaked out on a poster from her movie *Basic Instinct*. They had hung two identical posters of Sharon on their room walls.

On looking around Manas's room after picking up the schedule, Neel was surprised that Sharon Stone's poster was missing from the wall, leaving a light rectangular patch of vacant space. Manas explained, 'I am cold-shouldering Sharon Stone these days—pulled off all her posters from my room. There is a vacuum in my heart of late.'

Neel smiled as he said to himself, 'The vacuum in my heart is now filling up with or without Sharon Stone.'

INDUS LIBRARY, LUCKNOW

Sitting inside the Indus library, Kaya was reading a journal in a distracted manner. She raised her eyes every time she heard the sound of the door opening. Neel noticed that her eyebrows were plucked to perfection.

Neel sat—positioning himself not too close to Kaya, yet

not too far from her either—so that he wouldn't miss seeing her. Kaya had a pencil stuck behind the ear.

'Soon she will start chewing the pencil,' thought Neel.

He had picked up a book, *The Tao of Leadership*, by an American author named John Heider and pretended to read it. 'There is no better way to cement a relationship than a shared interest in books,' he thought. From the corner of his eye, he noticed a line of heads inclined in different directions around a long table in the reading hall. He saw half-bust images: receding hairlines, stern faces, T-shirts bulging with watermelons, pomegranates, guavas, and assorted fruits stacked inside. He quickly lowered his eyes and saw a swarm of feet moving inside the library. His gaze turned to chipped nails, pedicured toes, puffed-up ankles, dainty feet in dirty flip-flops, fat and plump steps like those of baby elephants.

His eyes were soon drawn towards Kaya's feet strapped inside red leather slip-ons. Her toes, shaped in a perfect oval and shaded in light coffee brown nail polish, stuck out like a tongue.

'If one ever desired to have a crush on a toe, this had to be the one,' Neel thought.

He imagined touching the toe many times over. He thought of feeling its smoothness with his fingers. Strangely, he imagined, the book he was reading could also be renamed 'The Toe of Leadership'. He chuckled.

Neel turned towards Kaya. When their eyes met, he gulped rather awkwardly. He wondered if Kaya was amused, but didn't think it was proper to look again. He flipped a few pages of the small and elegantly bound book he was pretending to read. Casually turning a new page, he came across the following advice:

> *Knowing how polarities work, the wise leader does not push to make things happen, but allows the process to unfold on its own.*

RISHIKESH ASHRAM, DAY 3
DRAUPADI TOO LONGED FOR KRISHNA

The storyteller said.

Which young woman would not think of Krishna as her lover? Draupadi too longed for Krishna. Yet, her desire for him remained submerged in the depths of their friendship. Wasn't he the most desirable match for any eligible princess among the Aryaputras? Tales about his legendary good looks and accomplishments had spread far and wide. Draupadi's maid, Nitambini, brought her news of all the exploits of Krishna. Was Krishna somehow aware that Draupadi nurtured a soft corner in her heart for him...?

In fact, Draupadi knew of Krishna long before she had met her future husbands—the Pandava brothers. She was also named Krishna by her father, Drupada, because of her dusky complexion. Stories of her beauty broke through word of mouth like the fragrance of her body. Legend had it that her exquisite body exuded the fragrance of a blue lotus that could be smelt from two miles away. Her suitors—princes and kings, the young and the old—fantasized about her. Born of a sacrificial fire, she was Yajnaseni, sharp in intellect and fiery in temperament. Her life was like an insatiable fire that was difficult to quench.

When she met Krishna, she looked at the man every maiden dreamt of with starry eyes. His dreamlike eyes and windswept crop of curly hair evoked more awe than desire in her. Krishna could almost read her mind. 'I know what is in your mind, sakhi!' he said.

Draupadi heard the word 'sakhi' spoken with such grace and affection that she began to feel Krishna's presence as a trusted friend. Krishna could communicate with her by just a handful of gestures. Just a flicker of his eyes, a twitch of his lips and a wry smile would speak volumes to Draupadi.

'I really know your heart's desires, sakhi. You have been born for a purpose much greater than marrying and rearing children. You have a life's mission to fulfil. A larger dharma. You are destined to be won over by a man who is Indra's own child and my own soulmate.' Krishna looked wistfully towards her as though he was reading the prophecy of a distant event.

'Who would be more eligible than yourself, sakha, to ask for my arm from my father, Drupada?'

Krishna said, 'Arjuna, who defeated your father and won half his kingdom, will win your heart and hand in a swayamvar. Even your father desires that mighty Arjuna, the third of the Pandava brothers, should marry you.'

Draupadi was still adamant. She said, 'How about the dreams that I have woven around you as my own? How deeply have I desired you as my husband? Don't you know that?'

Softening his eyes, Krishna said, 'You and I will remain friends and soulmates. I will show up for you whenever you are in distress. Count on me, my sakhi!' Having said this, Krishna slipped into a reflective mood again. He began to ponder why Draupadi would not have one but five husbands. Given the intensity of her life, her gift of intelligence and her blinding beauty—she would need the company and the power of the five Pandava brothers to keep her away from predatory men...

As Krishna had prophesied, Draupadi was won over by the mighty Arjuna in a rare feat of archery during her swayamvar. Krishna attended the event and wished Draupadi as any doting elder brother would do. However, as destiny willed it, she had to take all the five Pandava brothers as her husbands. Like the five fingers held by the hand, Draupadi united five Pandavas in an inalienable bond of love. Yudhishtira, the eldest of the Pandavas, and a firm believer in justice and truth, was reassuring like her thumb. Bhima, wild and volatile as the wind, was her index finger, fighting and settling scores on her behalf. Arjuna, like the middle finger, was the centre of her desire. He also balanced her fiery temperament with the coolness of his head. Nakula, the most handsome among the Pandavas, was her ring finger, a romantic partner. Sahadeva was the little finger, the youngest and treated as such, with affection and indulgence.

All the five Pandavas desired Draupadi and craved her for different reasons. Yudhishtira sought her for her straightforward nature. Bhima felt protective of her and sought her for her vulnerability. Arjuna loved her for her blazing beauty, and her focused and fiery eyes. Nakula fell for her hair and her exquisite shape. Sahadeva was besotted with her because of her caring nature. Yet, there was a sixth Pandava who was the most earnest claimant to her heart. His name was Karna. Only Krishna knew how Karna's obsession with her would turn him into an enemy of the Pandavas.

Yet, Draupadi was a lonely woman in the middle of all the male attention.

On that inauspicious day when Draupadi stood alone, clinging on to a single piece of cloth, defending her modesty in an open royal court, no one came to her rescue. Her husband, Yudhishtira, pawned her away in a mindless bout of gambling. The rascal Dushasan pulled her by the hair. Karna, her jilted suitor, called her a whore and Duryodhana teased her by exposing his bare thigh. The elders conveniently kept their mouths shut. Her five husbands hung their heads in shame and rage. Even as Bhima seethed in ineffectual anger, Dushasan crossed all the limits of decency and started to disrobe her. It was then that Draupadi turned to her sakha, Krishna, in a desperate cry for help.

Krishna couldn't turn a deaf ear to the entreaty of his sakhi. He kept his promise and showed up to rescue her. In a magical turn of events, Draupadi found her disrobed body wrapped up and clothed by Krishna who saved the day for her. The same bewitching lover boy that stole the clothes of the bathing gopis had restored to Draupadi her clothes and her dignity as a woman. In a dramatic twist of cosmic play, the love of one dear friend for another won that day.

AFTERNOON CLASS ON DESIRE

Keshav said, 'When not understood fully, desire becomes a state of human bondage. A man and a woman are drawn to each other by nature's law. A man carries within him the seed of life. A woman embodies the potential for the flowering of his seed. Together they complete the circle of life. A man looks for a beloved, a mother and a nourisher of his dreams in a woman. A woman desires a wild warrior with strong hands and an artist's heart. Maybe more!' He chuckled.

'A woman keeps longing for her perfect lover; a man yearns for his ideal beloved. A horizon of hope is created. It is an illusory horizon as the ideal lover is never out there—like a thirsty traveller chasing a mirage, a lover chases the perfect beloved. The only bridge that can take a human being to this non-existent horizon is desire. So, desire is like the mental connection between a human being and what he does not have. Desire is an energy that drives us towards our goal of fulfilment, yet very often desires remain unfulfilled. Desire is both the journey as well as the obstacle towards the realization of love.'

'So, how can the trajectory of desire be controlled?' a man with a severe face and glittering eyes asked.

'You cannot help desiring in so much as you cannot stop a shadow from showing up whenever you block a source of light,' Keshav responded.

'So how does one get rid of this shadow of desire?'

'You can only dispel desire through the clear light of awareness.'

'What is that?'

'A desire is the projection of the ego—the male ego and the female ego. Desire and ego cannot exist without each other. Desire is the outer appearance; ego is the inner shadow. Once you see that the ego is non-existential like a shadow, you will also see the futility of desire.'

'Yet, how does one really live without desire?' Anju asked.

'You cannot live without desire. Remember we are all born of desire. However, you can learn to let go of the feverishness of desire by a process of surrender.'

'Surrender to what?'

'To that all-embracing love that is clouded by the restless ego. When one lets go of the ego, a desire finds its natural path towards fulfilment. When the mind does not cling to its ego-centric desires, that which the mind was seeking manifests itself magically. This is possible because the pure mind is harnessed by the light of love. While desire distances, love connects everything together.

'When Draupadi in her deepest distress let go of the ego of a princess and surrendered herself to Krishna's grace, Krishna's love for her manifested immediately. Her desire to find a safe shelter was fulfilled. In her total surrender, the impossible became possible. On the contrary, the desires of Duryodhana and Dushasan to disrobe Draupadi were thwarted as their minds were deluded by their bloated egos. Desire and its shadow, the ego, stir the mind and disturb its firmness. It incites and heats up the mind to a feverish pitch leading the mind astray. Draupadi's ego was like a cloud blocking the sunshine of love. With her surrender, the cloud of her ego moved away. Duryodhana's ego functioned like a mirage, an illusion created by the sunlight hitting a hotbed of sand. The more Duryodhana chased this mirage, the more it receded from him.'

'Does desire fall off on its own with the dawn of the light of love?'

'Desire is a state of blind energy that has to be understood rather than controlled. When we understand the distortion that desire produces in our minds, the feverishness of desire automatically drops off. A bee buzzes frantically until it discovers the sweet heart of a flower. Then, it settles down and sips the honey in utter stillness.

'The world out there glamorizes the objects of desire with the haze of illusions. The mind colludes by chasing those illusions. When this falsity is understood, the falsity of the ego drops off by itself. It is like a dreamer who upon waking up discovers that the dream was not true. The dream automatically fades away.'

INDUS CAMPUS, LUCKNOW
DESIRE AND FEAR

Neel was reflecting on the terrible encounter in the city with a street gang just the day before. The three of them, Manas, Kaya and Neel, were crossing a narrow lane near Kapoorthala market in the city to help Kaya with some shopping. The gang of rowdies picked on Kaya and started following her closely. They had come within striking distance of the trio.

It was clear that the attackers had malicious intent. Neel sped ahead in distinct panic. Manas, in a surge of courage and indignation, pushed Kaya behind himself and stood between her and the gang. Manas's eyes smouldered as he stared directly into the tallest of the lot with a slender poker face and a slight moustache. Neel had started to feel guilty that he had not offered to help Manas and stopped in his tracks. The lanky poker face whipped out a knife with a sharp blade that flashed in the fading sunlight. He shifted a wad of tobacco from the right cheek to the left rather ominously. Neel, scared and shivering, looked down and whispered to Manas not to say anything provocative that would enrage the assailant.

The poker face, with a rust-coloured beard, threatened to chop off Manas's and Neel's 'little nuts' if they dared take him on. Those words fell on Neel's ears like a sharp axe. His hands involuntarily moved towards his crotch in a defensive posture. But to his surprise, Manas betrayed no fear and kept his gaze fixed on the poker face. Meanwhile, Kaya, gathering some courage, let out a shriek that was loud enough to be heard across the lane. A face popped out of the balcony of a house on the first floor as a woman looked out to see what was happening. More doors and windows opened. Sensing public reaction, poker face and his gang slowly began to retreat. When the trio emerged out of the lane breathing a collective sigh of relief, Neel did not fail to notice a glint of admiration in Kaya's eyes for Manas. Neel wondered why that same Manas who found it difficult to look Kaya in the eye in class was now exchanging glances with her.

'Was Manas, my bosom friend, betraying me?' Neel thought aloud dipping a crunchy butter toast inside a cup of tea. That old jab of pain seemed to come back in the pit of his stomach. While on his way to attend the Management Accounting class, Manas sensed that Neel was ignoring him.

In Malhotra's class Neel sat at a distance from where both Manas and Kaya were seated.

~

Meanwhile, the first-year MBA students had to use a whole artillery of flattery, feigned attention, and feminine charm to keep Professor Malhotra from conducting his surprise quiz that day. Thanks to a cleverly crafted students-led strategy, disaster was averted for the time being.

The class trooped out. Neel would carry some leftover food for his favourite among the stray dogs in the campus. The mixed breed was called Drucker. He named the dog after the world-famous management guru Peter Drucker. Neel's Drucker always had this tendency to look condescendingly at the neighbourhood dogs. He would, true to his canine nature, bark out his argument in a rising crescendo of disapproval. When every other dog would stick its tails behind its hind legs and give up the fight, Drucker would look at the sky and howl a victory sound with an air of smugness about him.

Through sheer instinct, Drucker knew exactly when Neel would show up to feed him dinner. He would peacefully wag his tail as his dinner was served on an aluminium foil paper. When dogs are well fed, they do not display the desperation that their counterparts who have to compete for crumbs do. Neel remembered that Keshav often said that competition led to the best products, but sometimes it also brought out the worst in animals and people.

Drucker felt the extra tenderness with which Neel caressed him that evening. Dogs read human emotions much better than humans themselves. Each time Neel felt betrayed or let down in the human world, he would return to his pet to soothe his nerves. Swamy, his roommate, told him once that repeatedly checking in on loved ones was a sign of obsessive compulsive disorder. Neel dismissed it as one of those fancy new terms that Swamy had picked up.

Neel imagined he was caressing Kaya's slender neck with his fingers. The dog smell made way for a French perfume whose fragrance he recalled from the memory of his last meeting with Kaya. His fingers touched the wet part of Drucker's mouth, but he was too full of Kaya not to have imagined her liquid lips. Neel's hands were electrified by the sheer touch of Drucker's wet snout—the meeting point of his nose, mouth and jaw. It was not merely a celebration of the senses; it was a celebration of meaning. Falling in love affects us in ways that the line between the sensory and the imaginary world blurs.

Neel slid his magnetized fingers below the ears of Drucker imagining them to be Kaya's earlobes.

'You are lucky, Drucker,' Neel whispered to the dumbfounded dog. 'Kaya would soon be touching you in the way I have caressed your face. The tingling skin of a third being will unite our shared craving for human contact.'

There was something formidable about the engineering mindset. Nine out of ten of those who pursued their MBA programme in Indus came from an engineering background. For them, everything in life had to be explained as a cause-and-effect equation. X loves his dog and touched it. X also loves Y. So when Y touches X's dog, there is a shared touch point. Neel realized that was precisely how engineers learned to think. Meetings led to interest, which led to greater communication, which in turn led to further meetings, which led to affection and that led to desire and love!

Of course, engineers always remember to insert the if-then conditional loops at a variety of points in that structure. But the crux of the matter was that there was no scope for abstract romance and everything eventually fell into a neat formula. So the engineers thought.

Before he went to bed that night, Neel wrote in his diary:

MY TOP FIVE TEACHERS

1. SILENCE
2. DRUCKER
3. (Keshav's) CLASSES/MANAS
4. LOVE
5. KAYA

Neel realized that his desire for Kaya was fraught with the fear of losing her. He fell asleep wondering if he were to write down the truth, would that order be reversed.

RISHIKESH ASHRAM, DAY 3
POST-DINNER CONVERSATION ON KILLING DESIRE

'Where do our desires eventually take us, Keshav?' asked Anju.

'They pretty much bring you back to exactly where you were before your desires took possession of you. Think of the hold of desire as a fiercely spinning top. The top whirls like a man possessed. When the spinning and fretting is over, the top topples over more or less at the same place where it began to spin. The top hadn't gone anywhere. Like the top, all desires take us for a spin.' He laughed.

'So, do you kill your desire then?' Sardar queried.

Keshav responded, 'No way. Desire is life itself. Life propagates itself through the fulfilment of desire. Trying to kill a desire is trying to chop the hand off for getting rid of a sore thumb. What irritates us like a mass of ailments is not desire itself but the frustration of non-fulfilment. When fulfilled, desires lead to a greater life. When not fulfilled, they lead to continuity of frustration.'

'So how should we desire so that it would be fulfilling?' Neel reflected.

Keshav continued to elaborate. 'All desires signal a longing to go back to the source of all desires—which is our original, unbounded life—a life full of possibilities. To be free from all constraints is the sole purpose of this life. We deny this unbounded life to ourselves as we are stuck in our own delusions. Listen to the story I am about to tell.

'A frog was hopping about under a tree looking wistfully at a swan that was flying by. It asked, "What is it that you see beyond the forest?"

'"Oh! I see the boundless, shoreless ocean ahead," said the swan.

'"Really?" asked the frog. "How far is that ocean? How does it look?" The frog's desire was whetted.

'"Some distance from here. When you see water and nothing but water everywhere, you will know that you have reached the ocean," replied the swan and it glided across the deep blue horizon.

'The frog then travelled some distance and came across a small puddle of water that overnight rain had caused. All he saw was an expanse of mud water and thought this was indeed the ocean. It splashed around in the muddy water for a few days. Soon, the sun dried up the puddle leaving nothing but mud behind. The frog was devastated to learn that this was not the ocean at all. However, when the illusion was broken the frog had a renewed thirst for the ocean.'

'How do desires find fulfilment then?' asked Kaya.

Keshav said, 'You don't drop desires. The only way you fulfil your desires is by killing your own illusions that desires produce in you. Do not mistake the puddle for the ocean. When illusions end, the same desire that was an enemy in your progress will become an ally and a friend. You learn from every thwarted desire that it was an illusion and not the reality one was chasing!

'All your desires grow like a tropical tree from a solitary seed of an idea. You can call this seed the idea of "I". The longing to gratify that "I" thought is the root of all desires. The deeper you dig inside the "I" thought, you realize that "I" is not a real person but only a shadow of the impersonal and interminable life. In reality, there is nothing like "your" or "my" life as two separate lives. There is only one life and its many expressions—"you" and "I" are just ideas or concepts that have no foundation in reality. It is like the same river flowing through different countries and tributaries that are given separate names—"you" and "I" are separate names for that one river of life.'

'Can you explain this a little more, Keshav?' asked Swamy, sounding rather pensive.

Keshav offered to explain through an example. 'Look Swamy, what is it that you have wrapped around your body?' he asked.

'A shawl,' answered Swamy awkwardly.

'No, there is no shawl there,' quipped Keshav. 'The shawl is just a name that you impose on a piece of cotton or silk and call it that. If you cut that shawl in the shape of a handkerchief, it will be called a handkerchief. Isn't it? If you use that same handkerchief to mop the floor, it will be called a mop. So the shawl, the handkerchief and the mop are just passing illusions of forms imposed on the same fabric. That is exactly what desire is—an illusion of form, shape, quality and utility that changes over time.'

Swamy was shaking his head vigorously.

'Yet the whole world is divided and demarcated by the human desire to reinforce the "you" and the "I". Our land and sea, and even our airspace, are divided by nations and people. These are no more than accumulated you's and I's—do you see that?'

'If illusions bring happiness, why not be in them for a while?' said Neel, feeling quite agitated.

'The desire that tries to protect that illusory psychological centre called "I" will always result in misery. However, when that illusion is gone, our desires turn out to be our life's support system. This is like breathing. When you hold your breath inside your body beyond a certain point of time, the stale breath suffocates you. But when you let go of your breath and share the air with the universe, your breath works spontaneously as your ally, keeping you alive. A desire can find true fulfilment provided you know how to share your desire with many others.'

Then turning towards Neel, Keshav asked, 'So what made you organize this retreat along with Kaya? Search for the answer inside your own heart!'

He then added, 'You didn't travel because of planes, buses and trains. You travelled here on the wings of desire. Didn't that desire come from the "I" thought—"I" have to go to Rishikesh to solve a problem that "I" have? Isn't that true? Would you explore what happens to your desires when the "I" thought ceases to function?'

With this, the post-dinner conversation broke up.

7
Ecstasy

RISHIKESH ASHRAM, THURSDAY
DAY 4 OF THE RETREAT
ECSTASY: THE DANCE OF THE DIVINE

The storyteller described the ecstasy of Krishna's rasa-lila:

> It was a full moon night in autumn. A balmy breeze blew across the Yamuna. The river, no longer in the torrent of monsoon rains, gurgled as though it was trying to mimic a young woman's laughter. It was a sensuous, seductive night that lovers rave about and mystics meditate on.
>
> Krishna stood on the banks of the Yamuna, his heart revelling in the beauty of the full moon. He brought the flute to his lips and filled it with his breath of life. The haunting music drifted through the forest and reached the ears of the gopis. Strangely, the gopis were the only ones receptive to that mysterious sound. Perhaps their one-pointed devotion to Krishna made unheard melodies of the divine audible to them. Their minds were in a trance, as it were. A gopi who had put on one earring forgot to put the other on. Another one did not remember that her face was only half made up. The third one, who had put the milk to boil, left her task unattended and the burnt milk turned to a brown cake. An intense and agonizing fire of longing for Krishna was burning in their

hearts. They left their household chores and rushed to the sandy shore of the Yamuna to be near Krishna. Some of the gopis who were confined to their homes by their family now had their eyes closed in deep meditation.

When human beings experience ecstasy, they transcend the limitations of their physical and mental boundaries. They are no longer dominated by their egos. Humans sometimes break social norms in search of ecstasy. The gopis raced through the labyrinthine jungle awash in the moonlight. Their hearts throbbed and their breasts thudded in intense longing. They staked their homes, hearts and even their reputation to be one with Krishna.

Krishna welcomed them and yet asked, 'Why have you braved this fearful journey through the jungles to be here? Is it becoming of women of good breeding to leave their homes in the dark of the night? Is it not the dharma of a married woman to be with her husband at this hour?'

The grief-stricken gopis were on the verge of tears. Their eyes were downcast hearing those harsh reprimands from Krishna. One of them said, 'Haven't we given up all our material possessions and carnal desires only to be with you? Our relationship with our husband is bound by time. Haven't you taught us to serve the timeless spirit in them rather than their bodies? When you, Krishna, are the very embodiment of the love that is timeless, does it not make sense to come to you without inhibition?'

Krishna was moved by the love that the gopis harboured in their hearts for him. He was ready to play and engage in the rasa dance with them. He said to the gopis, 'I carry the debt of your unconditional love for me.'

Then, by the mystical powers of maya, Krishna expanded his form. Through his illusory powers, he multiplied his body like angled mirrors reflecting a person's image in infinite ways. They held each other's hands. He danced with each one of the gopis in an enchanted circle. At first, there was one form of Krishna between every two gopis. Then, there was one Krishna with each gopi. Like a child looking at his own reflection in a shimmering river, Krishna cast his many-hued magic in the forest grove of Vrindavan. The hearts of the gopis were intertwined with the lord of love. They rose above their mundane selves in ecstatic union.

Meanwhile, some of the gopis were so possessed by Krishna's beauty that they were dragging themselves down to amorous dalliance with him. Their faces were drenched in droplets of perspiration. Their bracelets and ankle bells rang with the chorus of humming bees. Their pride in being Krishna's consorts inflated their ego. It was then that Krishna vanished from their sight.

When they realized this, the gopis became restless and dismayed. They began searching for him. They looked for him in utter desperation. They called out the names of trees and plants—ashoka, tamala, mallika, champaka, malati, as though the trees knew the secret of Krishna's disappearance. They soon began to act out Krishna's amorous pastimes, imitating his moves. While searching for him, the gopis chanced on a pair of footprints leading to a secluded place. One of the footprints was Krishna's. The other footprint, they conjectured, was that of a lucky gopi. Was that gopi Radha? Was Radha's devotion so much greater than theirs that the lord of love gave her exclusive attention? After tracing the footprints, the gopis realized that there was just one set of footprints that had deeper impressions than the earlier one. They imagined that on Radha's entreaties, Krishna may have carried her on his shoulder.

When they moved closer, they found the gopi, whom they thought Krishna had carried on his shoulders, sitting under a tree and crying inconsolably. She lamented, 'The moment I became egotistic about Krishna's exclusive affection for me, he left me.' With their egos crushed, the gopis shed tears of penitence and wondered where they could find Krishna again. Those tears of remorse washed away their egos. It was then that Krishna reappeared. They began admonishing him in feigned anger for deserting them.

The evening merged into the night and the gopis gave vent to their wanton desire to consummate their love for Krishna. Their garlands and ornaments slipped away. They kissed his limbs and caressed his face. He reciprocated by dressing them up, his graceful arms encircling them in an affectionate embrace. There was a stillness about Krishna even as the gopis were frolicking and moving around him in circles.

Like an ocean does not become a river when rivers merge with it, Krishna was not defined by the carnal cravings of the gopis for him. On the contrary, rivers become oceanic when they merge with the ocean. The gopis found the unity of ecstatic love as they were completely absorbed in their thoughts of Krishna. The blood in their veins throbbed with the pulsations of eternity. They felt an unbounded and limitless ocean of love drowning their senses. Krishna's rasa—the essence of his love was limitless. One of the gopis sang out in an ecstatic voice:

> *This autumn night*
> *A sea of bliss wells up like Krishna's love*
> *His gaze falls upon the full moon*
> *The tide swells in Vrindavan*

> *The rippling Yamuna is curled up with his bliss*
> *We gopis are drunk in amorous play*
> *Krishna draws us to the deep water to cool our passions*
> *Krishna sprinkles us with a spray of blue*
> *We surrender to his oceanic love.*

One night of ecstasy seemed like the timeless night of Brahma, the Creator. Krishna emerged from the water and strolled through the fragrant forest. The gopis followed him like bees buzzing around a wild flower. Krishna urged them to return to their homes. Demurring, they obeyed him and trooped back, still in a daze, to their homes and husbands. Astonishingly, the gopas, the husbands and relatives of the gopis, had no clue about the events of the night. They were oblivious of the absence of their women. For the gopis, this was an unforgettable experience, a lifelong treasure of memories.

INDUS CAMPUS, LUCKNOW
THE DARK SIDE OF ECSTASY

The longing for ecstasy comes from a human being's inherent need to be free of the limitations of the body and the mind. Yet, Neel realized that the search for ecstasy in sex and alcohol in those institute parties left behind an emptiness that only love could fulfil.

After a gruelling fortnight, the institute's party was a balm for the heart. It was the place to let your hair down, get drunk on vodka, look through the mist of tequila and bash the system left, right and centre. Sardar quipped, 'I would especially like to see how the girls get high on orange juice, tap their dainty feet and dance their asses off to the beats of Bollywood numbers.'

Looking at Swamy wearing a cap to hide his closely cropped hair, Prasad chatted about how Manas too was experimenting with a new hairstyle.

Neel remembered that Manas and he had had a long conversation about his experiments with life. That expression was borrowed straight from Keshav's class notes. Manas was always the one to try new hairstyles, even if he looked horrible in them. He said haircuts always had a rejuvenating effect on him.

'I begin to see new patterns and new pathways in life after a haircut. In any case, I find cutting hair more productive than splitting hair over those management case studies,' he said.

Swamy, adjusting his cricket cap, said that he could not agree more.

Manas lived in a world completely different from the one unfolding in Indus. He bunked as many classes as he possibly could without much concern about grade drops. However, if there was one course of which he never missed a single class, it was Keshav's LOVE sessions.

'They are not just sessions, they are sensations.' Manas's voice would ring with considerable hope and happiness.

'Is Kaya showing up at the Insti party?' Sardar asked. Neel shook his head to signal he did not know and pretended that he couldn't care less. Prasad informed him that he saw Kaya going around the Chanakya guest house with a foreign visitor. She introduced him as some kind of a doctor.

'They seemed quite familiar with each other.' Prasad winked.

Neel pretended not to be interested in that subject at all. Yet, this petty information started bothering him like a sharp chip of stone stuck inside a shoe. In his mind, Neel had a mental archive of how Kaya appeared in different moods. He could not imagine that she would now be in the arms of some scavenging doctor, smelling of chloroform. 'The sight of a doctor clinging to Kaya like a stethoscope would be unbearable,' he thought.

Kaya was predictably absent at the 'Insti party' held on the rooftop of Sutlej Hostel. In her absence, Eva Reddy took centre stage as the prima donna. Swamy blurted out to Neel, 'Eva is here, snaring boys with heart-swinging moves over gin and tonic.'

The junta watched from their comfort zone, their arms close to their chest, fingers interlocked, a cigarette stuck in their mouth, rivulets of sweat streaming down their tense jaw. There was something about Eva that would make Neel shrink away from her. Her unseemly display of teeth, the whip-like ring in her speech, her beauty which had vacated the rest of her face and had taken long-term tenancy in her pouting lips. 'They were so swollen that they appeared to be stung by a beetle,' Neel thought. He wondered what the guys in Indus found so alluring about her. There was something that was strangely animal and subliminal in the way they looked at her.

The conversations twisted from sober to slutty. The loud sound of metal music drowned everything except monosyllable howls and subhuman voices. Sardar was ogling Eva in between bites of marinated tandoori chicken. She brought an ancient thirst in his throat. A mist of desire flamed his drunken eyes as he watched the swirl of her sari and her twisting torso, which was half-exposed. Sardar was mesmerized by her curls and curves, her convex hips and concave lips, and her smouldering smile. Eva's mouth was arched like a flycatcher and her undulating bust, evocative and wavy, had completely swept Sardar off his senses.

Neel was reminded of his marketing lessons in the MBA class. Desiring was about classifying human bodies into categories—lips, hips, eyes, earlobes, waist to chest ratio—and then assessing the attractiveness of each category according to the desires and opinions of the onlooker.

Energized by alcohol, Sardar's imagination was morphing Eva from plain to pretty. He slurred at Prasad, 'She appears somewhere in my mind between Kimi Katkar and Angelina Jolie.'

Prasad completed a quick scan with his eyes and grinned his consent. Eva, however, was simmering in barely suppressed anger with Neel's utter indifference to her affectionate glances. 'Why does he turn so cold and aloof on seeing me?' She let Sardar wind his arm around her waist as they danced clumsily to the beat of 'Twist and Shout' by the Beatles. Prasad was pinching his nostrils with two fingers before downing a shot of vodka. He said he detested the smell but loved the after-effects.

'Buffoon!' said Neel as he wondered whether he should also get drunk.

Neel was looking down from the rooftop towards the Godavari Hostel gate. A gulmohur tree in full bloom was casting its shadow on the street. A solitary sodium bulb was blinking bleakly at the entrance of the hostel where the chowkidar sat on a stool. He was jiggling his legs out of sheer boredom. Drucker, the dog, was sniffing around for food. Neel was craving for a glimpse of Kaya. It was then that a car suddenly pulled up near the Godavari gate.

'Wasn't that Professor Keshav Mitra's Indigo?' Neel's eyes narrowed. He saw Kaya step out of Keshav's car and rush towards her hostel. She seemed unsettled and disturbed. She didn't even turn around to say bye to the driver of the silver-grey car as it pulled away quickly. 'Who was driving the car?' A feeling of suspicion crept over Neel as he impulsively grabbed a shot of vodka and gulped it down.

'Who was driving Keshav's Indigo? Was it Keshav himself?'

He watched from the corner of his eye as Sardar and Eva were sneaking quietly out of the rooftop party. Eva flung a lingering glance at Neel who seemed lost in his own thoughts.

'Is he watching me go away with Sardar? What is eating him up?' she wondered.

Neel was feeling desolate like an unclaimed notebook left behind in an empty classroom.

∽

The next evening, on their way to the library, Neel happened to meet Kaya. They exchanged polite and measured hi's. Kaya's hair was somewhat dishevelled. Her bright and sparkling skin looked slightly tanned.

'Missed you at the party yesterday,' Neel said. Kaya just said 'Yeaaaah.' The prolonged vowels in that expression were simply a means to fend off Neel's inquisitiveness. Neel smiled wryly, thinking, 'I want you to know that I really missed you, but I do not wish to show my hurt and anger towards you.'

Kaya noticed the expression on Neel's face. Then, almost abruptly, she came near Neel and brought her lips close to his.

Neel thought, 'Oh! Where did this come from?' He had his teeth clenched and flapped his lips like a fish out of water. His eyes hovered on her face, lips still twitching, not sure where to plant the return kiss. In these few seconds, Kaya guided him deftly with magical manoeuvres of her mouth and tongue. She smelt of a mixture of Wills filter cigarettes and chewing gum. The taste got better after the first few tentative kisses. He soon probed her mouth like a schoolkid licking an ice cream cone. Neel felt that he was not just kissing one white woman but the entire Statue of Liberty. The suddenness of it all took his breath away. Neel felt giddy!

Kaya looked demurely into Neel's star-struck eyes and asked, 'Your room or mine?'

Neel, feeling uncoordinated and tingling all over, blurted out, 'Room 101.'

Kaya and Neel were soon sneaking past the gates along Periyar Men's Hostel, one following the other, avoiding eye contact with the security guard at the hostel entrance. Neel closed the door behind him noiselessly and watched Kaya under a shaft of soft neon light. She was dreamlike, edgy and alluring! It was as though the spirit of a Sharon Stone poster had come alive in three dimensions.

Neel's heart raced and he said to himself, 'Ah! Such devastating beauty—freckled white skin, aquamarine eyes, sharp nose, quivering cleavage like the Grand Canyon—enraptured!' He felt gawky.

Feverishly, Kaya held Neel close in her arms while the rising crescendo of desire egged him on. 'This upturned nose is mine, the succulent lips are mine, those fine cheekbones, golden hair, the goblets springing like two large scoops of vanilla with soft pink cherries on top—all these are mine too.'

Kaya's breath got warmer. Her skin was burning. Neel could smell the citrus scent of lemon and grapefruit. He knew that Kaya wore a different perfume each day of the week. She ran her fingers over his two-day-old stubble. Neel inhaled the fragrance of her dishevelled hair late into the night before he drifted off to sleep. His heart was humming with a sweet and sensuous delight and he felt as though he was floating in the air!

When he woke up Neel saw a faint dark bruise on Kaya's right shoulder. The bruise looked like it was quite an old one.

'What is this?' Neel asked as she turned on her side.

Kaya dressed up hurriedly, tied up her messy hair and left the room quietly without answering his question.

RISHIKESH ASHRAM, DAY 4

The bougainvillea blossomed wild and carefree around the ashram landscape. The blooming of purple, magenta and red was like the threads of ecstasy weaving a floral carpet in the air. Keshav looked around and made his way towards his seat. It was nine o'clock. You could synchronize your watches trusting his punctuality.

'Acharya Keshav will now speak about the theme of the day, Ecstasy,' announced the storyteller.

Swamy has checked the meaning of ecstasy on his smartphone. He was sharing with Neel that ecstasy originated from the Greek word 'ekstasis' which meant standing out. He said ecstasy was a form of trance that enabled people to transcend the boundaries of their ordinary life. This blissful trance is produced by various means, both material and non-material in nature. When a person was in ecstasy, his external senses, seeing, hearing and feeling, ceased to function normally. The consciousness of time and space suddenly seemed to disappear.

'Why is the rasa-lila called so, Keshav? Is it a form of dance?' Kaya was curious to know.

Keshav cleared his throat and said, 'Rasa-lila is the dance of ecstasy. Rasa is that which flows. Lila is a play of the divine that makes everything in existence flow. Rasa is fluidity. It is the taste and flavour of existence. A true rasika, one who has lived the rasa, experiences what we call the flow of ecstasy. Krishna does not give a discourse on divine ecstasy—he simply sings and dances it.'

'How does someone reach the state of ecstasy?' Neel was curious to know.

'Ecstasy is the disembodied energy that can be accessed through the body. Music and dance put the body into an elemental state that breaks the boundaries of our body-mind complex. The body is nothing but a composition of the five elements. The mind is a composition of thoughts. The body-mind complex is held by a boundary drawn by the ego. Krishna transported the gopis to the heights of ecstatic bliss where boundaries blurred and inhibitions broke down. An inspired artist, a warrior possessed by furious energy, and the ordinary cowherd girls of Vrindavan who fled their homes in moonlight, all of them experienced the same state of divine ecstasy. Rasa-lila is a journey from me-centred love to love that is boundless.'

'Is ecstasy an emotion?' Neel asked.

Keshav said: 'Through ecstasy, one rises above all inhibiting emotions such as likes, dislikes, anger, possessiveness and fear. The ecstatic human almost stands apart from his conventional thoughts and emotions. It is an altered state of consciousness, where time stands still and space expands to embrace infinity. It is like a return journey to our natural state, which is blissful. Bliss is not a passing emotion; it is the very core of our existence!'

Eva asked, 'Why were the gopis drawn towards Krishna?'

Keshav said, 'It is through the feminine energy of prakriti or nature that the pure intelligence of purusha manifests everything in creation. Prakriti and purusha are just principles, and not two different genders. Purusha is the unmanifested energy and prakriti is the manifested energy.

'Take the example of a man drinking a cup of hot tea. The cup seems to burn his lips. Actually, it is not the tea or the cup that burns his lips, it is the energy of the heat invisible in the tea that burns them. Like the inherent heat in the tea, the invisible animating principle of purusha makes prakriti experience the world as hot or cold. Krishna is the purna purusha, the complete and pure awareness that animates the feminine prakriti. It is the feminine principle of prakriti through which purusha expresses itself just like the heat in the tea makes your lips experience the warmth.'

'That is understood. Yet I fail to see,' said the former nun narrowing her feline eyes, 'how the erotic leads to the ecstatic.'

Keshav's lips perked up into a smile. 'The sages discovered many devotional road maps to reach the divine. Devotion harnessed the power of bhava or human emotions. Sometimes the devotional path would take the form of vatsalya bhava, to love the divine as the mother loves her child. Yashoda's love for Krishna was rooted in the emotional state of adoration of a mother for her child.

'The second path of devotion is that of sakhya bhava, to love the divine as a friend. Arjuna's love for Krishna glowed with the warmth of friendship.

'The third and perhaps the most exquisite path of devotion is madhurya bhava, to love the divine as a sweetheart. The love of the gopis for Krishna was through madhurya bhava, the feeling of ecstasy. Through ecstasy, carnal lust is transformed into transcendental love. In the ecstatic peak of madhurya bhava, the pleasure potency of the divine love permeates and lifts the devotee to a state of boundless bliss. The erotic is embraced and transmuted into the ecstatic. This is a lot like the process of alchemy of transmuting a base metal into gold.

'The rasa-lila of Krishna is the culmination of madhurya bhava, the emotion of the beloved for her sweetheart.'

Anju asked, 'What happens to a human being in the throes of ecstasy?'

Keshav said, 'Imagine those Sufi dervishes whirling in circles in a sama ritual. They go round the axis of divine love, which is the ultimate goal of all forms of love. When the Sufis surrender their nafs or their egocentric personal desires to the rhythm of music and dance centred on God, love takes wings and expands. The Greek God Eros, from whom the word erotic comes, could cast his spell of enchantment on mortals and transport them to the realm of ecstatic love.

'When a human being experiences ecstasy, as the gopis did, the following symptoms appear: their voice dries up, they get goosebumps and tears stream down from their eyes. Tears are pure emotions. They express what words fail to communicate. Ecstasy numbs us with its exquisite, quivering ripples of delight unknown to our ordinary sense-based love.'

'But, why would it take an erotic experience forbidden by

custom and society to experience ecstasy?' the former nun persisted.

'Remember that the gopis had staked everything, including their reputation to respond to the call of Krishna. It was Krishna who reminded them of their obligation to their families. Yet, the gopis rushed to respond to that primordial play of Krishna's flute unconcerned about their husbands, homes and hearth. The dance of the divine cannot be confined to man-made structures.

'The divine expresses itself not in the dry rules and laws of the society alone. The divine pulsates in the form of rhythmic energy, in the choreography of movements in nature and in the enigma of attraction between polarities: man and woman; the terrestrial and the celestial.

'Dance is the original expression of the ecstatic universe. Atoms dance in their orbits; molecules move in rhythmic measures to create the structure of this tangible world. Those who are possessed by this elemental dance experience this rasa—silent fluidity of the intangible world. This is the world of ecstatic perceptions. There is an inkling of the presence of the divine outside the apparent boundaries created by civilization.'

'Can the erotic naturally transform into the ecstatic?' the nun said, probing further.

Keshav said, 'Eroticism is blind and luminous at the same time. The blind part of it is carnal and lustful; it is involved in procreation and recreation. The luminous part is a reflection of the divine and is involved in creation. The creative play of Krishna's flute is the perfect rasa, the transcendental beauty that softens the glare of lust into the glow of love. Love is a return to the origin of life. The erotic becomes lust when it is pulled down to the gross pleasures of the body. The same erotic principle is transformed into love when it is harnessed in the aspiration for the divine.'

EVENING SESSION

The ceremonial evening aarti at the Rishikesh ashram was performed by the purohit with great fervour. He sprinkled sacred water on everyone around him; many had been watching the ceremony with their heads bowed and hands folded. He then went about his business of distributing the prasad, consecrated fruits, sweets and assorted offerings made by the devotees. Sometimes cash, wristwatches, gold rings and ornaments were also offered. The purohit was keen on favouring the devotees who made generous offerings with an extra helping of the prasad.

In the order of hierarchy, the devotees were the first ones to receive the prasad followed by the senior monks, local visitors and then the rest of the retreat crowd. Kaya was diligent in accepting and acknowledging her share of the prasad with a sincere namaste to the purohit. She bowed her head.

The purohit simply smirked. He had his reservations about women being allowed to stay inside the ashram. Yet, he kept his opinion to himself as he knew that it was Keshav's decision to alter the traditional rules by allowing women to participate in most ashram activities. Manas's parents had arrived at the ashram late in the afternoon. Neel personally went to the railway station to fetch them. Neel had been in regular touch with them over the years. Manas's mother Mohini found some kind of solace through Neel, perhaps a substitute for their deceased son. The old couple were quietly offering their prayers to the deity. The purohit gave them a red hibiscus picked up from the feet of the Krishna idol and rubbed a dash of red vermilion on their foreheads. Long after the devotees had dispersed, Manas's father and Neel conversed with the purohit, discussing matters in whispers and with a visible sense of urgency.

The purohit closed the temple door and made his way to

the classroom where he was supposed to arrive before Keshav. This had become almost a ritual of the retreat, the storytelling by the purohit followed by an informal conversation in the retreat group with Keshav. That evening, however, the purohit arrived slightly late and Keshav, a stickler for time, had already begun to tell the story himself. He gestured to the purohit to sit by his side and said that he would be the storyteller for the evening. It was the story of ecstatic love and the adventure of abduction.

THE STORY OF A BRIDE WHO PLANNED HER OWN ABDUCTION

'What is that one quality that a woman values the most in a man?' Keshav asked in his usual provocative way. There were murmurs all around. Some giggles, muffled conversations and conjectures followed.

Keshav answered his own question. 'The quality a woman most desires in a man is trust. A woman needs to trust a man's ability to protect her children, her honour and shield her from her emotional vulnerabilities. This is part of a woman's evolutionary biology. Rukmini was passionately in love with Krishna. She addressed Krishna as Achutya, the infallible being, who never betrays the trust reposed in him by his devotees.' Keshav paused for a while and then started narrating Rukmini's story.

> Dark-eyed and exquisitely beautiful Rukmini was the only daughter of Bhismaka, the ruler of Vidarbha. Of the five sons of Bhismaka, Rukmi was the eldest. Bhismaka's palace was often frequented by Narada, one of the great sages, who sang praises of Krishna describing his power, grace and valour in great detail. Sitting by her father's side, Rukmini would hear stories about Krishna.

Her imagination would conjure up his divine beauty. Rukmini's mind was resolutely fixed on him. Without ever meeting Krishna, she gave her heart away to him. Bhismaka and his entire family were keen that Rukmini marry Krishna, whom they all endorsed as the most suitable man for her. But there was one in the family who was vehemently opposed to Rukmini's marriage with Krishna. This was her own brother, Rukmi, who was jealous and upset with Krishna. Ignoring the protest of his father, he arranged his sister's marriage with Sisupala, the prince of Chedi and a sworn enemy of Krishna.

Not deterred by her brother's insensitivity towards her feelings, Rukmini decided to write a love letter to Krishna, the lord of her heart. She wrote:

'O Achutya, having heard of your many qualities, your beauty, knowledge and character, I have fixed my heart unabashedly on you since my childhood.

'You can only be compared with yourself in character, lineage, wisdom and understanding. Which girl of marriageable age would not covet you as a partner? I offer myself to you to accept me as your wife. You may wonder how a well-bred girl from an aristocratic family can be so open in professing her love for a man she has only heard of. I cannot consent to marrying Sisupala, that small-minded prince of Chedi, when I have already surrendered myself to you with utmost devotion. How can a jackal like him appropriate that which is meant for a lion of a man that you are?

'I urge you to come with your army when the marriage ceremony is about to begin. You should visit Vidarbha unseen. After crushing the army of Sisupala, you can abduct me and marry me according to the rakshasa rites that permit the kidnapping of the wife. On the morning of the wedding day I would be in a grand procession leading to the Ambika temple to offer my worship to the goddess. That is the most opportune moment to meet me and take me away.'

Rukmini concluded the letter by saying, 'In case I am not able to achieve my heart's desire, I will fast unto death. I would be willing to be reborn and wait for a hundred more lives in the hope that you will take me as your wife. Please do not abandon someone who has been devoted to you all her life and trusts you completely.'

Rukmini couriered her love message through a kind and helpful Brahmin who delivered it personally to Krishna.

When Krishna heard the message that the Brahmin read out to him on reaching Dwarka, he was ecstatic. He held the Brahmin's hand and said, 'Just as Rukmini dotes on me, I too have desired her ever since I heard the sage, Narada, describe her to me. I have heard that her skin glows like gold and her hair is shiny as a beetle's back. Her eyes are dark and wide, and they quiver like a shy deer. I imagine her teeth resembling a row of jasmine buds and her neck as shapely as a conch shell. Although I have never seen her, I visualize her walking swiftly as a swan on her soft feet.'

Krishna had no time to wait since the marriage of Rukmini was supposed to be solemnized only two days later. He summoned his charioteer, Daruka, who yoked his favourite horses for the journey to Vidarbha. Krishna took the Brahmin along with him as he left for Vidarbha to rescue Rukmini from the clutches of her brother Rukmi and his friend, Sisupala.

Rukmi was aware that Krishna and his brother, Balarama, had secretly entered the city to disrupt the marriage of his sister. He ensured that the procession taking Rukmini to the temple was heavily guarded.

As it was preordained, with pomp and festivity all around her, Rukmini emerged from the Ambika temple having offered her prayers to Goddess Durga. All the princes assembled outside the temple premises were so enchanted with her beauty that they dropped their weapons from their numb hands and their eyes froze on her. Rukmini walked through the milling assembly of her suitors, indifferent to their wanton gazes.

A breeze blew away the dark hair fluttering on her face. It was then that her eyes fell on the majestic Krishna standing on the edge of his chariot, extending his right hand to pull her up. The chariot closed up towards her in the blink of an eye. Rukmini leaned in towards him. Krishna grasped her hand and pulled her up, placing her beside his seat on the chariot. Krishna then spurred his horses and drove away with Princess Rukmini while his adversaries stood there like bystanders. Cheering lustily, the citizens of Vidarbha loved what they saw.

Rukmi and his allies, led by Jarasandha, were unable to bear the shock and felt ashamed that a cowherd would walk away with a princess who rightfully belonged to Sisupala. Their army chased Krishna's chariot but was held back by Balarama and the Yadava army who were there to support Krishna. Rukmi, angered beyond control, persisted with the chase. Krishna confronted Rukmi and broke his sword into many pieces. On Rukmini's entreaty, he did not kill her brother but he cut his hair and shaved his moustache off as a stern reminder of who the victor was.

Krishna was like a lion walking away with his prey from a pack of desperate and whining jackals. Rukmini looked back through the trail of dust that Krishna's chariot raised as it drove furiously towards Dwarka, the capital city of the Yadavas.

Rukmini, the princess of Vidarbha who had planned her own abduction by her beloved Krishna, was soon to become his wife.

'That's quite some story!' Kaya remarked. Neel nodded in agreement. They were expecting Keshav to say something more and he did not disappoint.

'Ecstasy breaks down social barriers and mental roadblocks that come in the way of love. Imagine the depth of attraction that Krishna and Rukmini had for each other and the strength of the resistance of a society that came in the way of their marriage.

'Rukmini's unwavering devotion to Krishna moved Krishna's will to accept her as his own. By eloping with Rukmini, Krishna was only achieving the inevitable. The erotic energy of life, polarized into the feminine and the masculine, eventually unites in the realm of blissful ecstasy. The wise seers of India called it Hladini Shakti. When love transcends the polarities of the body and reaches a state of spiritual unity, it is experienced as spiritual bliss. Krishna met his paramour and his wife, Rukmini, as an extension of his primordial bliss, his Hladini Shakti.'

The group dispersed in a daze.

8
Absence

**RISHIKESH ASHRAM, FRIDAY
DAY 5 OF THE RETREAT**

The purohit was describing Krishna's journey from the village life of Vrindavan to the city of Mathura to fulfil an important mission.

> When he turned sixteen, Krishna's sojourn in Gokul and Vrindavan was over. Life amidst the pure-hearted, God-fearing villagers of Gokul was full of adventures. Krishna confronted all the demons that threatened his life and the lives of the residents of Gokul. The demons, like Putana, Vakrasura and Trinavarta, and the serpent, Kaliya, poured out the poison of hatred on him. The lord of love, who had conquered all the demons inside him, vanquished those that showed up on his path outside. Kamsa, who wanted to kill Krishna at birth, hated him the most. He conspired to invite Krishna and Balarama to the Dhanuryagna, a tournament of the bow, in Mathura. Kamsa sent Akura to Mathura to fetch the boys from Vrindavan. His plan was to get the brothers crushed to death by a fierce elephant or get them killed in a wrestling bout with his pet wrestlers, Mushtika and Chanura.
>
> It was Krishna's day of parting. Early in the morning, the gopis spotted Akura's chariot in front of Nanda's

house. Yashoda was weeping disconsolately with her arm around Krishna. He tried to comfort her in vain. The foster parents who had nurtured the divine child went through the pangs of separation. Krishna embraced each one of them. He told them his brother and he had to obey Kamsa's royal command, failing which his uncle would devastate Vrindavan. Krishna did not know where he was going. Yet he knew that he would never come back to Gokul and Vrindavan again.

The pain of separation is always greater for those who are left behind than the one who is leaving. The gopis went numb at the very thought that their pristine playmate, their soul's companion since childhood, would be lost to them. He would no longer play his magical flute on the sandbanks of the Yamuna under the soft moonbeams. Would he be lured by the city lights of Mathura and forget them forever?

One of the gopis said, 'What will it be like for us when you are gone? It does not matter if Kamsa kills us. We are ready to perish with our eyes fixed on you and our lips uttering your name. Do not abandon us, Krishna!'

Krishna tried in vain to console the gopis. His band of gopas, who were partners in mischief and merrymaking with him, were relieved by the fact that since their foster fathers would be travelling with Krishna to Mathura, they might be able to persuade Krishna to come back to Gokul with them. Krishna took leave of them and bid farewell to the cows he herded in the forest. Those cows, meek animals, who could not express their feelings, stood watching Krishna with their large, soulful eyes. Krishna wiped his tears with his forearm and hugged them goodbye. Finally, he stretched himself at the feet of his mother and took final leave of her.

Balarama climbed on to the chariot first. Akura

helped Krishna sit beside his brother. He then climbed on to the driver's seat and whipped the horses to pull the chariot away. Yashoda and Rohini stood stunned, covering their eyes as they could not bear the sight of the chariot moving away, towards the city of Mathura.

When the gopis realized that Krishna had indeed begun his journey to Mathura, they cried and tried to stop the chariot. Simple folks, they were; they spoke among themselves, 'Just see how cruel-hearted Krishna is! How could he leave us like this and vanish?'

Krishna stretched out his hand and asked them not to follow him any longer. They stood still watching as the chariot with their beloved Krishna in it was fast disappearing from their view. Krishna had a last lingering look. His Radha was not there among those who stood to say goodbye. Krishna had played his most intense flute song for Radha. Thereafter, he gave the flute away to her and promised that he would never play the flute again. They knew that for them there was no parting as they belonged inseparably to each other like fire and its capacity to burn.

Meanwhile, Krishna's chariot sped away, until it was not visible any more. The residents of Gokul still kept looking at the cloud of dust raised by the chariot's wheels and the speeding horses. It seemed to them that the heart of Vrajabhumi was torn asunder and life in Gokul and Vrindavan had turned to ashes with Krishna's going away.

Keshav gently interrupted the purohit's narrative to explain the significance of parting in love. He said, 'Love cannot be contained like the water in a lake. It will cease to be love. Love contained will stagnate and throttle the beloved with its sterility. Krishna's attachment to a place is not unlike the river's attachment to a particular part of the land mass in the course of its journey...

The river encounters everything on its path and is attached to nothing that comes in its way.

'Krishna's parting from the gopis and his foster parents did not mean that he disengaged from the past. He engaged in everything with the fullness of his being and then moved on when it was time to do so.'

'If the absence of Krishna is so painful for those he leaves behind, why does he even part from those who love him?' Kaya's face flushed intensely as she asked that question.

Keshav said, 'Love is not an emotion. Love is our own existence. To savour the existence of love, a human being oscillates between the appearance and the disappearance of love—between abirbhava and tirobhava. Separation, described as viraha, is as necessary to love as distance is to enchantment. Distance leads to a greater enchantment. The familiar becomes stale. A bright full moon appears after a dark new moon. The waxing and waning of the moon is only a terrestrial phenomenon as seen from the earth. In reality, the celestial moon neither waxes nor wanes. It is the changing position of the earth, relative to the moon, that gives it the appearance of waxing and waning. Krishna's love is like the hide-and-seek game that the moon plays with the onlookers of the earth. He hides so that he can be sought even more intensely by his beloved.'

'What does the emotion of parting feel like?' Neel asked.

'The point of parting with a loved one determines the intensity and depth of love. The gopis experience the depth of this love in separation. The gopis do not have or need a theory of love.' He chuckled. 'They are simply in love. They have a feeling of love—however painful or pleasurable that feeling may be. During the rasa dance, Krishna's momentary disappearance plunges the gopis into the depths of despair. They rise to the peak of delight when he appears again. Just like a full moon appears and disappears with the passing of clouds, the gopis feel Krishna through alternate bouts of separation and union. The groves of Vrindavan are replete with the dance of delight as Krishna multiplies himself to be with each gopi. The same Vrindavan turns into a bleak and despairing landscape in the absence of Krishna.'

'Is viraha, the emotion of absence of love, part of love itself?' Kaya asked.

'Viraha is not about wallowing in pain and loss. Viraha is a form of penance. It is the scorching feeling of the burning of the ego that paves the way for love to descend on us. Viraha precedes true union like a fast precedes a good feast. Viraha then is the process of purification of the body and mind; and the burning away of the ego that clears up the path to the divine. Love as attachment is a generator of illusions. Only the detachment of viraha can bring the lover back to the reality of what love really is. The detachment, which is letting go of the illusions, leads to non-attachment, which is the nature of love itself. Like the sunshine that falls equally on hills and valleys and warms them without getting attached to either, the very nature of pure love is to be non-attached to any particular form.'

INDUS CAMPUS, LUCKNOW
WHAT HAPPENED TO MANAS?

Neel's sleep broke at the horrible sound of the alarm clock. There was no sign yet of Swamy's coffee. He heard a buzz of human voices drifting down the corridor. There was the sound of footsteps rushing towards Room 102, next to his. Everyone was calling out Manas's name in hushed voices. What had happened to Manas?

Neel jumped out of his bed. There was a sizeable crowd at the entrance of Manas's room. Heads were popping over each other to look inside.

'This morning,' the warden said with a grim face, 'Manas was found dead in his room in the hostel.'

Neel stood there dumbfounded. His heart skipped a few beats. He was too shocked to react.

When his hostelmates entered his room, they found Manas's body hanging from the ceiling fan by a nylon rope.

His parents had been informed and they were on their way from his home town to claim his body for cremation. The eyewitnesses said that his laptop had online images of different ways to hang oneself. Was it the pressure of a high stakes MBA? This guy was on the verge of making a life! God knows why he gave up so easily. Was there a suicide note? Was it a suicide or...?

They noticed copious notes from Keshav's classes that were stuck on the wall next to Manas's bed. One of them read:

A life of experiment is worth a thousand times more than the world of second-hand experience.

Another one stared glaringly at Neel:

Learn to die for your desires
If you want them fulfilled.
Bury those desires as seeds in the soil—
One day they will sprout in a burst of marigolds.

Neel was shaken. Those lines were excerpts from Keshav's LOVE class notes that Manas had borrowed from him a couple of days back. He was trying to tell me something yesterday on our way to the class. 'Why did I ignore him?' he asked himself. A cold chill crept up Neel's spine.

When the local police scanned Manas's internet search history, hours before his death, they found a site that had put Sharon Stone's best pictures on sale on the net. Manas had placed an order for a couple of pictures to be delivered on Neel's birthday!

When Neel heard this, he wondered, 'Why? Was this yet another of Manas's many experiments to immortalize his bond of friendship? That crazy Manas, who for hours was planning his own death, set aside a few precious moments of his life to plan a birthday gift he knew would surprise me!' Neel's eyes were hazy with tears. The police interrogated Neel for possible clues to Manas's suicide but found no leads. They came to the conclusion that Manas may have been acting out of severe depression because of a sharp downturn in his grade point averages in class.

Neel knew Manas had the habit of writing a diary once in a while. When his room was being cleared and his belongings were being packed in a box, Neel noticed a blue Moleskine notebook where Manas wrote his last words after he had just finished watching the movie *Troy* on his computer:

> If they ever tell my story, let them say that I walked the corridors of the business school with giants. Students come and go like the cycle of seasons, the pages fall off a calendar like dried leaves of a spring gone by, but some things like hope and love never cease to be. Let them say I lived in the time of Keshav, the enlightened one; Neel, my buddy from many lives in the past—this life would be worth a lot less without his love and friendship. Sardar and Swamy, my two sparring partners; Prasad, the world's most unassuming court jester, and Kaya, Eva and Anju, the tamer of mighty men. Let them say that I lived in the time of Malhotra and Drucker.

Then there was a quote from Henry van Dyke, a former professor of Princeton:

> *To: The lesser mortals of the class.*
> *Use what talents you possess; the woods would be very silent if no birds sang there except those that sang the best.*

Neel couldn't hold back his tears any more as he read these concluding words—farewell, silent birds!

∽

The faculty tea room was abuzz with how Keshav's experimental classes were aiding and abetting an alien culture in the campus. A few faculty members led by Professor Erol Sequerra were at the forefront of opposition to his LOVE classes.

'What's this melodrama happening in a business school? What's the point of a misplaced idealism that draws students away from real studies and coveted careers?'

Surprisingly, his biggest critic, Malhotra, was not one of those opposing Keshav's course. Malhotra just listened, pensively, to Professor Sequerra's tirade against Keshav. He somehow recognized that it was the oppressive burden of relative grading and the culture of perform or perish that drove students to appreciate whatever Keshav had to say. Why wouldn't Malhotra think like that? His wife Mridula had asked him if they'd had a son like Manas, would they have forced him to get into a school that was so formidable and alienating for a young man. The Malhotras, who were a childless couple, had pondered silently over that question during breakfast.

The teaboy informed the faculty that Manas's parents had arrived from his home town in Odisha. The faculty and a motley group of students reached the hostel gate to escort and console the elderly couple who looked quite lost. When they met their dead son, the mother broke down in sniffles and sobs. Soon the sobs turned into a wail.

'Who killed my son?' The father, a doctor in a government hospital, wore a wooden expression. His gaze was frozen on Keshav who was holding Manas's mother close to himself, consoling her. The father said in a rasping voice, 'He was never the kind of boy who would want to die like this.'

'How much did a father really know his son?' Neel wondered.

'Why did this happen to us?' Manas's father asked Keshav.

That question whirred relentlessly like the blades of the ceiling fan from which Manas had hanged himself. Keshav silently escorted the parents to the Administration Block for completing some formalities.

The next morning, it was business as usual, except for that one short typed notice on the programme noticeboard. It read:

> **Professor Keshav Mitra will not teach the LOVE course for the next two weeks. The pre-scheduled classes will remain suspended until further notice. Those who have enrolled for this course may opt to attend other courses in this period. The inconvenience caused to the students is deeply regretted.**

The news spread through winks and nudges in the Indus community. There was a condolence in the Faculty Council meeting at which Keshav was absent. There was a rumour that Dean Nataraj Nandy had decided to temporarily suspend Keshav's course and set up an enquiry committee to see if the LOVE course was having any adverse impact on the students' lives. Some said it was a voluntary decision by Keshav to take some time off for himself, away from the campus. Whatever the truth was, many students felt that ultimately they were the ones who would be losing out on a great learning opportunity if the course was aborted.

∽

In the late hours of that night, Manas's parents spent time in conversation with Keshav. Manas's father, in his early sixties, was stocky and muscular with dark eyes and a thin moustache that had turned white. His mother was tall and ageing gracefully. They now carried their sorrow at the loss of their only child with a sense of despair that sat like a cold fog inside their hearts.

Manas's body had been cremated in the Gomtinagar crematorium by late night. His body was prepared to be fed into a raging fire struck on sandalwood. Since his parents couldn't bear to perform the last rites of their deceased son—how could they for they were supposed to precede him in this procession of life and death—it was decided that his best buddy, Neel, would put a sandalwood stick doused in rarefied butter into that pyre. Neel was surprised to see Professor Malhotra, of all people, among the bystanders. Manas was not one of his favourite students! Malhotra's eyes glowed with an unusual softness that no one in the class knew he possessed.

Neel fed the fire not just to Manas's body but to the entirety of who Manas was—the way he walked; the manner in which he imitated Malhotra and pulled off pranks at will; his wild darting eyes; his constant search for an opportunity to experiment with life; that look of hurt on his face when Neel turned his face away from him. The bright orange plastic cord with which he hanged himself, a floral shirt he bought from Goa, his beautiful mouth, high cheekbones—they were all within the grasp of this raging beast called death. If one had to see insatiable desire, one had to look at the twisted tongues of the fire consuming a whole human being. When Manas's charred body finally turned into ashes, there was no way to be sure as to whom they belonged to.

Neel wondered what the parents went through when they

were grieving the death of their son or daughter. 'Did they relive moments from the past, recalling instances when they feared their little one could die one day? Finally, when that dreaded moment arrived, did they feel cold and distant, as though they had anticipated such a tragedy even before its actual occurrence? Or did they become too numb to express emotions? What happened to those desires that parents held for their children?'

Neel looked at the old couple. Their eyes were glistening before the dying embers of the ritual fire. 'Would they now switch off from the world with all its cruelties and its grim reality? Would they relive the memory of their son through the eyes of other parents luckier than they were? Would they embrace this death as a preparation for their own mortality?'

Neel reflected on the many facets of Manas's self: playful, reflective, impish, lovelorn, bored and sometimes boisterous.

Kaya was looking intently at the dying embers that reduced Manas to ashes. The truth of what Keshav taught in his LOVE class now dawned on her. Those lessons had circled back and she could almost hear Keshav speaking. 'If you go to the heart of it, self-belief is a misleading thing. Which is the self that you would believe in? In our human experience, we are an assortment of many selves. We are the carriers of multiple identities. We believe in a multitude of selves. Only in death do we come to the realization that one who has a beginning must necessarily have an end. That which is born will surely die one day. Our many identities, fuelled by our desires, create a stubborn illusion of permanence. They are like many castles built on sand. The tide of time flattens all those sandcastles until they become one with the trillions of nameless and formless grains of sand.'

It was finally time to say farewell. To the gathering of Manas's friends in the crematorium, Keshav said, 'When we think of death as the end of life, we read the script of existence upside down. When this script is turned around, death appears to be that silent bed of sea, from which rise those boisterous bubbles of life. Death is the beginning that hides, in its depth, life's most enduring secret. Death is that restful seed that writes, in the dust, the vision of a whole forest. Dying and living are like sleeping and waking.'

Then he looked around slowly, making eye contact with everyone present, and said, 'For those of you who loved Manas, I have just this to say: Love leaves a treasure that neither this beautiful appearance called life nor the painful disappearance called death can steal from you!'

Neel trudged back to Periyar Hostel late that night thinking of Manas and their days together. He found himself silently repeating Keshav's words. 'Manas would have loved to etch these words on a stick pad,' he thought.

> *Love leaves a treasure that*
> *neither this beautiful appearance called life*
> *nor the painful disappearance called death*
> *can steal from you!*

RISHIKESH ASHRAM, DAY 5
HOW KRISHNA LIBERATES MATHURA

Keshav gestured to the purohit to carry on with the story of Krishna's next adventure in Mathura.

> After that memorable encounter with Kubja, Krishna and his brother, Balarama, were ready for the next task of taking part in the bow tournament organized by Kamsa. Krishna and his companions from Vraja reached the pavilion where the tournament was supposed to be held. Krishna made light work of stringing a magnificent bow on display. He then broke the bow effortlessly as though

it was a piece of straw. Kamsa's security, who was sent to kill them, was easily put away by the brave brothers. Soon their story spread all over Mathura. After dinner that night, the two brothers slept peacefully on a cart. In contrast, a terrified Kamsa couldn't catch even a wink of sleep.

Kamsa's reign of terror had reached its darkest night. Since the day of Krishna's birth, Kamsa had killed thousands of babies fearing they might be his annihilator in the future. His pale green eyes would gleam with hatred. He seeded deceit and revenge in his kingdom. The prisons of Mathura were full of those who even showed signs of rebellion. He poured a narcotic potion into the water of Mathura city that kept its citizens in a state of perpetual drowsiness. Able-bodied men, who dared to speak up against the king's tyranny, were brutalized and their dead bodies were thrown in the city's gutters. Women were violated by Kamsa's courtiers whose perverted tastes sent shivers down the spine of Mathura's residents. Terror was the weapon of the tyrant, Kamsa, and fear was the pervasive instinct for survival in Mathura.

Citizens of Mathura, who had heard about the dark blue boy of Vrindavan and his amazing exploits, hoped and prayed that one day he would deliver on the prophecy of Kamsa's end. In their heart of hearts kindled the flame of their love for Krishna—their deliverer. They decided to walk, run and even crawl to see the wrestling bout planned by Kamsa in the stadium.

The next day, at the entrance of the tournament arena, redolent with the sounds of trumpets and bugles, Kamsa's men let loose an intoxicated elephant named Kuvalayapida to trample the brothers who had come to take part in the wrestling bout organized by Kamsa.

Seeing the elephant coming towards them, Krishna walked up to the mahout and whispered to him, 'Would you care to take the elephant away from this public place so that he does not block the entrance.'

The mahout refused to move away, and as directed by Kamsa's men, spurred the elephant to charge at Krishna. Fleet-footed, Krishna played around with the elephant, making it spin around like a top. The elephant tried to grab the blue speck of a boy with its trunk but Krishna escaped with a dexterous move. The elephant dug its tusks into the ground and Krishna effortlessly climbed on to the head of the elephant and broke a tusk with no more than a twist of his wrist. With the same tusk, he killed the groaning elephant and the mahout. Then perching the same tusk on his shoulders, Krishna and his brother entered the arena of the wrestling match.

A packed stadium watched the wonder boy spellbound. Each one present in the auditorium saw Krishna according to their own understanding. The huge and mighty wrestlers saw Krishna as the spectre of death. The noble among the citizens saw him as the crowning glory of mankind. All the women adored him as he was the lord of love. The gopa boys, who had accompanied him all the way from Vraja, thought of him as their 'own boy'. The elderly men and women thought of Krishna as their own son and their hearts swelled with filial love. The wise saw in him the cosmic incarnation of the lord of the universe. The yogis perceived him as the supreme truth. Each one saw the blue boy in the light of their own perception.

Kamsa saw in Krishna the premonition of his own death. Kamsa's fear of Krishna made him think of his nephew while he was talking, walking, sleeping and even breathing. He was afraid of confronting Krishna, knowing that his nephew could emerge from anywhere—from under his throne, or the corner of his palace. His fears drove him to aggression and vengeance towards Krishna.

Inside the stadium, an anxious Kamsa, perched on a grand chair, raised his hand and signalled the commencement of the wrestling match. The huge-looking wrestlers, Chanura and Mushtika, now strutted towards Krishna menacingly.

Krishna, with a smile of mischief, said, 'Chanura, I am just a small boy and you are so huge. You are a veteran of many fights whereas I am just a village bumpkin who has only fought in street brawls. A wrestling match should ideally be between two equals. How can I fight you?'

In a sinister voice, Chanura said, 'You are not a kid. We just saw what you did to that elephant outside the stadium. Come on! I will fight you and Mushtika will take on your brother, Balarama.'

The packed audience roared their complete disapproval of this treachery and unequal fight staged by an unforgiving Kamsa. Soon, Krishna and Balarama started sparring with the wrestlers. Arms tangled with arms, legs intertwined with legs, chest thumping chest—the youngsters matched the veterans move by move. Suddenly Krishna, in a burst of energy, lifted Chanura above his head, whirled him around as if he was some kind of a plaything and smashed him on the ground. Balarama ended the life of Mushtika with a swerve of his left hand. Another pair of wrestlers came forward to challenge the boys and met with the same fate. Seeing the superhuman strength of the boys from Vrindavan, the rest of the wrestlers fled the scene.

Kamsa had by now started to panic. He masked his fear through bravado and started screaming his orders to catch the boys. He had lost his head. 'Arrest Nanda...

kill their crooked father, Vasudeva. My father, Ugrasena, seems to have switched to the enemy's side. Get him too.'

Kamsa's soldiers tried to grab Krishna but he slipped away. Eluding their grasp in the blink of an eye, Krishna was on the high platform where Kamsa was strutting around. Kamsa grabbed his shield and sword and ran towards Krishna. Like an eagle catching a snake, Krishna caught hold of Kamsa and threw his crown to the ground. He then threw him off the platform into the wrestling arena. He ran down and jumped lightly on the body of Kamsa. At that instant, Kamsa looked into the eyes of the lord of love, whom he had hated for years, and died.

The crowd that was cheering lustily fell silent for a moment. No one could believe that a tyrant, who had tormented the whole of Mathura for twenty years, would die in an instant without any resistance.

Krishna then met his parents, Devaki and Vasudeva, and freed them from years of suffering and imprisonment. Ignoring the demand of the elated Yadavas who wanted Krishna to be crowned the king of Mathura, he freed Ugrasena and coronated him as the king. His foster father Nanda, knowing that Krishna would never return to the verdant Vraja village again, returned sad but delighted that their little Kanha had proved himself to be a real man among the boys.

The purohit had a way of retelling Krishna's story, and would often end the tale with a dramatic twist. Keshav thanked him and gestured to the audience for questions.

A wizened, old professor from Israel clutching on to the hand of his grandson said, 'Tell us more about love and fear.'

Keshav answered: 'We are the light of love. Fear is love that wears a mask to hide itself. The lover fears the absence of the beloved. But how can this fear arise if there is no love between the two of them? It is because of the grand fear of love's inescapable laws that the planets move in their orbits and the seasons shift in persistent cycles. The sun shines, the moon waxes and wanes, and the sea ebbs and flows. Behind the mask of the grand fear lies the grander design of love.

'If you look with fearful eyes, the world of love would seem like a chasm between two mountains. If you look through the heart of love, you will behold a safe and supporting valley in place of the fearful chasm.'

Then, he started reciting the lines of a mystical poem that he was fond of.

> *Crushed grapes shrink from each other in fear*
> *Only to flow together*
> *In the distilled wine of love.*

The professor, who was still holding his grandson tightly in his grasp, asked, 'Did Kamsa still die in the fear of Krishna or was it the love of Krishna that killed him in the wrestling match?'

Keshav said, 'Love in practice is nothing but remembrance. The true lover remembers his beloved as often as possible. Kamsa did not just remember Krishna; he was simply obsessed with Krishna ever since he heard the prophecy that Krishna would be the agent of his annihilation. He looked for Krishna in every nook and corner of the prison where he had imprisoned Devaki and Vasudeva. He thought of Krishna while he was awake, or dreaming in his sleep. Kamsa's fear of Krishna erupted in anger and rage as he began to kill all newborn baby boys in Mathura, suspecting them to be the newborn Krishna. The fear and anger simmering within Kamsa is nothing but the explosive potential of love that he seeks but cannot find out there.

'Life didn't go Kamsa's way and his desire to get rid of Krishna was thwarted. And thwarted desire turned into vengeance. Kamsa's evil deeds to wreak vengeance on the citizens of Mathura were nothing but the distortion of love.

'Kamsa lived in fear. Yet, just before dying at the hands of Krishna, he saw a glimpse of love in his sparkling eyes that had the depth and intensity of an ocean. The evil in Kamsa was destroyed by Krishna's love. There are two ways to destroy your adversaries. One way is to hate them; the other is to love them. Through hatred, you can subdue the adversary; but when you love them, you kill the enmity between the two of you.

'Try to understand this. Kamsa was never at peace with his evil mentality. Someone who holds a lump of burning coal that he wants to hurl at his enemy ends up burning himself first. Krishna was not just killing Kamsa. He was liberating the man from his self-created prison of anger and hatred.'

IN MEMORIAM: MANAS

Twenty years after his tragic death in Indus, Manas still surfaced in group conversations. The old students, some of them friends of Manas who had met his parents years back, met the ageing couple, now into their eighties, in a large guest room in the ashram where Neel had made arrangements for their lodging. The post-dinner conversation with Keshav along with Manas's former friends veered around what Manas was looking for in those days at Indus.

'He was clearly feeling suffocated in the business school milieu and he had desired a life of greater adventure than getting and keeping a job,' speculated Eva.

'Exactly, precisely and totally, I second that! Manas had envisioned an ideal future with such unbounded freedom. He couldn't hold himself back from killing himself to get away from the unbearable situation in which he was in,' Swamy chipped in.

'What brought Manas to the point of self-extinction?'

Neel was looking down, focusing on the lines on his palm. Kaya had fixed her gaze on Keshav, looking for an answer.

In a solemn voice, Keshav said, 'The unconscious part in us fails to see that our desires are nothing but the shadows cast by our own life. Manas was very close to an illumined life and yet his desires were hounding him. He desperately wanted to rise above his desires, and shine above the competitive rivalries and petty jealousies. As they say in India, the darkest place is inevitably under the lamp that is lit up to dispel darkness.'

'Another castle of empty words,' Neel murmured. His jaw tightened as he felt a sense of anger creeping up inside him. 'How does one understand the heart of a son when he has not been a father himself?'

After a brief pause, Keshav asked Manas's parents, who had been sitting quietly by his side, if they were comfortable. Seeing all of Manas's friends, their wounds seemed to have opened up.

Neel remembered the lost look on their faces when they had come face to face with their son's death. He had seen how difficult it had been for them to embrace the inauspicious, to accept death—more so when the victim happened to be their son.

NOTES ON ABSENCE FROM NEEL'S DIARY

Neel still preserved the learning diary of the LOVE classes that he took twenty years back. He read Keshav's words exactly as he had then uttered them:

In the field of management, when all the numbers are crunched and all the data is mined, the undiscovered mystery will still be a human being. Management is that art by which you convert man into men, and men into a herd of sheep, and finally a man into a machine.

Almost the entire class had broken into a roar of applause.

Manas had shared his notes on Keshav's classes with Neel. In those handwritten words, he described how the absence of love ruled the corporate world. The corporate dark matter surfaced in ruthless competition, mindless production and meaningless verbalization of success mantras. The absence of love showed up in the corporate balance sheets where furniture and machinery were considered assets and people as liabilities and expenses. While in the rest of existence life was about cooperation and symbiosis of life forms, in business schools, it was all about cut-throat competition, kick-ass rivalry and treating each other as targets. There was no love lost in the competition. The romance of wealth creation was lost in the furious number-crunching of the world of enterprise.

9
Devotion

**RISHIKESH ASHRAM, SATURDAY
DAY 6 OF THE RETREAT**

'Devotion is the deepening of your presence.' Keshav's voice was sparkling and lucid like a waterfall. 'When devotion becomes deep enough, you have faith.' Then looking skyward, with his eyes fixed on an eagle whirling on the top of the temple spire, he said:

> *Birds fly as they have faith in their wings.*
> *Humans fly with the wings of faith.*

It was now the purohit's turn to read out the story of the lessons in devotion from Krishna's life.

WHAT KRISHNA'S EMISSARY UDDHAVA LEARNT FROM THE GOPIS

Uddhava was a dear friend and cousin of Krishna. He was the disciple of Rishi Vrihaspati, the foremost guru of the devas. Uddhava was a handsome man with long arms, large lotus eyes and a sharp intellect. He was proud of his erudition and had developed the arrogance of a young man of knowledge who was also good-looking. Krishna picked him as an emissary who would visit Vraja and meet those he had long left behind in Gokul and Vrindavan.

Holding Uddhava by the hand, Krishna pleaded, saying, 'My friend, I want you to go to Vrindavan to meet my foster parents, Nanda and Yashoda, for they must have been yearning to see me ever since I left them. I also have a message for the gopis who must have been feeling lost since I moved to Mathura, leaving them in the lurch.'

Uddhava agreed to go but wondered why Krishna always talked about those illiterate village women who fed him butter and simply frolicked with him. 'What is so special about those gopis?' Uddhava asked.

Krishna smiled and said, 'Go and find that out for yourself!'

When Uddhava arrived in Vrindavan, the sun was about to set. He was charmed by the serenity and rustic beauty of Vrindavan. Lamps were lit in households, bees hummed, birds cooed and cows lowed in leisurely contentment. The gopas and gopis of Vrindavan, the simple cowherd boys and girls, were singing in praise of Krishna. They were narrating the plays and pranks of Krishna and Balarama during their fifteen years of sojourn in Vraja. Krishna was the light of their eyes and the song of their lives. Uddhava was surprised by the outpouring of their devotion to Krishna.

He soon reached Nanda's house. Delighted to meet him, Nanda began recounting stories of Krishna as a boy with great affection. He introduced Uddhava to Krishna's foster mother Yashoda, and the villagers who had gathered there.

'Uddhava, tell us, does Krishna still remember us?' asked Yashoda.

Uddhava said, 'Yes, he does remember you as much

as he remembers to wake up every day. Krishna asked me to tell you to think of him as the Self that resides in all. Krishna is unborn and undying. Physically, he may appear like any other man. Yet, his identity is not defined by his body and its extensions. He is that transcendental Self that is unattached to any place or person. Yet, he pervades every place and person. He is not swayed by likes or dislikes, high or low. The world is simply his playground and he sports with all at will. This Krishna does not belong to Vraja alone. He belongs to all who love him. He hides in their innermost Self.'

Nanda and Yashoda, along with the village boys and girls who had gathered around them, quietly listened with unblinking eyes, although they were unable to make much sense of Uddhava's high philosophy. They spent the entire night talking about Krishna.

In the early hours of the next morning, the gopis spotted Uddhava. He resembled Krishna from afar, so much so that they rushed towards him mistaking him to be their long-lost friend. When they came close, they were disappointed to find it was someone else. Uddhava said that he had a message for them from Krishna. Without waiting for Uddhava to deliver his message, the gopis poured out to him all their grievances against Krishna.

'We know you have come to meet Krishna's parents. What else would Krishna be bothered about in Vrindavan? His love for us is seasonal. Like a bee discards a flower after drinking the honey and birds fly off a tree when all its fruits are devoured, lovers abandon their women.' They began to drift into furious monologues forgetting Uddhava's presence.

'Krishna must have been seduced and won over by those clever damsels of Mathura. We are simple-minded girls, unable to match their wily ways.'

Then, turning to Uddhava, they said, 'Tell us truthfully, does Krishna ever remember us? Do not try to lull our anger with your clever wordplay.'

Uddhava saw these women weeping. He was moved by the depth of their love and devotion to Krishna. Uddhava meandered into deep philosophy as he tried to explain Krishna's way of life to the gopis. He said, 'You see, Krishna is everywhere in and around you like your own existence. How can you or anyone else, then, experience any separation from him? Is he not established in your own Self? He cannot stay away from you. Why don't you meditate on his formless existence?'

'Meditate? How? With what instrument do we meditate? We are not educated, you see!' The gopis expressed their helpless desperation.

Uddhava showed off his knowledge, 'Meditate by concentrating your mind.'

The gopis giggled. 'But our mind no longer stays with us, you see!'

Bewildered, Uddhava asked, 'Where have your minds gone?'

They said, 'We have just one mind each and that has run away with Krishna!'

Uddhava fell utterly silent.

The gopis continued, 'From where does one get a spare mind to meditate on the formless Krishna that you speak of. By the way, where did you say this formless Krishna lived? We have worshipped our blue boy, Krishna, with our hands and loved him with our hearts. He decorated our hair with his own fingers and caressed us with his own limbs. Ever since he left, Vraja has turned to ashes for us.'

Uddhava now played his trump card. 'Krishna has

not forgotten you even for a moment. You are always in his mind. In fact, he asked me to deliver this message to you.' He then read out Krishna's unwritten love notes. The gopis listened with their eyes wide open and ears perked up.

'My beloved gopis, the reason I had to part with you was to ensure that you would never be separated from me. Parting of bodies only makes the hearts grow fonder and the souls thirsty. Parting is to love what a storm is to fire. If your love is a flickering flash fire of lust, the storm of parting will put it off. But if your love is like the unwavering flame of devotion, the storm of parting will turn it into a blazing, all-consuming and purifying bonfire. That is why I have kept myself hidden from you. You will look for me everywhere until you find me in the depth of your own hearts. Then your minds will become completely saturated with my presence. Do not grieve. Your devotion is only deepening my presence inside your hearts.'

The gopis were ecstatic as they heard Uddhava deliver Krishna's message to them. Uddhava himself began to experience the devotion that the gopis had for Krishna.

He wondered, 'It must have taken them several births and thousands of years of evolution to reach this state of exalted love and devotion.'

Uddhava now clearly understood why Krishna had sent him to Vraja. The pride that Uddhava had acquired about the supremacy of his bookish knowledge got tempered by devotion and pure love. He touched the feet of the gopis in reverence as he took leave of them. He bid farewell to Nanda, Yashoda and the gopas.

When Uddhava returned to Mathura from Vraja after spending a few days there, he described to Krishna what he had experienced. Krishna listened rather dispassionately to the story of the gopis' devotion that Uddhava narrated. Then he smiled that enchanting half-smile of his and moved away saying, 'I have a promise to keep. I must visit Kubja, the beautiful woman who once moved with a hump. She is waiting for me in her home.'

Nothing was too important to gloat over and no one was too insignificant to ignore as far as Krishna was concerned. He dealt with all the aspects of life with equanimity.

The story of Uddhava was over. It was now time for questions.

'How does one reach the state of devoted love that the gopis experienced for Krishna?' Marsha, a scholar and a former student of Keshav from Sweden, asked.

Keshav said, 'Faith is the seed of devotion, and knowledge is the fruit. Faith is deep-seated knowing without conflict or contradiction. The seed of a tree knows its potential for growth just as the bird knows about its potential to fly. When faith finds a congenial environment, it grows like a tree from the seed. When the tree bears fruit, this knowing of the seed is validated in the knowledge of the growth of the tree.'

'What is the difference between belief and faith?' Marsha asked again.

'Belief is only a mental affirmation based on a good reason. A mental affirmation is not adequately convincing by itself. The body may often reject the mind's assertion. The body may offer its subtle resistance to the mind's belief. Faith is total acceptance of the head, the heart and the entirety of the body. There is no prayer that goes unanswered in the realm of faith. The eagle pushes its newborn out of its nest on sheer faith. After an initial struggle, the eaglet learns to fly as that faith in flying is sown inside its body. The eagle does not worry about what would happen to the eaglet when pushed out. That would ruin its faith.'

'Was Radha's love for Krishna based on her devotion to him?' Kaya asked.

Keshav responded, 'Devotion is the ancestor of knowledge. Radha knew that she was an integral part of Krishna because of her devotion to him. Radha's devotion was the fragrance of Krishna's love. She offered him not just her sensuality or her body. She merged her own identity with that of Krishna. Of the 16,108 queens that Krishna was supposed to have, no one quite rose to that exalted state that had been attained by Radha and those gopis. Radha's devotion was inseparable from Krishna's love like water is inseparable from its fluidity. That is why the name of Radha always comes before Krishna's. The world remembers them as Radha-Krishna. If Krishna was the purna purusha, the complete being, Radha was the purna prakriti, the whole of nature that manifests that being. Water cannot manifest without flowing. Krishna cannot manifest himself without Radha. Her devotion merged her with Him and in Him.'

Eva asked, 'What is the meeting point of devotion and love?'

'Listen to this ancient story,' said Keshav. He then began his narration.

'Krishna was restlessly pacing around in his palace in Dwarka with a severe and persistent headache. The royal physician diagnosed it as a rare flu caused by a viral infection. He was perplexed as there was no known remedy for this disease. However, Krishna intuitively knew about an unfailing remedy. The cure he suggested was rather unusual. He said, "If my devotees agreed to allow the dust of his or her feet to be rubbed on my head, I have a chance to be cured." Narada Muni, a great devotee of Krishna who was visiting him around that time, was mortified to hear about the bout of headache that the lord of love was suffering from. Krishna requested him to bring the dust of the feet of a true devotee.

'Narada thought to himself, "I am his greatest devotee and I utter his name day in and day out. Yet, how can I offer the dust of my feet to my lord! That would be the height of sacrilege." Narada rushed to the devotees and several wives of Krishna with a request to offer the dust of their feet to alleviate the divine being's suffering.

'They moaned, "How can we do that? Wouldn't that pave our path to hell? How can a doting wife insult a husband like that?"

'Narada went about asking almost everyone whom he considered to be a devotee of Krishna in Dwarka. Yet no one would dare violate the dharma of a devotee that put the divine on a higher plane worthy of worship. Placing the dust of their feet on a divine being's head would be adharma, a violation of a sacrosanct principle. Narada returned to Krishna, crestfallen.

'Meanwhile, Krishna was feeling more feverish and his headache was intensifying. He looked at Narada's solemn face and asked, "Have you tried speaking to Radha and the gopis in Vraja?"

'"What! Those wanton village girls who romanced with you in Vrindavan? What would they know about devotion?" Narada retorted.

'"Just give that a try as a last resort and see what they have to say." Krishna smiled mischievously.

'Narada reached Vrindavan and met Radha and the gopis who were surprised to see him. Narada explained the situation and asked for their help.

'Radha spoke on behalf of the gopis, "We are not exalted devotees of Krishna as much as you are, Narada Muni. We do not know much about dharma and adharma, the sacred and the profane. All we know is that when Krishna suffers, we also suffer. If something as little as the dust of any of our feet helps Krishna recover, we are happy to give that to you.

Here, take whatever dust you can gather from us. Even if this means risking our passage to hell, it will not deter us from this act of love for our beloved Krishna."

'Narada was both astounded and delighted. He took the dust of the feet of the gopis and brought that to Krishna in Dwarka. Krishna reported that his headache was gone and the fever came down soon. He turned to Narada with that mischievous smile that refused to leave his face.

'He said, "Did you see that true love and devotion are both unconditional and identical. Love, in all its purity, cannot be sensed by the head or the five senses alone. This love can be grasped only through pure devotion which is a quality of the seventh sense. The gopis have shown you through their simple action that love and devotion are one at the root. The gopis will be remembered as my greatest lovers and my most earnest devotees in the times to come."'

With that story, the class came to end.

INDUS DAYS, LUCKNOW
END-TERM EXAMS AND AN OFFSITE TRIP

Passing an examination in Indus was a passport to getting a job. The ringing of the bell, signalling that the last end-term examination was over, spelt freedom. The Consumer Behaviour paper was the last examination of the course. Two hours of arrested energy, paper shuffling, racking the rusted brain, vomiting on paper whatever one has committed to memory. Finally, the ecstatic release that evening!

In the lawns between Periyar and Godavari Hostels, students lit a bonfire of class notes and course materials. Thirty copies of *Management Accounting* went up in spiralling smoke. The hearts of every student crucified by excruciating courses lifted with every wisp of smoke. Then it was the turn of *Consumer Behaviour*. Thereafter, *Statistical Methods*.

'Let the living cremate the dead. Hail horse sense!' cheered Sardar lustily.

'Oh! What joy and jubilation, exultation, exhilaration, ebullience,' said Swamy as though he was reciting a mantra from *Roget's Thesaurus*.

Prasad had some great news for Neel and the rest of the gang. Keshav was back on campus and Director Jalebi had agreed that he would be allowed to take the last two classes of his LOVE course offsite.

'So are we travelling out of campus this weekend?' Anju said, looking at Prasad, rather hopefully.

'Yes! Yes! Yes... We isz!' Prasad blurted out, tossing his hair as well as English grammar over the top of his head.

༄

'The distance between Agra and Lucknow of a little over 200 miles would take a whole day to cover given the condition of the road after the monsoon,' said a boy with a squeaky voice, handing the travel brochure to Kaya.

Gulu Sheikh, the driver of the bus, held a betel nut in his mouth. He promptly took over the narrative as the expert guide: 'The Expressway is under construction, you see. Once that is done, we will fly on these roads. The condition of the local government is like the current road. The government functions unpredictably with many twists and turns, and cuts. As a result, you can expect regular bumps on the irregular road. However, I assure you that we will negotiate the bone breakers with utmost ease, we are now ready for take-off, Inshallah!'

The bus was abuzz with loud music. Kaya had a tour map spread on her lap and wanted to know which of the three places they would be reaching first.

'Agra! The city of the Taj Mahal, madam. We will go to Mathura and then Vrindavan via Agra.'

'Oh God!' Swamy could not help but react. He had not missed the pun.

Neel and Kaya sitting on adjacent seats just smiled away as the driver Gulu tested the three horns, rubber, plastic and metal, in quick succession. He created a strange cacophony that got all the campus dogs barking. The bus rumbled to life like a mild earthquake. Gulu Sheikh, who was a failed pilot, was rejected by an aviation academy in the course of its rigorous test. He regretted it forever that he could not get a pilot's licence. For him, a bus running at full speed on the highway was a lingering fantasy for rolling a plane over a runway!

Neel looked out of the window and saw that Drucker, who had spotted him sitting by the window, was chasing the bus well past the main gate. Neel flung a small packet of biscuits that he had bought for himself for the journey, knowing that there may not be anyone who would feed Drucker over the next few days. There was a desolate look on Drucker's face as the bus sped past him. Kaya noticed a pall of sadness grip Neel's eyes. He was terribly sad about leaving Drucker behind.

OFF-CAMPUS, AGRA
FIRESIDE STORIES AND A LOVE CLASS

They reached Agra in the fading twilight. The atmosphere was a festival of the senses. Gulu parked the bus at the entrance of Hotel Clarks Shiraz.

It was close to a full moon night. Keshav had ensured with the travel agent that the group had an opportunity to see the Taj Mahal by moonlight. India's most visited monument was situated on the southern bank of the Yamuna river, on the fringe of the city of Agra. It was a mausoleum of white marble, symbolizing the love, loss and longing of Shah Jahan, a Mughal emperor, for his wife Mumtaz Mahal. Like the many shades of love, the colour of the Taj varied depending on the time of the day. The effect of light, as the day gradually progressed into night, was indeed breathtaking. In the early morning hours, there would be a pink rose tinge to the structure. In the daytime, the exotic markana marbles looked dazzling white. During the evening, the Taj wore a golden glow. At night, in the moonlight, the Taj Mahal was at its bewitching best. The white marble mausoleum was awash in silver moonlight with an ethereal tinge of blue.

The tourist guide was narrating some facts about the Taj Mahal with his practised melodrama. For a while, the guide excused himself for his evening prayers. Keshav took over and began talking to his students about how the human love that created the exquisite Taj plummeted into the depths of despair.

'Unrequited love becomes a prisoner of the ego's attachment. Shah Jahan's pride as the emperor of India and his thirst for fame turned out to be his prison walls. This attachment is a carrier of illusions. Shah Jahan realized this in the last days of his life as a prisoner of his son Aurangzeb. His fame, youth and imperial power would fade away like a mirage.'

Keshav was ecstatic as he gazed at the mystic Taj glistening in the soft glow of the moon like a pearl. It was like a lover's heart frozen in marble.

As the special tour of the Taj came to an end, there were talks of organizing a campfire night, which always came with the promise of exchanging love stories.

A large fire was lit on the Shiraz hotel lawn as the whole group sat down in a full circle for a pre-dinner conversation. Kaya and Neel sat on opposite sides of the fire. Keshav sitting in the middle said, 'Let's call this the Mumtaz Mahal night to commemorate Shah Jahan's beloved wife.' Thus it was decided that that night only the ladies would share their stories and the men would listen.

Keshav said, 'Take a few moments to recall some stories or some songs that moved you the most in your life.' The women fell silent, each one retreating into the seclusion of their fondest memories.

The bright moon played hide-and-seek with tufts of clouds that flitted past. Grilled vegetables, kebabs and assorted beverages went around on brass plates carried by two waiters dressed in white livery with rust marks on them along with missing buttons.

Mridula, Professor Malhotra's wife who had joined saying she too wanted to be a part of the trip, was sharing the story of a sixteenth-century Indian princess, Mira Bai. She translated one of Mira's many ecstatic songs that spoke of her love for Lord Krishna. Although she had been besotted with the image of Krishna since she was a little girl, Mira's marriage was arranged with Rana Kumbha of Chittorgarh by her father, Ratan Singh. Her life was a raging battle between duty and devotion. Her heart yearned to express her ecstatic love for Krishna even in the face of persecution by her family who felt that she was not behaving in a courtly manner, as was expected of a princess.

Mridula sang some lines from a song composed by Mira.

I am insanely in love
And no one understands my plight.
Only the wounded
Can fathom the torment of the wounded.

Then Mridula went on to tell Mira's story. 'Mira's sister-in-law, Udabai, slandered and gossiped about her. She said Mira was cohabiting with other men in her room. Her husband Rana, infuriated by these stories, stormed into her room with an open sword. However, he was surprised to see Mira playing with an idol of Krishna, whom she accepted as the only man in her life. Folklore has it that her husband and his family attempted to kill her twice, once by sending her a basket with a venomous snake and another time by mixing poison in her drink. She miraculously survived on both the occasions. Her defiant love and her talent as a poet shone through her soulful songs.'

Mridula burst into a rapturous song again.

> *I stay drunk in the ecstasy of love, no matter how hard I try to be sober.*
> *Rana, who would not tolerate my free spirit, gifted me one basket with a snake crouching in it.*
> *Mira wrapped the snake around her neck, it was like her lover's necklace!*
> *Rana's next offering was poison: 'This is a drink for you, Mira.'*
> *She drank from that cup of poison uttering his Holy Name in her heart,*
> *The drink turned out to be the nectar of a new lease of life!*

Circling back to Mira's story, Mridula said, 'The royal princess finally left her palace and lived as a hermit in Vrindavan writing songs and visiting devotees who were drawn to her ecstatic love.'

> *Nothing belongs to me except Krishna.*
> *My dear parents, I have explored the world*
> *And found nothing worthy of that love.*
> *I remain a stranger in the crowd of my kin*
> *And an exile from their company.*
> *When you offer the Great One your love,*
> *Be ready to orbit his lamp like a moth giving in to the light.*

When Mridula ended reciting snatches of Mira's song, a hushed silence fell on everyone. Keshav was soaking in the depth of pain and sorrow that was lurking in a vivacious woman's heart stuck in a passionless marriage. He sat motionless with his eyes closed. Sangma, the librarian, too sat transfixed with hands folded in front of him.

The last story of the evening was shared by Kaya. With her eyes fixed on the dying embers of the campfire, she spoke in a voice that wobbled a little in the breeze: 'This is the story of a monk who fell in love with a princess. She said, "I understand your passion for me. But you have to wait a hundred nights outside my home before you can propose to me." The monk took his prayer rug and sat outside her home in all earnestness. One night passed after another, the monk sat there braving the heat of the day and the harshness of the night. He barely ate and his skin turned pale. The monk sat steadfast on his prayer rug with hope in his heart and the lord's name on his lips.

'Finally, it was the ninety-ninth night and the sky looked brighter than ever before. The full moon shone majestically. The monk was almost close to his goal of winning the heart of the princess. Then as the wind blew gently, he got up and decided to leave.'

Neel's gaze froze on Kaya for a while. He looked at Keshav who sat cross-legged and still with an indescribable serenity on his face.

The story session was over. The night got darker. It had been a promising night of poignant reflection, a night to savour the solitude of stars. Everyone retired to their rooms, ready to crash.

MATHURA AND VRINDAVAN

Early next morning, their first stop was Krishna's birthplace, popularly known as Krishna janmabhoomi. It was located in the middle of the city of Mathura. The red stone structure of the janmabhoomi temple stood out from the adjacent buildings including the dome of a mosque. They filed past a huge posse of gun-wielding police officials to enter a cave-like prison walled with stones. The prison cell was called garbha griha.

'Ironically,' Neel thought to himself, 'Krishna's birthplace continues to be heavily guarded even five thousand years after his death.'

The police officials were there to ensure that law and order prevailed on the premises. A mosque named Shahi Idgah stood close to Krishna's birthplace. The tourist guide told them that an ancient Keshavnath temple had been razed to the ground by Aurangzeb, the sixth Mughal emperor who had imprisoned his father Shah Jahan; and a mosque had been built in its place in 1669. Neel saw that Gulu Sheikh did not enter the temple premises. He got down from the driver's cabin, and inhaled a prolonged puff of a Charminar cigarette before snuffing it out with his shoe. He then offered his prayers at the Krishna temple standing up, with eyes closed and hands folded in a reverential gesture.

The birthplace was converted into a temple where celebrations began after midnight coinciding with Krishna's birth. To the southeast of the temple was a large water tank with steep cascading steps. This tank was called Potra Kund.

'The tank, it is said, was used by the mother of the boy to wash the first clothes of baby Krishna,' the guide said, adding to the mystique of the tank.

Keshav looked at the rippling green water. So did Kaya, standing some distance away from him. Keshav was reminded of his own mother and how diligently she used to hand-wash his school clothes. Kaya was thinking of someone who was closest to her heart and who even washed baby clothes for her.

From Mathura, they drove to Vrindavan. On their way, they had a sumptuous lunch at the majestic ISKCON temple that was built by a great Krishna devotee, Srila Prabhupada.

Kaya remembered the porter at Logan airport mentioning Prabhupada's name. 'How things come full circle,' she thought.

The narrow by-lanes of Vrindavan were resounding with greetings of 'Radhe Radhe!' The incessant chant of 'Radhe!' drowned the hi's and hello's that the tourists were prone to saying. Everyone, including taxi drivers and shopkeepers, addressed customers with a 'Radhe Radhe!' and in the same breath, they haggled over price and tariff. The locals of Vrindavan believed that the doorway to Krishna's heart was by pleasing Radhe. They trooped out of the janmabhoomi towards the most popular Krishna temple.

Milling crowds standing in dense queues thronged the Banke Bihari temple. The guide explained that 'Banke' meant 'bent', and 'Bihari' meant 'rejoicer'. 'This is how the dancing Krishna, with his characteristic tribhanga or tri-bent pose—hands holding a flute; a raised hip; and one leg bent in a rhythmic pose while rejoicing—got this name Banke Bihari.'

Keshav told Kaya that a sage had once seen this temple's statue of Krishna, in his tri-bent pose, in a lucid dream. The fluidity of Krishna's dancing form and his large eyes indicating his heightened awareness of life got reflected in the image of Banke Bihari. Kaya noticed well-fed rats scurrying around the floor of the temple. She could also see a large crowd of monkeys brawling outside the temple gate over food. Some ingenious monkeys were trained by professional muggers to steal the spectacles of unsuspecting tourists, the tour guide warned. They were accordingly taught to return the glasses in exchange for a hefty ransom paid by their owners. The guide instructed everyone to remove their glasses and put them in their pockets.

Nidhivan was the last stop on their way back to Lucknow.

The guide, splitting each word to explain its meaning, said, 'Nidhi means treasure and van means forest. It was a forest grove where the wealth of divine love was treasured.' He continued. 'This forest and the temple were believed to be the meeting place of Radha and Krishna. They rested, slept and performed rasa dance at this place along with the gopis. This place was also connected to Goswami Haridas ji, the founder of the Banke Bihari temple. It was here, in the lush forest of Nidhivan, that Haridas ji dug out the idol of Krishna that is worshipped as Banke Bihari. The forest grove was surrounded by residential houses. There was a temple of Radha Rani known as Radharani Shringaar Ghar—the dressing chamber of Radha. The shrine made of marble had a bed inside, which was decorated with flowers by the priest every evening.'

The guide's voice became sombre as he described what happened to Nidhivan as the sun went down. 'After sunset, Nidhivan becomes a forbidden place. No one is allowed to stay inside the grove. The frolicking monkeys, chirping birds, and even ants leave this place. Many believe that the spirits of Radha and Krishna descend on Nidhivan to perform the rasa-lila every night. The trees transform themselves into gopis swaying and dancing in the breeze. The gods and goddesses watch from their abodes. Some hear the sound of bangles and anklets. Yet, no one can ever testify with his eyes, for any witness to the transcendental love play is condemned to turn blind, deaf or dumb forever. Those who stayed back have either been found dead or have lost their minds. What happens at night in Nidhivan is beyond the reach of the human senses.' His voice sounded almost conspiratorial.

Keshav said, 'If the Taj housed the grand spectacle of human love, Vrindavan was redolent with the fragrance of love that was divine. The human love of Taj was like a glittering pool that reflected the evanescence and romance of the cool moonbeams. The divine love was like the open air, refusing confinement, forever renewing itself from the staleness. The rendezvous of Radha and Krishna culminated in a love that was transcendental. It was meant for those lovers whose thirst for love was too deep to be quenched by mere sensory contact. Here was a state of ecstatic love that many silently crave, but very few actually get to experience.'

Neel saw Kaya listening to it all with her eyes closed. It seemed as though Keshav had hypnotized her.

It was now time to leave. An exotic and exhausting journey through love's many faces and manifestations was gradually coming to an end. Over the course of these days, Sardar was getting closer to Eva. He began to see those enchanting qualities of her head and heart even without the aid of alcohol. Prasad and Anju were inseparable ever since he proposed to her during the Taj visit. Kaya and Neel sat alone by themselves next to the window seats on the same side of the bus. Neel sat behind Kaya and peered in the same direction watching the night falling in the village. He smelt the fragrance of a new woody perfume that Kaya was wearing that night.

Was she smelling of parijat, Indian night jasmine? Neel thought she was.

Mridula's much-touted affair with Sangma turned out to be a one-sided longing and infatuation of a world-weary assistant librarian.

The city of Vrindavan and the Yamuna quietly flowing by were receding behind the speeding bus in the haze that was wrapping up the night.

KESHAV LEAVES INDUS

Neel recalled one of Keshav's classroom conversations on organizational commitment. Keshav had said that it was possible to get someone committed to an organization by paying money and other material benefits. But great organizations required devotion, not just commitment. It is very difficult to buy devotion! Did Keshav ruin his own life by his extreme devotion to what he believed was the truth?

The enquiry committee probing factors leading to Manas's death was headed by Dean Nataraj Nandy. The committee submitted a report in a closed envelope to Director Jalebi. The committee praised Professor Keshav's popularity as a teacher but questioned the efficacy of the LOVE course in the context of a management school. Professor Keshav Mitra was asked to modify the content of his Leadership of Voluntary Enterprises course material if he wanted to continue teaching that. He was asked to write a note of apology for some of the controversial statements he had made in class that were not in keeping with the ethos of Indus.

Keshav explained why he could not stop teaching what he knew, in his heart of hearts, to be the truth. He said that as an academic, he was devoted to truth and not convenience. He took full responsibility for the unintended consequences of his teaching methods on his students' minds. He then gently placed his resignation letter on the table of the director, leaving the man totally speechless. He politely said that he would remain devoted to the well-being of his students. But his resignation from Indus was non-negotiable and he would be leaving the campus within the next couple of days.

Keshav soon drove out of the red-brick building of the school towards the main exit. His eyes swept over a blur of bougainvillea that he had helped plant over the years as part of the campus beautification project. A pall of sadness settled on the face of staff and a few colleagues who had gathered around the main gate to see him off.

Neel noticed that Kaya was looking wistfully at Keshav's silver-grey car. The small Indigo moved around the corner of the library building leaving a trail of dust behind. In that haze, Neel's eyes turned misty. He saw Kaya was crying. Neel held back his tears knowing he was a clumsy crier. It wasn't so much Keshav's departure as it was the sense of loss of Kaya's love that hurt him the most.

3

After Keshav left Indus for his sojourn in Rishikesh, Kaya was no longer the same person. Neel noticed that she became more introspective and kept to herself. Their accidental non-meetings turned out to be cold and were reduced to formal exchanges. Kaya was planning to leave for the US by the end of the term. Before that, she wanted to make a trip to Haridwar and was wondering if anyone from the class would be interested in accompanying her.

Neel was completing his assignment on the Microsoft case study for the Business Communications class. The course on communications had really proved to be effective in his real life. Neel kept nodding his head, feigned a thoughtful pose and kept changing his body posture as proof that he was very much in the class even though he was mentally elsewhere. He discovered that there was a strange magnetic attraction between gravity and his upper eyelid. He tended to get into a trance-like state with his head nodding off from time to time. The Microsoft case study was tough enough to soften his ego. Neel realized that he wasn't quite the enlightened multitasker that he assumed himself to be. He still had a lot to learn from his seniors.

One of his seniors informed Neel that paying attention in class actually works. Every time a professor blinks multiple times, he is sending a coded signal that the topic being discussed in that minute is important for that exam. Neel was astonished at the power and accuracy of that insight.

The class was taken by a guest professor from the corporate world, a former vice president, who said that he was still in his thirties but looked like a weather-beaten fifty-year-old. There were dark circles below his eyes like a hidden half binocular.

'How do they age so quickly in the profession?' Neel thought to himself.

The VP was describing how he was poached out of his

erstwhile company by a persistent headhunter. 'You see, by the late twenties, I was a blazing star in the corporate sky. I had everything that an MBA graduate could dream of. But nothing was satisfying as you still did not make as much as the highest paid guy in your batch. Everything in our world is relative, you see!'

Neel couldn't agree more although he detested the guy.

The VP's class was reaching a crescendo. 'Happiness was not in fame, salary or love...' he roared on.

Neel found out that happiness lay in rediscovering a long-lost chewed-up ballpoint pen. He was scurrying around the hostel and looking for the pen that had Kaya's teeth marks on it. Then he realized that it was tucked inside his laptop case. He sent a text to Kaya: 'Hi! I can accompany you to Haridwar if you allow me to. Do let me know.'

Just when the communications class was about to end, class participation reached its peak with many students raising their hand, waiting for the professor to hear them out and address their queries and doubts. The guest professor happily overshot the class time by a good ten minutes. Neel had his eyes on his smartphone to see if he had received a reply to his last text message.

While he was coming out of the class, Neel saw a blue blip on his phone. It was a response from Kaya.

'Well, yes, thank you! Do book us a couple of train tickets to Haridwar and from there to Delhi. You can see me off at Delhi airport, only if you can and your time permits. Cheers, Kaya.'

Neel felt a bittersweet emotion rippling through him. 'You know that this is the least I can do for you,' Neel said to himself. He liked how he rehearsed that line with his throaty voice laced with longing.

TRAIN TO HARIDWAR, 2000

Kaya's memory flashed back to the train journey to Haridwar with Neel almost twenty years back.

Kaya and Neel left for Charbagh railway station in Lucknow to board the 13009 Doon Express. The man sitting at the information desk gleefully reported that the incoming train which was usually late by a couple of hours every day was just one hour late in arriving that evening. The coquettish female voice in the public address system announced the delayed arrival without any trace of regret. The railway station with its jostling families and their heavily stuffed suitcases, colonial coolies in scarlet dresses, the strong stench of urine, and tea vendors crying "Chai-garam" and pouring the saccharine tea from a large aluminium kettle stretched Kaya's senses to its limit. As the train chugged in at the station, way beyond the appointed hour, she was shocked to see a bearded man wearing a lungi and a kurta jump inside an unreserved compartment through the window of the train. His family ran alongside the moving train pushing his baggage inside with the same alacrity with which they pushed the man in.

Luckily, Neel had a reservation in a two-tier air-conditioned coach for Kaya and himself. The compartment reminded Kaya of getting inside a submarine. It was dimly lit, painted in blue and covered by grey windows. Steep iron ladders connected the lower sleeper berths of the train with the upper berths. There was a musty smell of stale window curtains combined with the aroma of spicy food. Neel helped Kaya with her bags as she climbed to the upper berth. A man wearing oversized sunglasses was lying down on one of the lower berths. He was watching Kaya step up the ladder, as though she was some kind of a zoo animal trying to climb a tree. Kaya thanked her stars that Neel stood close by to shield her from those searching, invasive eyes.

The train moved from the station with a huge jerk, stirring up all the passengers inside. Neel was perched on the upper berth parallel to that of Kaya. They spoke in sign language to each other. Neel warned Kaya not to drink too much water as it would be a challenge for her to use the toilet at the end of the compartment. Kaya had already noticed a small queue of people in front of the toilet. She pulled up a blanket over herself and closed her eyes as the rattling train gathered some speed. Kaya wondered if she would ever come back to Lucknow again.

Her train of thought was interrupted by the man with the sunglasses. He was conversing loudly with a co-passenger, whom he was trying to impress with his wheeling and dealing as he talked about the political bigwigs in Lucknow.

Kaya overheard him saying, 'I had lunch at the governor's house last Sunday. It was a beautiful lunch prepared by his delicious wife.'

Kaya pressed her mouth with her hand trying to suppress her laughter as she wondered what the governor of the state would feel about his seventy-year-old wife being referred to as a sumptuous delicacy. She was often surprised by the creative use of the English language by Indians, especially when it came to expressing their innermost feelings.

The old companion who had been listening to the man as he went on with his bragging session soon started to recount his recent visit to the emergency ward of a hospital for a surgery. 'Believe me,' he said, 'the doctors had to push a cathedral inside my bladder!' There was anguish in his voice as he recalled the incident.

What! Kaya's jaws dropped—pushing a cathedral inside! Then she realized that the old man was referring to a catheter. She laughed uncontrollably, struggling to muffle the sound with her blanket. Neel looked at her bemused.

Kaya could not get a wink of sleep in the sleeper

compartment. She thought of her own loneliness in that small apartment in Downtown Boston. It was not as though she did not have people in her life, but they were not the kind of people who fulfilled her need for close companionship. India fascinated her because of Keshav. He was the one who taught her how to love without attachment. He had taught her that love was that fullness of being that required no other anchor to support itself. Not to be attached was not being indifferent. It was about loving without wanting, without hankering. Neel had dozed off by then. Kaya could see his face in a shaft of light as the train passed a station. She thought about her relationship with Neel.

'What does he look for in me?' She felt that Neel wanted her for her exclusivity, an exotic American blonde who scored head and shoulders above the other women in the campus. This love aroused passion and bloated the ego, but left her with a sense of non-fulfilment. She knew that with Keshav leaving Indus, Neel and she would be drifting apart to two different continents. Keshav was her reason for falling in love with India and the people here. His absence felt like a missing baby tooth that one probes with the edge of the tongue long after it has gone.

The man with the sunglasses was snoring. He was like this one-man philharmonic orchestra. His snores would rise to a high octave and then calm down with a temporary lull. His co-traveller, the Cathedral, had pleaded with him to stop snoring, but his entreaties fell on the deaf ears of the snoring man—or perhaps his dense nose. The only way to stop a snorer is to snore back. That's exactly what the Cathedral was doing. There was a jugalbandi, a duet, of two snorers: one like the whining of a mosquito and the other like the full blast of a wild buffalo. The two of them were evenly matched in a mutual combat of snore-full deterrence while the rest of the compartment was turning and tossing in agony on their sleeper seats.

HEARTBREAK IN HARIDWAR

The Doon Express finally arrived in Haridwar very early in the morning. It was an ancient city sacred to pilgrims. Here the Ganga exited the foothills of the Himalayas. Kaya stepped out of the railway station accompanied by Neel. She had learned that Haridwar or Hardwar (sounded like hardware to her) was the gateway of Hari and Hara, Shiva and Vishnu. Her attention was drawn to a colourful, imposing bust of Shiva perched in the shape of a Shiva lingam right in front of the station.

Neel hired an autorickshaw to take them to Haveli Hari Ganga, a heritage property on the banks of the Ganga with beautiful courtyards, dazzling interiors and intricate floor designs. The property, owned by a cousin of Neel's friend, was a welcome relief from the claustrophobic train journey for Kaya. They were there for the day. Kaya wanted a dip in the river flowing close to the hotel. She accompanied Neel to the bathing ghat to take a dip. A priest with flowers and a scented stick offered to do a puja for the couple for just fifty rupees.

'This,' he said, 'is a 50 per cent discount for off-season seekers.' He promised that this puja was meant to liberate the souls of three generations of ancestors.

Kaya could not bear the heat of the marble floor of the ghat on her bare feet.

She cried out, 'Oh God! Oh my God!' The priest mistook her discomfort as a sign of spiritual fervour and remarked, 'These Western women—very God-loving, no?' Neel just smirked.

After a dip in the cool waters of the sacred river, Neel and Kaya sat for a while feeding fish with the balls of flour that a little boy was selling. It was decided that they would drive straight to the Delhi international airport from the hotel in the evening. Kaya had read and heard a lot about the mystical evening worship along the Ganga by priests and wanted to see that before she left for the US.

The flowing Ganga appeared magical against the setting sun. From the temples in Har ki Pauri, priests holding giant candelabras came out of nowhere. They worshipped the river with a hypnotic chant:

Om jaya gange mata!

The flames they lit exploded into the sky and the images rippled in the flowing water.

Kaya saw Neel was completely preoccupied with his thoughts. She realized that she had no access key to his personal world. Neel was locked up inside his head. He was lost in his own grief. He was someone who worried compulsively. Unable to savour the moment with Kaya, Neel kept obsessing over her indifference towards him. 'Does she think of me as much as I think of her?'

They drove out of Haridwar towards Delhi, winding their way downhill through treacherous traffic. Their car passed a road sign pointing towards Rishikesh.

Kaya said, 'Keshav would be here close by in some ashram in Rishikesh. Don't know when we will meet again.'

Neel just nodded. He was thinking, 'Isn't she always lost in the haze of Keshav? Does she see me only in Keshav's reflected light?'

The international airport in Delhi looked blurred as Neel looked through his misty eyes at the vague mass of people rushing their luggage carts inside the airport. Kaya turned around and gave Neel a big hug. She poured into him all her love and gratitude in those few intimate moments. Neel inhaled the lingering fragrance of vanilla and lavender. He knew that her perfume would delay her departure from his memory long after she had boarded the flight.

'Thank you for being who you are, Neel,' she whispered.

Neel felt that those words cut through his heart like a knife.

'Travel safe,' he muttered, swallowing a lump in his throat.

'Will my absence hurt?' asked Kaya as she was about to proceed to the boarding area.

'Nope,' Neel said, faking non-attachment.

Kaya had tears in her eyes. 'I hate you,' she said.

Neel muttered to himself, 'I hate Keshav who is the reason why you are leaving me.'

She went into the airport, turning back just once to see if Neel was still there.

He was there but not quite fully there. He stood there for a while, looking at a strand of blonde hair clinging to his shirtsleeve; and then he watched it twirl in the air before it vanished.

10
Parting

RISHIKESH ASHRAM, SUNDAY
DAY 7 OF THE RETREAT

The morning walk from the guest rooms to the temple courtyard was a moving festival of blue.

Keshav had requested everyone to wear some shade of blue for what he described as Graduation Day.

The group photo session would take place next to the courtyard in front of the Krishna temple. The photographer arrived wearing a hat, and perched on it was a pair of dark sunglasses. In exaggerated theatrical movements, he began to assemble the retreat participants into a manageable bunch.

'Why don't you listen to me, machaan!' he said in exasperation.

All the ladies stationed in the first row began to compose their faces for the shoot while the men stood behind and decomposed under the rising sun. Prasad went and coaxed the photographer that his bald crown should be protected from the glare of sunlight as much as possible—so he should be allowed to stand in with the ladies in the first row. The ladies were no less amused. The boys from the back row let out a few catcalls. The blue-tinted lens of the camera was now searching for that picture-perfect moment.

Keshav, vibrant in a sky blue kurta and a purple scarf,

was standing right in the middle of the back row. Sardar was striking a solemn pose in defiance of the merriment around him. Swamy was straightening himself, holding his breath and pulling in his protruding belly. Strangely, Neel was standing slightly apart, at the right end of the last row, with a forlorn look on his face. His eyes were firmly fixed on the ground as though he was trying to bury himself there. The photographer urged him to get closer with a shrill voice. 'Arrey andar aao na!'

The group waited in a sort of studied, academic silence anticipating a flash.

Sardar could hear that familiar sinister rumble inside his stomach caused by an excess of mooli paratha at dinner last night. In that hushed atmosphere, even the rumble was heard like a loud glug of water pouring out of a slender-necked bottle. Eva, in the front row, giggled. Soon, the entire group went up howling like wild jackals. Prasad, uncertain about the reason for the laughter, asked the photographer, 'Kya hua re?'

The photographer went berserk, muttering under his breath, 'Saale, badtameez!'

Finally, when the photograph was taken it looked like a happy lot without much care. What was included were faces that were lulled into a sense of collective well-being. What was excluded were warts and wanton blemishes of life that weren't a part of this feel-good world. Photographs always do that.

The photographer presents the world in frames into which the photographed are condemned to fit and yet are desperate to get out of. The eye of the beholder stiffens and freezes us in time. The freedom to flow without inhibition was arrested in some way as each one in that group tried desperately to hold on to that elusive perfect moment.

On this last day of the retreat, Keshav said he would be present in the morning puja along with the purohit. The blue wave followed him wherever he went. Keshav walked across the courtyard with great intent. His eyes caught sight of a couple of seemingly dead sparrows lying by the side of the walkway to the temple. Their bodies lay stiff on the grass. Keshav asked the gardener to see if the sparrows still had life in them and whether they could be revived. He walked inside the temple hall. There was a special puja on Sundays when the largest number of devotees congregated to have darshan, lapped up the prasad and listened to the morning discourse that was always fascinating.

The purohit had arranged flowers, garlands, baskets of fruits and sweets along with a cola can tucked inside the fruit basket! Keshav noticed that the can was open and a stream of dark brown beverage was trickling down the edge of the basket to the floor. There were several dead ants lying and swimming around desperately along the liquid trail.

The purohit looked up and asked Keshav, 'Should we offer or accept a cola can as an object of worship?'

Keshav simply nodded. He kept looking intently at the patch of brown cola dripping out of the can and an ant writhing around until it was dead still.

Keshav quietly instructed the purohit to prepare to tell the story of Krishna's journey to freedom.

'The class will happen as scheduled,' he announced.

The purohit listened deferentially, his hands folded in a 'namaste'. Keshav then instructed the temple staff to close the temple doors and keep them shut until further orders.

'Fruits and sweets offered to the deity that morning could be distributed later, only after the permission to do so is given,' he added. He then drew the ashram manager by the hand and seemed to be giving him some confidential instructions.

The ashram's resident cat Arjun who usually circled and brushed his fur around Keshav's feet in the morning seemed pale and sick. He greeted Keshav with a mild purring sound. Keshav picked up Arjun by the skin of his neck, gently caressed him and asked an attendant to take him immediately to a veterinary doctor. He was deeply concerned about Arjun.

The blue wave moved from the ashram to the designated space for the talk.

INDUS CAMPUS, LUCKNOW, MARCH 2000
THE NIGHT BEFORE CONVOCATION

It was time to pack up, tie stuff together and sort the valuables from the leftouts. Neel cleaned up his hostel room starting with his reading desk and drawer. What emerged inside the drawer was a whole array of objects, keepsakes and memorabilia, perhaps fit for a museum. He made a list of the things that had to be discarded.

- Three chewed-up pencils—two of Kaya's and one of his own
- One silver hair clip
- The torn ends of three movie tickets (Manas's, Kaya's and Neel's)
- One packet of Wrigley's Double Mint chewing gum
- An amber pocket comb wrapped in a dark banana skin, rotten beyond recognition
- One torn shirt and a button
- An unfinished love letter

Neel ran his fingers over all his possessions before making a bundle out of them, and discarding it into the dustbin. Strangely, he also found a tissue paper that still smelt of sandalwood, a fragrance that Kaya wore some days. He neatly folded the tissue, inhaled it gently one last time and let it float out of the window instead of throwing it in the wastebasket. Each object he rediscovered was a key to some emotion that was locked up inside him.

'Keshav's words, for once, sound so true,' he thought. 'The universe of our experience has no objects; there are only different elements of the same subject. All our decisions, all our preferences are subjective in the ultimate analysis.'

Neel had read somewhere that letting go of things and some emotional spring cleaning tends to bring unexpected fortunes. Within a minute of this thought crossing his mind, Swamy knocked on his door. He had come to invite Neel to join a pre-convocation drink that his uncle, Prakash, was offering to all his friends.

Neel laughed and said, 'I am lucky Swamy—that was probably my unexpected gift.'

∽

Neel was intrigued to meet Prakash Uncle who had always been an integral part of Swamy's spirited conversations. He was least interested in another one of those 'C_2H_6O infusions'—the code name for surprise in-campus cocktail parties. 'In any case, thanks to Jalebi's reforms, the late night parties would soon be things of the past in Indus,' he thought. Those party lights would be replaced by CCTV cameras to catch smooching couples red-handed.

It was a dimly lit rooftop get-together of eager party hoppers. Swamy went ahead with his introduction. To the motley group of graduating students, he said, 'This is Prakash Uncle from Switzerland who has come all the way to see me graduate tomorrow.'

A portly, middle-aged man with gold-rimmed glasses and transplanted hair was reeking of what seemed like garlic. Swamy had shared with Neel every little detail about his uncle. Prakash was in his sixties, a divorcee who lived off a pension by the Swiss government. He was perpetually looking out for a life partner, even in his sunset years. He hung around nightclubs and parties with the eagerness of an owl hunting around for a good nightlife.

'Here is an undisclosed secret,' Swamy blared out.

'Prakash Uncle was the one who got me hooked to reading those matrimonials. Ladies and gentlemen, I urge you to meet the man who has devoted half his life to the pursuit of matrimonials. The printed descriptions of exquisitely beautiful brides fill his imagination with ecstatic possibilities. He can smell nuptial bliss in the newsprint that carries those matrimonials. Here is to Prakash Uncle, a happily unmarried man.'

Swamy swore and swallowed a large sip of single malt whisky.

Uncle Prakash belched discreetly, covering his mouth with his left hand and slurred, 'Soooorry!' He raised his glass and said, 'Excuse me for the garlic smell. I am devoted to garlic as a panacea for all my ills, including my weak heart.'

Swamy had foretold everyone that Prakash Uncle was given to spinning yarns about his many adventures in life that he never actually undertook.

'If there is anyone who can outdo Jalebi in spinning fantastic tales, it is my Prakash Uncle,' Swamy said, confidently.

Prakash was a lonely man. He paid for people to drink with him so that he could share his bizarre fantasies with them. He was particularly unstoppable after a couple of pegs. Prakash declared that he was a Swiss scientist (although Swamy told Neel that he was a school dropout) and made his fortune selling garlic as an ancient herbal product in Europe. He was prone to slipping in a big name or two to prop his stature up in front of his admirers.

Prakash had already started to shoot his mouth off.

'It was the month of June in 1975, I think.' Prakash Uncle faked a winning combat with his fertile imagination.

Neel knew that veteran liars used the alibi of a precise date to give credence to their lies.

'I was carrying an Indian herb, asafoetida, inside my wallet on a plane to Switzerland. What an impact that herb made.

Wherever I went, people made way. The waiter at the airport restaurant took my orders from a long distance. Inside the plane, pretty ladies held handkerchiefs close to their nose, children puked, and perfectly robust men looked for oxygen masks. The whole plane smelt of the herb. Conversations went nasal and were cut short by the intense aroma of that exotic herb emanating from my pocket. The aisle seat next to me was deliberately left vacant at the discretion of the flight attendants. Finally, even the pilot couldn't stand the smell any longer. By that time, the cockpit was reeking of asafoetida.'

Swamy's invitees were doubling up in laughter. Prakash Uncle, surprised by his own eloquence, lifted his thick eyebrows and carried on.

'The plane that had taken off from Chennai in India made an emergency landing in Kabul. Everyone slid through the emergency wing of the plane in their oxygen masks. It was reported that many passengers complained of suffocation after they deplaned. My wallet containing the herb was confiscated by a bomb squad. However, I had cleverly slipped in some stock of the herbal powder under the toilet seat in the plane. Fearing a germ attack, the Swiss government refused to allow the plane into their airspace. Our friendly neighbour, Pakistan, over which the plane flew, complained to the United Nations about a conspiratorial biological war that was launched by a Swiss scientist of Indian origin (that was me, you see) with a foul-smelling odour emitting out of a plane that had crossed their land. Anyway, I had almost brought India and Pakistan close to another war. I was deported back to India by the Afghan government. Once back in India I gave a suggestion to a high official in the Indian army that all it would take for India to push back the hostile Chinese was to have a million soldiers belch out asafoetida gas along the Line of Control. With their olfactory organs choking, the People's Liberation Army of China would retreat miles away from the Line of

Control. I was told that India's defence establishment pounced upon my idea as a brilliant war strategy. The only reason they have not implemented my dazzling idea yet is that the Chinese have access to more foul-smelling animal parts as deterrents.'

'Tell them, Uncle, what happened when you returned to Switzerland several years after that episode.' Swamy egged Uncle Prakash on.

Prakash was spinning again. 'Once back in Switzerland, I think that was May...the 25th...Wednesday... I was put under quarantine for one full year, and chemically treated and tested as though I had come from another planet.'

Prakash Uncle had to stop momentarily as several of Swamy's friends were choking up.

With renewed vigour, he started spinning another one. 'Once when I was invited to play poker with the Prime Minister of Morocco in Casablanca...'

Neel slid away quietly and stood alone in a corner thinking of Kaya. His heart felt heavy. He saw Eva Reddy coming towards him with a drink in her hand. She stood beside Neel and said, 'It is all right to cry if you feel like it. It will make you feel lighter.'

Neel looked at Eva's eyes for the first time in these two years. They were dark and comforting like the inside of a bird's nest. She made him sit down next to her. There wasn't the slightest tinge of that sensual yearning in her touch—rather a mellowed warmth of a trusted friend as she held his hand. She ran her hand through his hair with great affection and to his surprise kissed him on the cheek.

What Neel did then startled him even more. He did something that he was not taught to do in Indus. He sat down on his knees, buried his face between his legs, and began to weep.

THE CONVOCATION

The convocation procession began with three hundred noisy students filing past a festooned podium in their fluorescent blue gowns. They all sat in their pre-planned seating arrangement. Neel had requested the class representative to keep a chair next to him vacant. 'Here's where Manas would have sat down if he had been alive,' he said. This was followed by the velvet red line of faculty moving in their jaded dignity as academic midwives. Finally, the director and the board of governors led by the chairman and the chief guest for the day, Swami Shivganesh, who was a world-famous hatha yoga teacher with a huge influential network and following, entered the podium. Most were surprised to see Swami Shivganesh as the chief guest for Indus would usually invite a CEO or a minister to do the honours. It was revealed that Swami Shivganesh was Dean Nataraj's spiritual guru.

'Nataraj has taken to spirituality in a big way ever since he started aspiring to be the next director of Indus,' said Sangma who kept a tab on Nataraj's personal life.

Swami Shivganesh was almost bald except for a ring of hair from ear to ear, forming a semi-circle on the back of his head. He was known for championing cow protection. He was sharing his philosophy of education that embraced not just human rights but also the rights of all species—especially cows. His speech was brief and was met with a thunderous applause as he said, 'You, the cream of the world, now go ahead and milk your talent. Om Shanti!'

The swami had a fit of nervous laughter, bordering on hysteria, as he was escorted off the stage by Dean Nataraj Nandy who was, in turn, basking in the glory of his guru.

The students threw their caps in the air and savoured the moment of graduation. Director Jalebi, now out of his convocation gown, appeared like a featherless chicken. He started to shake hands with the graduating students.

Neel surveyed the leather-bound, rectangular graduate certificate that read, 'Neel Kamal Ray conferred the Master of Business Administration Degree from the Indus Institute of Management, Lucknow'. This piece of paper was a mute record of the two years of his life lived within the campus. This was soon followed by customary hugs and congratulatory curse words. Parents bloated with pride basked in the institute lawn for the ceremonial cup of tea (one cup per person, please!) organized by Jalebi.

Neel's brain did a quiet flashback on the journey that had brought him here—the journey of life thus far and the path that lay ahead. While appearing for job interviews for campus placement he would often come across hiring executives who would say, 'Tell me something about yourself.' What do I tell about myself? Which of my many selves do I talk about? I am someone who split into many shreds like a broken mirror. The story that defines me is like an illusion—a long-lasting illusion of heightened success and hidden failures. All that seemed perfect in theory such as 'competitive advantage' now morphed into a devotion to a distinguished career (a mission, mind you, not just a job). All those roles that I had assumed—thinker, writer and lover—suddenly fell out of place.

'I believe you will make it to Harvard one day!'

Who was saying this? Neel noticed that it was Professor Malhotra giving him a parental pat on the back. People whom you avoid meeting the most in the campus are surprisingly the ones who show up at unexpected times.

'Headed for Harvard!' Neel said to himself, wondering if he would meet Kaya there again.

Neel visualized a dazed Kaya waving at him from a distance at a hypothetical graduation ceremony at Harvard. Her father, Michael Johnson, demurely watching his son-in-law, this great achiever from India!

Neel wanted to go somewhere and lie down with his eyes closed, and finish watching the wonderful movie that was going on inside his head.

Before he vacated the campus room, he stood for a while before Room 102, the room Manas used to live in. He put his head on the door and whispered his farewell, his parting homage to their friendship. He was grateful to Manas for teaching him the little things, like lying down on the grass and looking at the large-hearted winter sky without a trace of cloud.

'Manas loved me selflessly, to the point of hopelessness,' Neel thought.

Then, he had to say his last goodbye to his devoted disciple Drucker whom Neel entrusted to the new caretaker, a first-year student who doted on dogs and fell in love with Drucker the moment she met him. Drucker got wind of Neel leaving the night before. He was squatting solemnly at the exit gate of Periyar as Neel was pushing the wrought-iron turnstile open with two huge suitcases.

Neel was struggling hard to break his bond with his biggest fan in Indus.

'You taught me all about undefined love and the purity of friendship,' Neel told Drucker. Drucker listened sitting on his hind legs, his eyes unblinking. He seemed to understand every word that Neel spoke.

I have seen many dogs in my life, but not one quite like you, Drucker. You reminded me of those carefree days in my childhood, the vivid smell of wild flowers and a sharp ear for sounds of life around. It is from you that I learnt the value of patience in love. You greeted me with the wagging of your tail, the twitching of your ears and a gentle lick that melted the tensions of the day. You taught me that it was all right to meet you with an unshaven beard, ruffled hair or stale breath.

'May I have a parting kiss, Drucker?' Neel sat down with

his eyes closed and turned his cheek towards the wet snout.

Drucker knew no second-guessing. He licked Neel's face generously.

Neel stood up. 'We may meet some place, some time on earth or in heaven. But, for now, let's go our ways, my Drucker.' Neel didn't look back as the hired taxi drove him away towards Lucknow airport. All he heard was that familiar heart-warming, heart-wrenching bow-wow rising above the spluttering sound of the engine of his cab.

RISHIKESH ASHRAM, DAY 7
THE UNDYING DECIDES TO DIE

The purohit was reading out the story of Krishna's final days on earth in a subdued voice.

> Krishna saw the imminent decline of his Yadava clan and had a foresight that the city of Dwarka would soon be submerged under the sea. He asked the Yadavas to go on a pilgrimage to purify themselves from their earthly entanglements.
>
> 'We will let the women and children go to Sangotra and the men will reach Prabhasa. They can observe fasts and prepare to face the calamity that awaits us.'
>
> Krishna knew that empires and people rose, only to decline later. Men and women were born only to die one day. This was the ultimate truth. Yet, the greater truth was that there has always been an undying witness behind the spectacles of life and death. It has always been that is-ness of life that is neither born nor dies. The present is, the past is and the future is playing out in this unblinking is-ness, like clouds on a clear sky!
>
> Krishna stood as a witness as the Yadava men, relaxed in their guard after a strenuous observance

of purification rituals, began to drink an intoxicating, homemade wine, maireyaka. Soon the drinking turned into reckless revelry with wine flowing like water down their throats. A harsh word spoken in drunken jest led to arguments. Arguments led to quarrels. The Yadava heroes were soon divided into warring groups. They brought out their swords, maces, bows and arrows and emerged from their camps in Prabhasa upon the open seashore. The serene shore was transformed into a slaughterhouse. The heroes charged at each other's throats with whatever they could lay their hands on. One after another, Krishna's kin destroyed each other. Satyaki, Aniruddha, Kritivarma, Pradyumna, Samba, Gada and Sarana got killed in the reckless and drunken frenzy.

Balarama, unable to bear the sight of the annihilation of the Yadavas, retreated to a distance. Krishna and Balarama looked at each other. In that instant, Krishna knew that Balarama would leave his body. By the power of his yoga, a silver serpent emerged from Balarama's mouth. The rest of Balarama's flesh morphed into a serpent. The serpent had a last lingering look at the dark form of Krishna. Soon, Balarama's physical body withered away and spiralled its way up to the sky in wisps of smoke.

Krishna was left alone. He knew that he had taken a human form and had to die like an ordinary human. He remembered Gandhari's curse. She was the mother of the hundred sons who were killed along with the mighty Kaurava army in the eighteen days of the war of Kurukshetra. Gandhari believed that Krishna could have averted the war but did not. Overpowered by anger and grief over the death of her sons, Gandhari had cursed Krishna with the destruction of the Yadavas in the same way her sons and the Kauravas were destroyed. Krishna smiled at the irony of it all. He could only watch the spectacle of cause and effect in human affairs, the unending chain of karma unfolding in front of his eyes. Bloodshed led to more bloodshed. That was the way of mortal life.

Walking away from his palace Krishna retreated into the depths of the forest and sat still under an ashwattha tree. He went into a meditative trance. The sky and the birds hovering above him saw his dark blue form shining like the smokeless lustre of a fire. He was dressed in two pieces of his favourite yellow silk. They adorned his body like molten gold. He had a smile on his lips. His mind was awash in a whole range of emotions. Yet he was distant from it all. With his garland of herbs, the vanamala, flying about, he was at peace with himself. With his legs outstretched and left hand on the lap, Krishna was resting under the tree.

As destiny would have it, a hunter named Jara was passing by. From a distance, he paused and looked at the yellow silk that was barely covering Krishna's foot and mistook it for the ear of a deer. No hunter wishes to miss the opportunity of finding a prey. Jara unleashed his iron-tipped arrow dipped in poison. The arrow seemed to have pierced his target with precision. Instead of a stricken animal's shriek that he was expecting to hear, Jara heard the sharp cry of a human voice. He rushed to the spot and found that Krishna was holding his left foot with both his hands. His brow was knit in pain and sweat was dripping from his forehead.

Jara realized what he had done and burst into tears. He asked, 'Lord, what have I done! I have committed a sacrilege for which I cannot forgive myself. Now tell me what to do to atone for my sin.' Krishna forgave his slayer, saying that he had done what was inevitable. 'Do not feel remorseful for you have rendered me a great service in helping me get liberated.'

The hunter could not quite comprehend what he had heard. He only learnt that Krishna was generous enough to pardon his crime. He left with a grieving heart. Tears drenched his eyes.

Meanwhile, Krishna's charioteer Daruka was frantically looking for him. He traced his path towards the forest by the scent of the garland of herbs that his master was wearing. Daruka was aghast to see Krishna down on the ground with the arrow stuck deep inside his flesh.

'What happened to you, my lord? Who did this to you?'

Krishna said, 'I do not have much time on this earth, Daruka. Listen to me carefully. You can inform my parents about the death of the Yadava clan and the demise of Balarama, my brother. After that ensure that no one stays in Dwarka because I foresaw that the city will be swallowed by the sea in a week's time. Instruct my friend Arjuna to escort all the women and children to Indraprastha. I have thought about you a great deal, Daruka. Set your mind on me in all earnestness, you too will soon find freedom as I have... Your last task, Daruka, is this—pull out this arrow from my foot.'

In between sobs, Daruka pulled out the poisonous arrow. He went around Krishna three times and left as instructed to fulfil his master's final wishes.

Daruka was the last person who had seen Krishna in his mortal form.

Krishna's eyes became serene. His face glowed with boundless gratitude. He remembered his days in Vrindavan. Those were the best days of his life, carefree and uninhibited. It was Radha who complemented the unbounded love that he always cherished. Radha was his aradhya, the one worthy of his worship. He remembered that when he was leaving his pastoral playground in Gokul and Vrindavan to go to Mathura, he had taken a last lingering look at Radha. Krishna knew that he would never come back to Gokul or play the flute again. He handed over his flute to Radha as a parting gift. Radha had lightened the burden of his obligation by not asking him to come back to Vraja to meet her. When Krishna closed his eyes for the final time, an ethereal light left his body, ending his tryst with his human form.

'Jai Radhe Krishna!' A chorus led by the purohit rose in the air. With the story over, the purohit closed his book, bowed his head and excused himself to run an errand. Keshav recited a few lines from his composition commemorating Krishna's passing away:

When I am long gone,
You may glimpse my fleeting presence
In the ripple of a river
In the sweep of the air
In the dust of the earth
In the blaze of the fire
Or in the vastness of space.
When you miss me in the five elements,
When you do not find me in the sixth sense that is your mind
Look for me inside your own heart—your seventh sense!
For I live there as timeless love!

In the backdrop of the rousing song, everyone heard a commotion in the temple premises. Some people were talking in agitated voices.

HOO-HA IN THE RISHIKESH ASHRAM

Even as Keshav was finishing his morning talk, the commotion in the ashram turned into a boisterous hoo-ha over something. The ashram manager ran breathlessly to Keshav and reported that a shop assistant who supplied food and beverages in the ashram had fallen sick with a painful stomach cramp. He had had to be hospitalized. The doctors said that it was a case of poisoning that could prove to be fatal.

Keshav turned to the purohit and asked him if he had locked the temple door where all the fruits and sweets and other offerings of the devotees were kept. The purohit nodded with a nervous vertical movement of the head. Keshav turned towards the manager and asked, 'Have you found out what that shop assistant was doing in the ashram before he felt sick?'

The manager reported that he had carried two cans of cola, one for Kaya and the other one for Keshav himself.

'But who ordered him to bring that?' Keshav enquired.

He turned again to the purohit and said with a hint of rising concern in his voice, 'When he brought me the can of cola, I asked him to offer it to Krishna, the lord of our temple. You know that whatever I eat or drink is first offered to Krishna. So, I asked the boy to keep this can before the deity as an offering. Something else came up and I got busy; but my mind circled back to the can of cola, and I started looking for him. I could not find him. He must have already left.'

The purohit looked down nervously.

The head cook scratched his head and said that some time ago he saw the purohit directing the shop assistant to the room where Manas's parents were staying. He also saw him giving the boy some money.

'Well, the purohit should know this then! Did Manas's parents attend my talk this morning?' Keshav asked with a steely calm in his voice.

There were droplets of perspiration on the purohit's face.

'No!' said the caretaker of the guest room. 'Manas's parents left this morning before sunrise. They said that they wanted to take a holy dip in the Har ki Pauri in Haridwar before catching the train to their home town. They must be on the train now.'

Keshav asked the caretaker to go to the hospital to keep a watch over the health of the shop assistant and get a detailed report for the ashram office. He learnt that his cat Arjun had died while he was being taken to the vet.

Keshav immediately announced a meeting of all the ashram staff.

The dazed students of the retreat decided to take a tea break. Some of them clearly panicked.

Swamy swore in front of everyone. 'It was an act of poisoning that was planned diligently, rigorously and painstakingly by the purohit. Did you not notice the nervous twitch on his lips and his shifty eyes?'

'Agreed!' howled Sardar. 'The purohit was itching to get even with Keshav for a long time for implementing some unwelcome changes including allowing women residents to live in the ashram.'

Eva said, 'The purohit was definitely eyeing the role of acharya after ousting Keshav.'

They wondered why Kaya had left for Dehradun so early in the morning.

Keshav chaired the office meeting in a large hall with the administrative staff of the campus. All eyes were on the purohit. The buzz in the hall subsided as Keshav began to speak.

He said, 'A few unexpected events have taken place in the ashram in the last seven days since the retreat began. There were many of my former students who were attending this retreat organized by Neel from thirty different countries. The retreat was organized in memory of one of my former students at the Indus Business School, going back nearly twenty years. His name was Manas. Neel also invited Manas's parents, who left the retreat suddenly for Haridwar this morning.

'However, I discovered through my contacts in Odisha that Manas's mother is a relative of the purohit. In fact, they are first cousins. Neither the purohit nor Manas's parents had shared this fact with me.' The purohit's face was turning pale as Keshav went on.

'I am not attributing the case of poisoning in the ashram to anyone. That is for the medical professionals and the investigators to find out. I had passed on a can of cola that was sent to my room by someone this morning. Obviously, the sender was aware that I occasionally enjoy a drink of cola, my old habit since my university days in the US. However, I was getting late for my talk and I did not have the time to go to the temple. I had asked the shop assistant to offer the can to the deity for the morning puja in the temple like all other offerings.

'I did notice that the tab on the edge of the can had a sprinkling of some granular salt-like substance. I wondered if it was some grocery stuff that may have gotten stuck on the can. I could also identify a faint but familiar fragrance coming out of that can. Someone using that fragrance had held the can in his hand. It was the fragrance of an aftershave lotion that I have some familiarity with.

'As providence would have it, the young shop assistant couldn't possibly resist the temptation of pulling out the tab of the sealed can to sample a sip of the cola himself.'

Keshav was interrupted as the medical officer attached to the ashram had brought a copy of the diagnostic report evaluating the shop assistant's condition. The report said that a granular, white, odourless, crystalline, poisonous powder called strychnine was laced with something that the young boy had taken either by inhalation, swallowing or absorption through eyes. It caused painful muscle spasms. Eventually, his muscles were fatigued and the boy couldn't breathe properly. He was in emergency care and his life was still at risk.

'That explains a lot of what happened this morning.' Keshav sighed.

'The little boy gave the partly opened can of cola laced with poison to the purohit, who kept it right inside the fruit basket as an offering to the deity. Some cola from the can was dripping out of the basket on to the floor. I noticed some dead ants around the spilt fluid. The ants trying to taste the cola died in the process. I suspected some foul play and ordered the temple doors locked until my talk was over. The sparrows chirping around the temple premises would have made a feast of the poisoned ants and eventually poisoned themselves. We saw two sparrows lying dead on the walkway this morning. Our cat, Arjun, may have licked the spilt cola and become sick with the poison. I am sad to say Arjun died this morning while he was being taken to the vet.'

The group assembled in the hall were in deep shock.

'The real question still remains. Who poisoned the cola cans and why?'

The purohit, who was shivering in his chair, abruptly spoke up. 'I didn't do it. I swear in the name of Krishna; I was not the one who would think of such a heinous act against humans or animals.'

'Then who?' asked the caretaker of the guest room, quick to defend himself when faced with a situation wherein he could become the target of growing suspicion. 'Wasn't the purohit the one who sent the shop assistant to buy rat poison for Manas's mother?'

'But that was because there was really a field rat hiding inside her ashram room that she needed to get rid of,' shot off the purohit with his eyes bulging in anger.

Meanwhile, the doorman said that Kaya had come back

from Dehradun with a foreign woman and was surprised to hear that someone had kept a can of cola outside her door. Having heard the story of what had happened, she asked for permission to join the meeting.

Keshav nodded his approval. He then asked the purohit if he had anything more to say.

Crestfallen, the purohit confessed that he had indeed harboured bitter feelings towards Keshav as he had altered several traditions of the ashram. The worst was that Keshav changed the rule that forbade women to stay in the ashram premises. 'Manas's mother, who is indeed my relative, told me all about Keshav and how she suspected his role in abetting the suicide of their son Manas.'

'Manas's father seemed to have forgiven Keshav. However, the mother, my sister, Mohini, was still unforgiving after many years. The untimely death of her son still rankled her. Unknown to me, she may have laced the cola can with rat poison.'

The purohit added that he had no idea that the cola cans would be poisoned. He remembered Mohini asking him frequently about Keshav's whereabouts and his relationship with Kaya.

'She had spoken about Keshav sneeringly. "What is he doing with this foreign woman who is of his daughter's age?"'

He then went on to tell the rest of his story. 'Last evening, I saw the shop assistant looking for Mohini as she had asked him for a few provisions. I gave the boy some money so that he could fetch whatever Mohini and her husband wanted for the trip to Haridwar early next morning to offer prayers for the departed soul of Manas. I had no idea she would poison the cola drink,' said the purohit. Keshav listened quietly. His unblinking eyes betrayed no trace of surprise.

KAYA SPRINGS A SURPRISE

Kaya showed up around lunchtime with a young blonde. She had such sparkling green eyes! Both Kaya and the young girl were looking for Keshav who was chatting with Neel and his friends about the day's dramatic turn of events. Spotting Kaya at a distance he said, 'Look, there they come!'

Kaya and the young woman had something startlingly similar: glittering green eyes, oval face and blonde hair tied in a ponytail.

A sad half-smile sat on Neel's face. He was quick to spot the resemblance in the way the two women smiled flashing their slightly uneven teeth.

'Meet my daughter, Radhika Johnson.' Kaya stared at Neel.

She waited to see Neel's reaction to her abrupt disclosure before she spoke again. Neel looked away uneasily.

'Radhika arrived this morning from Boston to spend some time with me before she goes to college.'

Everyone seemed to be in utter disbelief. No one expected Kaya to have a daughter tucked away in Boston. Even if she did, they would not have expected her to show up at the ashram.

Kaya gestured to Radhika and she lowered her head uttering a 'namaste'. Then she bent down to touch Keshav's feet.

Keshav brushed her hair with his hands and then drew her up to look at her eyes intently.

He said, 'You are a strong woman, Radhika, like your mother. And your eyes are a shade greener than hers.' Keshav chuckled. He noticed a faint dimple showing up on Radhika's right cheek as she flung a shy 'hi' to everyone around.

'Kaya will share her story with you all this afternoon,' said Keshav, anticipating the growing curiosity around the undisclosed life of the mother and daughter all these years.

'Let's all disperse for lunch. We will meet in the evening

for our last conversation session. There is too much happening for all of us today!'

Saying this, he drew Kaya along and asked her something about the cola can that was retrieved from outside her room.

Kaya and her daughter then retired to Keshav's ashram cottage to have a private lunch with him.

Neel shook his head in a daze and slipped away from the group saying he was going to take a walk outside the ashram.

'If a woman can hold a secret that long, she must be some kind of a goddess,' said Sardar looking at Eva.

'Sarcastic,' mumbled Prasad.

'Mother of all surprises!' Anju said, rolling her eyes.

'Don't tell me Radhika Johnson is for real,' said Eva with her trademark pout.

'Bizarre, bewildering, baffling, bemusing!' Swamy babbled, summarizing the collective confusion of the gang.

They all went to lunch huddled together, buzzing like a hive of agitated bees.

'Where is Neel?' Eva wondered.

But he was nowhere to be seen.

KAYA JOHNSON'S STORY

Keshav had invited all the batchmates of Indus to his ashram cottage for a cup of tea that afternoon. Kaya was already there laying the table with tea and assorted snacks.

'Radhika had gone out to the city on a trip,' she said.

Twenty years had rolled by, yet the whole ambiance reminded them of Keshav's tea parties in his faculty residence in Indus. They all settled down with their beverages and eatables.

Keshav smiled, looked at Kaya and nudged her. 'Now, your story, Kaya Johnson!'

Kaya took a sip from the cup. Her face caught the

slant of the sun. That afternoon Kaya was wearing a spicy fragrance, conjuring up a mysterious cocktail of cardamom and pepper. Swamy was wondering why Neel had to miss such a memorable get-together of the G-7. Swamy's memory went back many years and he remembered the lines Neel had shared with him about his infatuation with Kaya.

> *The sensuous asymmetry of her teeth,*
> *The unexplored mystery of gold, blonde hair*
> *Soft as ripe wheatgrass!*

Kaya's voice spiralled in the air like wispy smoke from her cup of tea.

'Hmm, where do I begin? As an undergraduate student in the university, I was trapped in an abusive relationship with a medical student, Mike. He was an alcoholic, a split personality—generous, when he was in a good mood, and possessive to the point of madness. It does seem like I have a habit of attracting such people in my life.

'I come from a conservative Christian family and it was impossible for me to face my parents when I bore Mike's child as an unwed mother. I was completely lost. I did not know where to go. I turned to a charismatic professor, who was teaching a Master's course at the university, for some counselling. He asked me if I really wanted to have the child.'

'My deepest impulse was to say "yes" yet I kept quiet. Keshav was then living in a small apartment rented out for the faculty of the university. Seeing my plight he was kind enough to offer me a spare room for free in his apartment until I found a secure shelter for an unwed mother. When my daughter was born, Keshav named her Radhika,' she said.

'He ensured I got some work part-time at the university as he took care of my daughter. He even helped me with the chores that included washing baby Radhika's clothes.' She chuckled.

'Before he quit his job at the US school and left for India, Keshav had transferred all of his modest earnings and terminal benefits to me to ensure that I was financially secure until I got a full-time job. I can never repay his debt. I was overwhelmed during his last Master's class at the university that ended with a flute song. I simply wrote a small thank you Post-it note to Keshav, promising myself that I would return to India with Radhika at least once in my lifetime. So here we are!

'My parents visited me at Keshav's request and eventually accepted Radhika as their grandchild.' Kaya's eyes had welled up with tears. She covered her mouth with her hands, unable to come to grips with the intensity of her emotions. Eva hugged her, trying to comfort her.

Kaya was concluding her story. 'Mike visited the Indus campus in Lucknow for a couple of days. He was repentant about his behaviour in the past. He pleaded with me and wanted Radhika and me back in his life. When I refused to go back to the once-abusive relationship, Mike flew into a rage and physically beat me up in the guest house at Indus. The scar he left behind stayed with me for quite some time.'

She raised her eyes looking for Neel. He was not there! She wished he could hear the truth of that old scar!

Kaya continued. 'I had to turn to Keshav again to come to my rescue. He mediated with Mike and asked him to leave me alone to enable me to make my own decision about my life. Keshav then drove me in his Indigo to my hostel that evening after he had settled matters with Mike.'

Eva's mind went back several years to the memory of Neel watching intently as she rushed out of the Indigo under those bleak night lights only to vanish into the girls' hostel. She distinctly remembered Neel muttering under his breath with his jaw clenched, 'Isn't that Keshav's car?'

Kaya went on. 'Radhika blossomed as a bright kid and a fine young woman and I lived a large part of my life only for her. I am deeply indebted to Keshav for being in my life. I had promised him to keep Radhika a secret until yesterday when he advised me to share the truth.'

Keshav looked at her and said, 'Kaya, do you see the intensity and the dignity of the struggle that has shaped your life so far? Our characters and identities are all forged by adversities. A few years after birth, we strive to be individuals. The first part of our life is invested in protecting and strengthening our individuality, thinking largely about ourselves. The second half of life is a quest for getting free from this claustrophobic, misleading individuality. The less obsessive we become about our false identities as individuals, the more we truly taste the freedom of that one indivisible life that flows through us. That is what makes for an enlightened individual—someone whose personal life is interdependent with larger life. To be responsible for life beyond your own life is the very perfume of enlightened living. To lose oneself in the love of the other is the essence of true freedom.'

He concluded with these words:

The first cry of freedom is to crave more love for oneself.
The final song of freedom is to desire nothing but love for all.
In between, the spirit that governs our lives struggles to be free.

One after another, everybody in the gang took turns to hug Kaya. 'Where is Neel?' Kaya enquired. No one in the group knew where he was.

THE MYSTERY OF THE POISONED COLA

Everyone was hoping that by the evening the mystery of the poisoned can of cola would be unravelled. The shop assistant who had suffered severe poisoning had finally recovered. In a statement to the police, he revealed that Mohini, Manas's mother, had ordered the two cans of cola for herself. However, he did not actually see her poisoning the can. She took the cans inside her room and had asked the assistant to wait outside so that she could pay him for the cola in cash. As the door was ajar, he remembered she was speaking to someone who was inside. After a few minutes, she returned with the cans and asked him to deliver one of them to Keshav and the other one to Kaya. She gave the boy a generous tip.

The shop assistant did as he was instructed. Unwittingly, he delivered the cola can to Kaya's doorstep. As luck would have it, Kaya had left for Dehradun to fetch her daughter before she received her surprise gift from the unknown well-wisher. The cola meant for Keshav had to be offered to the deity first at Keshav's request. However, the shop assistant could not resist the temptation of opening the tab of the can and taking a sip discreetly. Soon after, the poison started working.

Mohini had left with her husband saying that they were going for a purifying bath in the Ganga before heading home. The police recorded the shop assistant's statements and sent a lookout notice for Mohini and her husband.

That was that.

However, it was not clear who the man sitting inside Mohini's room was. Who was that mysterious man she was talking to inside her room before the poisoned cola cans were handed over to the shop assistant?

TWO MORE SURPRISES

Keshav called a meeting of the temple trustees that evening and announced that he would be taking leave to go on a solo pilgrimage to the Himalayas. He added that since he would be away for an indefinite period of time, it would only be appropriate that the trustees choose a suitable candidate to assume charge as the next acharya of the ashram. Until then, the purohit would hold charge. He also appealed to the trustees to forgive Manas's mother Mohini, and withdraw all charges against her. 'We can now speculate that Mohini, the boy's mother, may not have any clue that the cola cans were actually being poisoned by someone who was doing it without her knowledge. One can understand the grief of a mother, and therefore whatever she thought or did can be easily considered to be caused by a temporary loss of sanity. She may not be the one who plotted the poisoning of the cola!'

'Who did it then?' Sardar squealed. 'Was it her husband, Manas's father, who was sitting inside the ashram room when she took the unadulterated cola cans inside?'

'No, it wasn't her husband either,' Keshav said convincingly. 'I checked with the ashram guard who told me that Mohini's husband was taking his usual long walk outside the ashram when Mohini vanished inside the room with the cola cans to talk to a man sitting there.'

'If not her husband, who was that man in the room then? Who was plotting to kill Keshav and Kaya?'

Keshav said in his usual poetic way, 'A bit of a fragrance clings to the hand that gives a gift like that. I have forgiven the wearer of an aftershave that I smelt on the cola can. For the perpetrator of the crime, the only thing that was more painful than the memory of the loss of a dear friend was a possessive love. Without naming the person, all I can wish for him is that he may now be free from the poison of the envy that he nurtured for such a long time.'

'The man who plotted it used Manas's mother as an alibi, a cover for his misdeed. When his plot failed, he left the ashram with great remorse. Knowing him as I did, he must have prayed for the forgiveness of the Class of 2000 for what he had done. Let bygones be bygones.'

'What? Now I know who the man conspiring with Mohini was,' whispered the purohit more out of relief than shock. 'He was sitting inside the room using my sister Mohini as a shield for his devious plans! How could he even think of doing this?'

The Class of 2000 spoke in shrill voices charged with horror and disbelief.

As though this was not enough of an emotional roller coaster, Keshav's announcement of stepping down as acharya of Krishna Prem put everyone in the ashram in a tizzy. The purohit was disconsolate. With hands folded, he asked for Keshav's pardon for any ill will that he may have harboured.

Keshav said, 'Unburden your mind, Purohit, of all guilt as well as prejudices. Our common goal is freedom. Only a mind unburdened from likes and dislikes will see the light of freedom. A heart will feel the warmth and intimacy of love when free of guilt.'

'Why are you leaving us?' the purohit asked, almost imploring.

Keshav said, 'My relationship with Krishna has been lifelong. It started with the name that my grandmother gave me. In the course of living, my identity merged with Krishna's. I once sought Krishna's grace in knowledge, in the quietude of the academic world. However, I realized that arrogance and prejudices grew secretly in the sylvan shades of campus life. The intellect was blind to its own follies. So, I sought refuge in the realm of devotion as the acharya of the temple. The ashram gave me space to purify my heart. However, the one you know as acharya—Keshav—saw that the heart without the light of reason became dark and impure. A crooked heart seeks to satisfy desires; it will find ways to manipulate others and ensure that its wishes are fulfilled.

'Institutions often rob the goodness of a human being. Institutionalized knowledge is as dangerous as institutionalized devotion. Yet institutions are so necessary for mankind to strive together towards their chosen ideals. The business school taught me that when rationality follows a narrow and insular groove, reason becomes cold and works against our best intentions. From the ashram, I learnt that devotion without reason could twist itself into a self-centred dogma and mistrust. This is what is happening to our universities and our places of worship all over. The circle of reason has to embrace the ampler circle of love for humanity to thrive and prosper.'

Keshav's words sounded like a rousing valediction for the graduating class. He continued. 'My Krishna, whose essence is freedom, could not be confined to a university or a temple. He would cease to be Krishna then. The essence of Krishna is hidden deep within us as a lifelong yearning. He has seeded the longing in us to be free. Sometimes, we are too obsessed with our own emotional world or too entangled in our network of thoughts to be able to see with clarity that we are actually born free. The highest principle in us, higher than the limited perceptions of our bodies and narrow conceptions of our minds, is actually free. It requires our seventh sense to be aware of our inborn freedom. You have to learn, know and finally realize that you are truly free from all the bondages imposed on you, your physical and mental nature. All we need to do is drop our illusion that we are finite. Our mukti, our freedom, is nothing but the light of the knowledge that we are the infinite being hidden behind these finite knots of the body-mind. This is the solution to all our problems.'

Turning to his ex-students from Indus, he said, 'Simply become aware that you are building your own prison with those bricks of dogma and the mortar of attachment. Just this awareness will make those walls drop off. How? These walls are not made of concrete, but of conditioning of thought and feeling. You yourselves have to break through the walls of ignorance. No one else can do it for you. Only then will you receive the kiss of freedom.'

Then, Keshav handed over the key to the ashram office saying, 'Women and men are two wings of timeless love. Keeping women out of the ashram premises only means that we are still subservient to our unknown and unclaimed half. The community of Krishna Prem is a commitment to unconditional love. I would be happy if women like Kaya and her daughter Radhika feel at home here, just like every other member in the ashram.'

The purohit still had his hands folded. For the first time since Keshav had taken over as acharya, the purohit bent his knees and touched the ground in front of Keshav with his head. Keshav lifted him up and gave him a gentle hug.

KAYA WITHOUT NEEL

The setting sun was now a huge orange orb casting its mystic light on the Ganga. Kaya stood knee-deep in the river. Temple bells rang in the distance. The wicks of the shining brass candelabra were lit. The priests stood by the riverbank chanting a hymn to the sacred river. Ripples of emotions swept through Kaya: acceptance, rejection, affection, desire, ecstasy, absence, devotion and finally the hint of freedom. Her entire life flew past like a swift current in the river.

Kaya felt the painful void Neel left in her heart. A pall of sadness sat inside her. The sky was overcast. A faint drizzle fell on her in shimmering silver streaks. She tried her best not to cry. Neel's bearded face floated vaguely before her eyes on the dusky horizon. Even if she tried to forget him, his face would not go away; it was a disembodied face with stubble on the cheeks and a crooked yet enchanting smile. His eyes with their desperate, lost, pleading look seemed to spy on her from every direction. Kaya could imagine a speechless yearning burning inside him.

'He extolled my beauty in his verses, tormented my soul by his possessiveness. How could it end just like that? He who troubled me the most also learnt to love me recklessly,' she thought. Kaya was now talking to herself in halting monosyllables.

'Love you...miss you...hate you!'

She turned around against the sun to head back to the ashram.

With the sun on one side of the horizon and rain on the other, she saw the vague outlines of a rainbow. Radiant white light had spread itself in a palette of colours. There must have been a storm close by, she reckoned, as she hurried to attend the retreat class.

THE FINAL SESSION

'Our conversation this evening is about knowing that which enables every human problem to be resolved!' said Keshav as he began the session. The day's turn of dramatic events that spread through hushed voices and soft whispers had apparently not rattled him even a wee bit.

'Let's first focus on what is the origin of all human problems. It is nothing but ignorance of our real nature. Our real nature is that of a free being—a being that is independent of the mental world that we construct around it. Our mind, our emotions and our intellect are trained to divide the world in illusory shape, form, qualities and utility. All our problems start with the mind's attachment to a divided world of forms and shapes. The division is a creation of the cut-and-paste mind. Such a division is supported by the outward diversity in nature.

'As we look inward, we see that such divisions do not exist in the unitive reality of our awareness. The five senses and our mind divide us. The seventh sense which is our undivided awareness unites us. In the depth of awareness, we can sense our real nature as one interconnected being. When our inbound awareness becomes outbound, in a swift sweep of identification, the mind tags an emotional value to a world of likes and dislikes. The mind suffers when it cannot find what it likes. The mind also suffers when it is stuck to what it dislikes.

'This experience of our life is based on a false foundation of attachment to likes and dislikes. This indeed is the source of all our problems.'

'Keshav, if false knowledge is the problem, what then is the solution?' asked the Egyptian.

Keshav responded, 'If wrong knowledge is the problem, the solution ought to be right knowledge. Isn't that so? If what is false sits like a sharp shard of glass in your leg, you need another shard of glass that is rightly held in your hand like a surgical knife to take out the one that is stuck there. When the first glass piece is taken out, you throw it away along with the second glass piece, which has done its job.

'You cannot allow right or wrong knowledge to stick to you. You have to abandon both like the two pieces of glass.'

'Why is that so?' asked Swamy.

'That is so because knowledge is just a ladder, a means to reach the plane of realization. You do not hold on to a ladder once you have climbed to the place you wanted to go to. Unburdening yourself of knowledge disarms your ego that would otherwise raise its head soon with all its false perceptions.'

'How does the ego function in creating false knowledge?' Swamy pressed the question.

Keshav said, 'The ego functions through a monkey mind that gets drunk after being bitten by a scorpion. The monkey is a symbol of the restless mind that is constantly moving from one stimulus to another. The scorpion is the bite of jealousy. The ego survives by its constant need for validation of its likes and dislikes in the world. The ego thrives by comparison with others, asserting its need to be right and to prove others wrong. The drunken mind, inflated with its assumed knowledge, bloats up the ego. The drunken mind gets caught in power struggles.'

'How does one break free from the ego?' Anju asked.

'The ego always projects the mind outward. To break free from the ego is to turn the mind inward. When the mind turns inward a magical shift takes place within a human being. All saints and sages have called this inward journey the process of true awakening. It is the awakening from the slumber of ignorance. The power of the mind that was projected outward by the ego is now reclaimed by a serene seventh sense that has returned home to its own source.'

'What is this source of the ego?' It was Eva's turn to ask.

'The rishis named this source as the sense of our existence expressed by the words "I am". When we are identified with the outer world of likes and dislikes, our perception of who we are gets distorted by our contact with the world of appearances. "I am" becomes falsely identified with the body. The ancients called this the work of maya. We begin to believe in maya's story that says "I am the body". We cling to our "I am this body idea" as though we would have this body forever.

'Our stubborn clinging is one of the most amusing aspects of our false identity. Everyone knows that this body will grow old, wear out and die one day, yet no one seems to be able to let go of the "I am the body" idea. The body appears in time, and disappears in time. Our unbounded am-ness gets identified with the nature-bound temporary body. Likewise, "I am" gets falsely identified with our feelings, beliefs and possessions, all of which are transitory.'

'How does someone then get out of the false "I am the

body" idea?' asked Sardar.

'The rishis said one can loosen the grip of this false identity through discrimination and detachment—viveka and vairagya—just as you give up an old shirt and wear a new one! First, you discriminate that the old shirt has outlived its utility and then you discard it. I will tell you an interesting story to explore why a human clings to his false identity.'

Keshav smiled broadly as he began the story.

'A hygiene-obsessed boss looked at his shabbily dressed subordinate and said, "Duffer, why do your socks smell all the time?"

'The subordinate, browbeaten and scared, said: "Sir, I am sorry. I will surely discard the old pair and get a new pair for myself from the supermarket tomorrow."

'The boss shot back. "You may as well act on that. If I find you wearing that stinking pair again, I will have you dismissed."

'The next day as the subordinate entered the cabin with a file, the boss turned his nose up, and sniffed hard. Then, with his eyes narrowing and brow wrinkling, he said, "Gosh, that old foul smell again! Did I not tell you that you will be dismissed if you did not obey?"

'"Yes, sir" said the visibly shaken subordinate. "I did exactly as you had ordered. I went to the supermarket and got a brand new pair. That new pair is what I am wearing today. Please look!" He promptly pulled his trouser leg up and showed his boss a clean new pair of blue socks.

'"Then, where is that noxious smell coming from?" the exasperated boss asked.

'"Sir, it is probably coming from my trouser pocket where I am carrying my old socks as proof in case you did not trust that I indeed bought a new pair!"'

There was a roar of laughter. Among the audience was an American who was laughing so hard that his belly was shaking.

He was slapping his right thigh with his left hand in glee.

Keshav joined in the merriment and said, 'You can't get rid of this stinking "I am the body idea" until you deeply trust that you are indeed the awareness, the infinite, unblinking witness—in short, your seventh sense—behind the body-mind phenomenon.'

Kaya asked, 'What is the relationship between the awareness of "I am" and the experience of love?'

Keshav said, 'The love we experience is nothing but the movement of this unitive, undivided awareness through our body-mind, however fleetingly we sense this awareness. We do not possess love; love possesses us when we are aware. With this awareness, you can fall in love with just about anything: a blade of glass, the dust of the earth, a flowing river or a bird singing, an octopus in the deep sea—everything around you is linked to this infinite awareness. When you surrender to this awareness, that is your real nature, all your illusions, your anxieties, your fears drop off.

'Awareness is that which resolves all your problems at their source. The dreamer instantly resolves all the problems he experiences in a nightmare the moment he is aware that it was only a dream. Isn't that true?'

Most of the audience nodded.

'Look at Krishna's life and the problems he is beset with. His birth is a problem. Kamsa threatens his life at birth. His upbringing is a challenge for his foster parents. His love for Radha encounters societal pressures. He has to elope with Rukmini before he can marry her. Even his death is caused by an irreversible curse. Have you wondered how Krishna overcomes seemingly insurmountable obstacles to live a lifetime of adventures? Have you observed that Krishna never loses his capacity to love? He loves his pranks with his mother in Gokul; he loves his pastoral pastimes in Vrindavan with the gopis; he loves his exploits in Mathura and his rule in Dwarka.

Like Christ, he even loves the one who inadvertently kills him with his arrow. Yet, his love is devoid of all attachments. He never looks back at Vrindavan once he leaves Radha there. He remains dispassionate in joy as well as in sorrow...'

He resumed. 'Krishna lives life to the fullest and is yet not caught in the bind of duality, joy or sorrow, like or dislike, life or death. He is pure awareness that does not manifest itself through opposites. Only through the play of the opposites, dwandwa, does the universe of form and phenomenon take shape—man and woman, hard and soft, stillness and movement. The divine Krishna is never born, nor does he ever die because the divine is nothing but an undivided and deathless awareness. That is Krishna's original state. Although he is born in a human form and he lives the ecstasy and the agony of a human life, he is free and unbounded like the blue sky. We are just like that even in the human form—free like the unbounded sky. The only difference is that Krishna is aware that he is free while we are not. That's why we have all appeared in a bit of blue today to pay homage to the blue God.' Keshav chuckled.

Upon some reflection, he pointed out, 'Come to think of it, the sky is actually not blue but only appears to be so. In fact, there is no sky either. What we know as the sky is simply an enchanting emptiness, a magnificent void. Just as the sky is defined by the constellation of stars and planets, Krishna is defined by the relationship that his community of people has with each other. Without devotees, there is no trace of the divine! Krishna lives in the hearts of his devotees. He lives as a human among other humans without always revealing himself. Likewise, the one you know as Keshav hopes to live in the hearts and minds of his students.' He laughed gleefully.

'What an awesome analogy!' said Swamy.

Swamy remembered the first lecture of Keshav that he had heard at Indus. After the class, he was reflecting on the content of that class with his classmates over snacks interspersed with sips of ginger chai. Keshav's words then appeared like frothing, energizing yet transient bubbles of cola. Now, the same teaching felt as though they were waves from the depth of an ocean. The fizz of a dark cola drink was the surface intimation of its hidden allure. Behind the froth and fumes of life, there was a deeper mystery of our true nature. In Swamy's eyes, Keshav was still a mystery. What Swamy failed to reckon was that he himself had come a long way in these twenty years.

THE LAST DINNER

Kaya surveyed the generous spread of dinner along with Radhika. Being the first ones to arrive, they went sniffing around. Kaya was explaining to Radhika that Indians had more variety of vegetarian food than anywhere in the world.

The cook chimed in to help with describing some of that. 'This is freshly steamed fluffy dhokla with green chilli tempering served with an aromatic green chutney.'

Kaya's eyes lit up as she described the next thing on the menu. 'And, here is chaat masala to tickle the palate.'

'Very *testy*,' said the cook smiling.

'He means tasty.' Kaya winked and interpreted that for Radhika.

This was followed by malai kofta. After that was chole, onions, and tomatoes with ginger paste served with deep-fried and fermented bhatoora.

'What is this dumb biryani?' queried Radhika, rather amused.

'Well, not quite dumb, it is called dum biryani.' Kaya smiled. 'Dum is the Hindi word for breath or air. This biryani is cooked by choking the steam or the breath inside the pot that cooks the biryani to give it an exotic flavour.'

Then, there was luscious dal makhani, creamy lentils laced

with butter. 'Here is palak paneer,' said the cook, adding to the conversation again.

'Palak paneer is the romance of spinach paste with cottage cheese.' Prasad appeared from nowhere and started adding his little spice to the ongoing commentary on Indian food. 'Here you can see south Indian vada which is nothing but the American doughnut that has just woken up and has had no time to dress up.'

Radhika could not contain her laughter.

There were puffy and flat naans. Finally, Kaya spotted Keshav's favourite, piping hot and crisp wheat aloo parathas. They were stuffed with spiced, faintly sour, mashed potatoes and served with some tangy mango pickle.

After a good meal, there was kheer for dessert, and rasmalai, flat cheesecake dipped in sweetened milk that Radhika was told would melt in the mouth. All of them gathered around the dinner table.

Keshav announced that he was leaving early in the morning. This then would perhaps be their last meal together. There were some sighs and a numbing silence. Neel's reference was strangely missing in most of their conversation that evening; his name was mentioned only in whispers and hushed undertones.

Keshav, never one to let the situation turn grim as it just about threatened to, lightened the mood by saying, 'You cannot clean up all the organic vegetarian delicacies without the entire neighbourhood getting wind of the feast tonight.'

Kaya laughed until there were tears in her eyes. Eva was watching the similarity in the way both the mother and daughter sizzled when they smiled. She extended a tissue to Kaya.

Post-dinner, there were tight hugs, teary eyes and some restrained sniffles. Then, all of them gathered around Keshav and stood in a circle.

The purohit asked him for his blessings for the whole community. Keshav stood there silently for a while. The sound of a bat flitting around the ashwattha tree made a monotonous noise. And then Keshav said, 'Neel, who is not here today, and Kaya organized this retreat to pay respects to Manas. Manas's devotion to my teaching was rare and exceptional. He had faith in every word I said. He is the only one among you that almost reached that final frontier of love and freedom in his short lifetime. He is the one who understood the nature of this illusion of "I am the body" idea by which we define ourself. Yet, he chose the path of annihilation rather than that of transcendence of the self. Manas still lives among us in our urge to be free.'

There was an eerie silence.

Then he said, 'Many of you are going home tomorrow. You had come here to find answers to your questions and solutions to your problems. Some of you came here to transform yourselves. A few sought freedom. A handful came to experience love. You may think that you will be free tomorrow or sometime in the future.

'You can't be free tomorrow. Freedom must be experienced now and here. If it is not here now, it will not be there tomorrow either. Freedom is here at this instant, not sometime later or some place else. You cannot seek freedom out there because you are exactly that which you are seeking.'

Then he lowered his voice and said, 'If death came to you and asked you to leave all that you thought were your possessions, what would you leave behind here and now. Pretty much everything, isn't it? Your possessions, your likes, your dislikes, your reputation and all of that. Death will claim everything sooner or later except this one reality of your existence—freedom and love. The only way to escape the jaws of death is to go on this pilgrimage to the blazing shrine of love that is burning right now inside your heart and the flag of freedom that is fluttering here.

'Now if all of you were asked to say farewell to the person standing next to you, what would you say?'

Raising his voice to a more intense pitch, he said, 'Look into the person's eyes. Think of this night as though it was your last night on planet earth. How would you then greet the person standing next to you? Knowing that you may not meet each other ever again, would you look deep into the eyes of the person that you are standing next to and say a silent goodbye?'

Everyone turned around and followed the instructions given by Keshav.

His voice now rose like a swelling wave. 'How does it feel to say goodbye to a friend on this earth for one last time? Would you not go to the depth of your heart to explore the love you can bring to this last encounter?'

With that last question melting into the air Keshav slowly walked away towards his room, taking each step deliberately as though he was deeply in love with the earth he was stepping on. He walked to his residence with his hands folded signalling that the weeklong retreat was over.

11

Freedom

For Kaya, it was just that kind of a day. A morning that melts your moods into the lightness of being. It was a day when nothing could go wrong; nothing could make you unfree.

The sun sprinkled liquid gold on the rippling riverbed. A soft breeze felt like a whispered secret. Intermittent waves splashed on the sailboat tethered to the bank of the Ganga on the ashram side. Neel had already left the ashram. Kaya and her Indus classmates were waiting for Keshav to take a boat ride with them to the other shore. From there, Keshav would move on to his next destination, the Himalayas. He had no plans to return to the ashram again.

Kaya held Keshav's hand for support as he stepped on to the wobbly boat. That touch, warm and caring, felt like the commencement rather than the end of a journey for Kaya. Keshav had nothing more than a cloth bag as his belonging.

'Is that all you need, Keshav?' asked Sardar, as he helped with the bag.

The boat, unhinged from its anchor, began to move. Keshav sat on the edge facing six of his students.

His voice drifted away as the speeding wind scattered the words he uttered: 'You have to learn to lighten your burden and go on this voyage of freedom, unafraid and alone. Now, listen to this ancient story.'

A stream meandering through pebbles and rocks came upon a desert. The stream was terrified to see that it was drying up in the blazing heat of the desert. 'Will I perish here? What will happen to me when I am gone? Will I be able to cross over that steep mountain ahead and become a youthful flowing river again?' These were the thoughts that were buzzing around in the mind of the stream. Then, a gentle breeze began to blow. The breeze said to the stream, 'If you hold my hand I can carry you across the desert and beyond the mountain.'

The stream did not believe what it had heard.

'I can understand the wind blowing over the mountain, but how can a heavy stream do that?'

'You have to lighten your burden! There is no other way,' said the wind.

'How is that possible?' The stream was intrigued.

'Well, just stop clinging to the earth and allow yourself to be vapour!'

Soon enough the stream realized that it was floating in the air as vapour.

The wind was favourable and the vapour wafted in the air and became a cloud that crossed the steep mountain and burst out in rains on the other side of the mountain.

The stream that decided to unburden itself now became a river.

Keshav's words drowned in a hushed stillness before he spoke again. 'To be free, one has to learn to live without clinging. To be absolutely free is to receive the bounty of the invisible giver.' Then like a poet reciting a verse, he said:

Clouds flowing freely like white sails
Swell with the wind's charity
And unleash their wealth of rain
On the thirsty earth.

Keshav's words stirred his students' minds. Yet, it was in his silent presence that they found answers to their most pressing problems of life.

Kaya was thinking about one of Keshav's riddles that she took a long time to find an answer to. With this one sentence, he had taught her the most profound truth of life: *Knowing your original nature resolves all your problems at their source.*

At that moment, a northerly wind, open and free, caressed Kaya's face and made the Ganga gurgle like a living being. The river spoke to her in a strange voice. She recognized that her life was an unending series of experiences, bitter and sweet. Where she was born; the Roman Catholic school where she had spent some time; her first big crush; the silent horror of an abusive relationship; the dullness of the first job; the chores of a single parent. Crossing the river now in Rishikesh appeared like a movie from an exotic world. A palm-leaf boat gliding through the swelling river stirred the currents of life in her. They were too deep for her to fathom.

This life was far away from the haze of street lights in downtown New York. During that unseasonal rain, she clung to Keshav as they rushed to catch the outbound metro. She smelt his manliness. Yet it was his serenity that had truly enchanted her. He held her, then pregnant with her daughter, in a caring embrace. Keshav helped her recognize something in her own nature that was unmoved by whatever happened around her. The stillness within her helped her rise above her experiences. She became a quiet witness of the ups and downs in her life. This indeed was her original nature. It was unblemished, tranquil and clear like a crystal. A thrill of recognition crept up her spine as she remembered Krishna's words from the Gita:

> *Under my watchful gaze*
> *All actions are performed by the laws of nature.*
> *The ignorant deluded by the ego thinks 'I am the doer.'*

The boatman, exhausted with the effort of rowing, had large sweat patches on his shirt. For a while, he relaxed his hands on the oars and let the boat glide gently downstream.

Swamy was watching Kaya's face glow with an unusual brightness. There was a new depth in her eyes he had not witnessed before.

Keshav asked Swamy if he had made any progress in his lifelong search for someone to marry. Swamy shook his head, saying, 'That has been precisely, poignantly and persistently my problem.'

Keshav chuckled as he said, 'If only you could give up the allure of that exclusive mate that you often described so eloquently. If only you could focus on the unity rather than the exclusivity of life around you, you could find the right partner.

'You see, all of nature including human nature strives towards this unity. Look at your own body, Swamy. Your body's survival is not based on any exclusive body part. You could survive without a leg or a lung or even half a colon. Your life depends on the unity and rhythm of relationships between different parts of the body. Once you lose the unity of rhythm, you go out of sync with life itself. The trillions of cells in your body seek unity of purpose inside that one body. Love is only a name we give to this invisible unity of life.'

'How do you live in a relationship without drawing boundaries that include as well as exclude?' asked Swamy.

'You have to carefully observe nature to find an answer to that. Look at the myriad life forms that thrive under this flowing water. At least five hundred known species of fishes like jellyfish and shellfish can genetically mutate in as little as ten days to change their gender. When a male fish is removed by a fisherman, the largest female of a species immediately senses his absence and adopts full male breeding behaviours the same day. The vast range of flora and fauna—green grass, red roses and white lilies—have inclusive characteristics; they have both male and female reproductive systems. Nature defies exclusion and classification. Boundaries in nature are constructs of the human mind. In life, nothing can really be excluded.

'Do not put human beings into categories. Life cannot be categorized without exclusion. That which you exclude, excludes you—whether people or planet, the same truth holds.'

Swamy's bewildered face was reflecting the vulgar quest for exclusivity in his love life. Like Uncle Prakash, he had wasted his life in the pursuit of the enticing 'other'. In the process, he had left behind very important aspects of his identity in relative isolation.

Swamy's mind zoomed back to his closest friend Shyam from his schooldays in laid-back Mysore. How he watched him from his vast palatial veranda. Shyam was lost in the babble of schoolboys around a mobile ice cream cart. A cockily turned cricket cap sat on his dark, long hair glistening with oil. How he missed that choreography of emotions creeping up on Shyam's face as they stole glances at each other. He recalled how his mother, pouring filter coffee from one steel cup to the other, watched them from the corner of her eye. She was sadly a prisoner of this polarized world where the queer and the sexually uncategorized had no status and little place for expression.

Swamy recognized how his mind was shaped by his upbringing in a conservative small town. A mind that traded freedom for safety, separated him from Shyam. He could not take the plunge into a messy and uncertain love life where boundaries made no sense. He couldn't forget how Shyam cried wordlessly with his hand on his mouth and his hair thrown back when Swamy announced that he was leaving Mysore after his engineering studies. He told him that it was all over between them. The mist of sadness that descended on Swamy that day had stayed in his heart for so long.

For the first time, recalling those moments in Mysore, he felt utterly alive and free. A tear dropped from the corner of his eye. It felt like a bout of rain that had washed away the fog inside his mind.

Swamy saw the river flowing below him. The rippling water was in a state of constant churn. Wave after wave the river changed its faces—renewing, replenishing itself as it coursed along.

'If one cannot relate to someone exclusively, will that not end in a diminishing of desire?' Eva asked, holding on to Sardar's T-shirt. They had been living together for years without committing to marriage.

Keshav said, 'Not really. Desire as much as you possibly can, but do not become attached to a desired outcome. Desire is your own projection; outcomes are decided by the larger universe. If you are obsessed with outcomes, you will become a hostage to your expectations.'

The water suddenly became choppy as the boat began to swing uncontrollably from left to right.

'Yet how do you do that in practice?' Sardar raised a query rising above the mild panic that had set inside the boat.

'Here is how: learn to surrender your multiple-choice mind to your singular and choiceless awareness,' Keshav said, holding firmly on to the stern of the boat to stabilize himself.

'When you simply observe the constant chatter of your mental activity, you invoke the gaze of choiceless awareness. Unlike your mind that is constantly tossing about like a boat, your awareness is still and singular. This awareness is able to organize life in and around you with utmost order. When the mind faces the gaze of awareness, it goes back to its own source like a snake retreating into a hole under the supervision of a snake charmer. At the source, you don't need to choose any more. Whatever happens from the source happens for the best.'

The wind was now gathering speed.

Keshav started speaking aloud so that his words could be heard over the background noise.

Experiment for a day in the whole year when you choose nothing. See how the day feels. Write on your calendar in bold letters, NOTHING TO CHOOSE.

'Let the day just unfold. Let it simply happen. Try not to judge anything that happens that day. That's not going to be easy, but try it. Become like a sailboat that moves with the wind. You will be surprised to discover an intelligence that is utterly free from your chattering mind, beginning to operate through you.

'Listen to what Krishna has to say.' Keshav then recited a few lines from the Gita. Recalling Krishna's words of advice to Arjuna on the battleground of Kurukshetra, he said:

> *Eating, walking, sleeping, breathing,*
> *The disciplined man who knows reality*
> *Should think "I do nothing at all".*

Prasad turned towards Anju and said, 'That's how I really like to be. Do nothing.'

Anju scoffed at him, 'Lazy bum! Living off your wife as usual!'

Keshav laughed out loud. The boatman looked at him, startled.

'No, Prasad. This is not an invitation for doing nothing. This is an invitation for undoing your little ego that claims the doer-ship of everything.

'You still have to do your bit. In fact, nothing in this phenomenal world is spared the urge for action.'

'How can one do that undoing?' Anju asked as her eyes grew large in excitement.

'Find out that little "I" thought, Anju, that always grows in your mind like a fungus. Root it out before that one "I" thought becomes a dense growth of illusion and ignorance. That's the best way to find true freedom. Live through the experiences of life without buying into the illusions created by the "I" thoughts around the ego.

'Learn to float on the river of experience like a hollow boat. If the water begins to come inside the boat, you will drown. The boat is your body-mind complex. The water outside is the flow of life. The same water, when it trickles inside the boat, becomes the burdensome ego that wears down your body and mind.'

It was a beautiful day. The boat had almost reached the other shore. The sun shone with an unusual brightness.

Prasad and Anju, like the rest of the Class of 2000, felt as though a dusty mirror that they had carried inside themselves had been cleaned up. The mirror was covered by layers and layers of ignorance and false perceptions. The cleansed mirror reflected their original nature. It shone brilliantly revealing the depth of their souls. The mirror showed them who they really were and the illusory nature of who they were not.

Each one of them sitting on that boat recognized that the solutions to all the problems of their lives could be found in the source. The source was what each one could see in a flash inside the mirror.

Keshav stepped out of the boat. The head trustee of the temple, who had come to receive him on the other shore, gushed in gratitude, saying, 'Whatever way I can be of help to you, Keshav ji, for your onward journey, I would be delighted to do so.'

Keshav looked him in the eye and said with considerable grace, 'Right now you can help by stepping aside a little so that I can clearly see the happy faces of my students and say a brief goodbye to them.'

Prasad and Anju had their hands folded in a namaste. Eva had a wistful look on her face. Sardar was fumbling for words. Kaya had her eyes frozen on Keshav in rapt attention.

Keshav said: 'I missed Neel on this wonderful boat ride. But he and I will catch up soon. This indeed is a small world. So, farewell my co-travellers! Whatever I have given you has been a result of all that I have received from this life, and I believe that I have lived a life of abundance. Remember to love this life inherent in all forms and shapes. You will then be a true servant of love.'

Having said this, he bid the trustee goodbye and walked away with his shadow trailing behind him.

Kaya could hear that voice still spinning inside her head.

'Where are you going?'

NEEL WAS GOING SOMEWHERE

The same day, Neel was thinking of Kaya as he was leaving Rishikesh on a train towards an unknown destination. His eyes were swollen red as he had had little sleep the whole night. His mind was frozen on Kaya.

Neel now saw Kaya like time sees eternity. She was a voiceless and ethereal presence devoid of flesh and blood. He saw her in the pure whiteness of the floating clouds; in the flamboyance of a wild flower and in the fragrance of the wet earth as his train chugged past a small village.

Pure desire, when freed up from its obsession with a particular form, returns to its own source and becomes an impersonal force of nature. Desire, free of all compulsions, endows everything with serene beauty and enchantment.

Neel said to himself, 'How I ached for you, Kaya, like a child in pursuit of a butterfly!'

With an unlit cigarette in his mouth, he soon stepped out of the suffocating air-conditioned coupe and pushed open the swing door. The crusty door screeched and kept swinging behind him. Neel's mind had gone numb and was desperately trying to slam the door on his dimly lit past. He stood precariously on the moving train compartment's exit stairs as the wind kept striking him hard in the face. The train, with its coal-black engine and match-box-shaped compartments painted in magenta, was moving smoothly. The engine swerved around a bend, flashing back beams of the morning sun.

He tried to light his cigarette cupping the matchstick in his hand. The matchstick flashed for a while, as though kindling the memory of an old wound, before dying out.

Neel now thought of Manas and what would have prompted him to commit suicide. To put one's life voluntarily at stake, and die for one's ambitions and desires was perhaps the most courageous thing to do. Neel remembered the animated conversations he heard in the café where Sardar was talking about Kaya's growing fondness for Manas. 'You know how she looked when he was complimenting her for one of her assignments.' Although Manas was a dear friend, Neel had then felt a sharp jab of envy in the pit of his stomach.

He remembered that he had ignored Manas the whole day. He sat sullen and sulking inside the stuffy hostel room watching a long vertical crack on the wall next to his bed. Manas had promised to get a glitzy poster of Sharon Stone to cover the crack for Neel. He remembered Manas saying, 'I would rather have Kaya's photograph in there.'

Was Manas too in love with Kaya then? Or, was it not Keshav's teaching that prompted him to commit suicide?

Neel was too close to the edge of the exit door of the train. He thought, 'Was it better not to be alive if one had betrayed one's own potential?'

The hollowness of reality as perceived by his mind was much more vivid to Neel than the allure of a better future.

A train was coming from the opposite direction on a parallel track with an ominous whistling sound. Neel was about to release his hand clutching on to the exit door. He would allow his body to be cut into pieces so that he could free his mind from the burden of guilt he was carrying inside his head.

He held back for a moment remembering Keshav's words in the Indus class, 'The mind's search for freedom is a stubborn mirage. The mind is a serial killer. It offers the promise of freedom in the shape of illusions. To be free is to turn back on this illusion producing machine with all its phantom promises.'

Neel's entire life flashed before his eyes as he edged forward with one foot on the footboard and the other in the air. The train from the opposite side was hurtling towards him at a monstrous speed.

At the count of ten, Neel was ready for the plunge.

He unclutched his hands and let go of himself...

In the suffused light of the dawn, a jacaranda tree swept past him in a blur of blue. The tree was shaped like a man's face—a half-smile flickered over that face! Neel's head spun like the earth hurtling in space—it was a face that was all too familiar. A peacock with its iridescent wings took off from the tree against the sandy sunset. A shiver crept up his spine. His heart felt light like a floating feather.

It was then that he sensed an invisible arm gripping him from behind. He heard a calm voice that sounded somewhat familiar. 'Life always gives you a second chance.' The man who spoke these words drew Neel in. He said, 'I have fooled around attempting those mental death dives many a time in my younger days.' His face was half masked by a coarse blanket that he wore like a hood over his head. Yet his right eye shone like a piece of burning coal.

Meanwhile, the train came to a halt at a junction station with a loud metallic screech. There was the buzz of anxious passengers and clanking of cola bottles carried by a cold drink vendor who was running a bottle opener rapidly over the surface of the cola cans into a lyrical trrring-trong. That was some attention gripping melody for parched throats.

The unseen traveller stopped the vendor and bought two cans, one for himself and one for Neel. He handed the cola can to Neel who accepted the gift without a murmur.

Neel exclaimed, 'It seems you are getting off the train here. If I may ask, what is your name?'

The man laughed like a child and without turning back said, 'I have many names. Some know me as Krishna. You can call me the Seventh Sense!'

Acknowledgements

*My deepest gratitude to
The Living Krishna
The one who visits our hearts and minds as love and light!*

I also want to thank Aditi Chatterjee, Anasuya G. Nair, Anees Salim, Baishali Mitra and Shashi Tharoor for nurturing and supporting this work with their talent, generosity and kindness.

I am deeply grateful to Dibakar Ghosh, Editorial Director of Rupa Publications, without whose support this book would have been a much lesser version of the current one.

I also want to thank the Rupa team—Amrita Chakravorty for the cover and Pallavi Ghosh for her deft editing.

Glossary

Aarti: Sanskrit aratrika, in Hindu and Jain rites, the waving of lighted lamps before an image of a god or a person to be honoured.

Abirbhava: Manifestation. Indication by gesture and action.

Acharya: Late 18th century from Sanskrit a-ca-rya 'master, teacher'.

Adharma: unrighteousness. Antonym of Dharma 'righteousness'.

Agarbatti: Incense stick, used as a part of religious ceremony.

Aloo Paratha: Bread stuffed/mixed with mashed potatoes.

Alphonso Mango: A juicy, nutritious mango originated in India.

Amico: Italian for 'friend'.

Aradhya: Someone worthy of worship.

Aryaputras: Sons of noblemen; 'arya' means 'noble' and 'putra' means 'son' in Sanskrit.

Ashram: A retreat for spiritual aspirants; a place where one strives towards an ascetic or spiritual goal.

Ashwattha: Sacred tree.

Avatar: Incarnation of a deity on earth in a human form, an animal form, or a partly human and partly animal form; 'ava' means 'down' and 'tar' means 'to cross' in Sanskrit.

Bharatanatyam: An Indian classical dance form originated in Tamil Nadu.

Bhatoora: A puffy, leavened, deep-fried Indian bread.

Bhava: Emotion.

Bhodro Chhele: From Bengali, meaning a gentle and well-bred boy.

Bread Pakoda: A common street food made from bread slices, gram flour, and spices.

Chaat Masala: A spice powder mix originating from South Asia to add flavour.

Chai Garam: Hot tea; a Hindi phrase associated with tea vendors at railway platforms.

Chakra: Each of seven centres of spiritual power in the human body.

Chapatti: A type of flat, round bread made without yeast.

Chedi: An early kingdom in India.

Chillum: A straight conical smoking pipe traditionally made of clay or a soft stone.

Chole: A dish made of chickpeas.

Chowkidar: Watchman, Guard

Chutney: A thick spread in Indian cuisine.

Ciao: Italian greeting used while meeting or parting.

Daal-Chawal: A basic meal of simple lentil curry, and rice.

Dada: Informal term for an elderly figure.

Dal Makhani: A dish made of lentils, spices and butter.

Darshan: Sight and insight; an opportunity to see or an occasion of seeing a holy person or the image of a deity.

Devas: Gods.

Dhaba: A roadside food stall.

Dhanuryagna: Competition of stringing of the bow.

Dharma: Righteousness, duty, cosmic law; it is a key concept in Indian religions such as Hinduism, Buddhism, Jainism, Sikhism.

Dhokla: An Indian dish, visually similar to cake, made by steaming batter of gram flour.

Dhoti: A garment worn by males consisting of a piece of cloth tied around the waist and extending to cover the legs.

Dupatta: A long piece of cloth worn around the head, neck, and shoulders by women from South Asia.

Dwandwa: Dualism; an important concept in Indian and Buddhist philosophies.

Garbha Griha: Inner sanctuary or altar room that contains the main deity of a temple; Sanskrit; translates literally to 'womb chamber'.

Ghat: A mountain pass.

Goddess Durga: A major deity in Hinduism associated with protection, strength, motherhood, destruction and wars.

Goddess Katyayani: An incarnation of Goddess Durga who slayed the tyrannical demon Mahishasura.

Gokula: Name of the cowherd settlement where Krishna grew up.

Gopas: Cow herder in Sanskrit.

Gopis: Wives of Gopas, milkmaids, unconditional devotees of Krishna.

Guru: Teacher, imparter of knowledge, a spiritual guide.

Hladini Shakti: Energy of bliss, pleasure-giving potency; it is the highest stage of divine love.

Insha Allah! : An Arabic phrase that means 'if Allah wills it!'

Jai Radhe Krishna! : A slogan celebrating Radha and Krishna.

Jalapurusha: A person who moves in water.

Jalebi: A sweet made of a coil of fried batter and steeped in syrup.

Janambhoomi: Lord Krishna's birthplace; the prison house of Kamsa.

Junta: Mass of people.

Kama: Desire or passion.

Kanha: Yashoda's pet name for Lord Krishna.

Karma: Law of Cause and Effect.

Kauravas: The 100 sons of Dhritarashtra, the King of Hastinapur, and Gandhari from the Mahabharata.

Kebab: Pieces of meat or vegetables grilled on a long thin stick or slices of grilled meat.

Kimi Katkar: An early 90s Indian actress famous for her beauty and acting style.

Krsna: Sanskrit name of Krishna.

Kurta: A loose collarless long shirt worn by people in South Asia.

Kya hua re? : What happened?

Lakshman Jhula: A suspension bridge across the river Ganges in Rishikesh.

Ma: Mother.

Machaan: Tamil; informally means dude. If it is a relative, it represents brother in law.

Madhurya Bhava: An intense form of devotional love where the devotee regards God as the lover; relationship between Radha and Krishna.

Maer Dibbi: Bengali phrase for 'I swear on my mother'.

Maharaj: Great King; Sanskrit.

Maharishi: An honorary title for a great Hindu sage or spiritual leader, a teacher of spiritual and mystical knowledge.

Markana: A part of Jodhpur state in British India, it is home to some of the world's most renowned marble sites.

Maya: The divine power of illusion that projects the world of multiplicity and conceals the transcendent unity.

Mooli Paratha: A popular Punjabi whole wheat flatbread made with unleavened dough and filled with spiced grated radish stuffing.

Mukti: Liberation, Enlightenment; a fundamental concept in Hinduism, Buddhism, Jainism and Sikhism.

Naag Champa: An Indian fragrance said to purify any environment of its negative energy.

Naan: A type of leavened bread, typically of teardrop shape and traditionally cooked in a clay oven.

Nafs: Arabic word for 'ego'; an important concept in Sufism.

Namaste: An Indian greeting used while meeting or parting, literally translated to 'bowing to the divine in you'.

Nataraja: 'Lord of Dance' in Sanskrit; Lord Shiva in his form as the cosmic dancer.

Om jaya gange mata!: A salutation to River Ganga worshipped as a mother.

Om nama bhagavate vasudevaya!: Sanskrit phrase meaning 'I bow to Lord Vasudeva (Lord Krishna)'.

Ore baba: An expression of shock or surprise in colloquial Bengali.

Palak Paneer: A dish made of cottage cheese and spinach in a thick paste.

Pandavas: The five sons of Pandu, king of the Kuru kingdom, from the Mahabharata.

Parijat: Night-flowering jasmine, a species native to South and Southeast Asia.

Pashmina: A fine variant of spun Cashmere.

Prakriti: (Feminine) In Sanskrit, the basic cosmic material that is the root of all beings, represents creation and divinity.

Prasad: A devotional offering made to a god, typically consisting of food that is later shared among devotees as consecrated food.

Pravachans: Recitation of a scripture or text by monks or scholars in Hinduism and Jainism traditions.

Prem: Unconditional love that leads to total devotion and surrender.

Premayogi: The embodiment of love that is infinite.

Professoressa: Professor in Italian.

Puja: A form of ritual prayer showing reverence to Gods in Hinduism and Buddhism.

Purna Prakriti: The complete and perfect woman.

Purna Purusha: The complete and perfect man.

Purohit: Priest

Purusha: (Masculine) In Sanskrit, self, consciousness, spirit of conscious energy that governs life and reality; combines with Prakriti to create the world.

Rakshasa rites: Demonic rites with which marriage is performed by abducting the bride.

Rasa-lila: The blissful dance of love with the gopis.

Rasmalai: A type of dessert.

Rishi: Seer, sage.

Sabdhane theko: Bengali phrase for 'take care of yourself'.

Sakha: Friend (masculine).

Sakhi: Friend (feminine).

Sakhya Bhava: A form of devotional love where the devotee regards God as a friend.

Salwar: A pair of light, loose, pleated trousers worn by women from South Asia.

Samadhi: The highest state of mental concentration that people can achieve through meditation while still bound to the body. In yoga, it is regarded as the final stage.

Samosa: A snack consisting of vegetables, spices and sometimes meat, wrapped in a triangular pastry and fried.

Sankalpa Shakti: Determination, the power of primordial will within us, a tool to shape meaningful intentions and guides our journey towards inner transformation.

Sari: A garment consisting of a length of cloth elaborately draped around the body, traditionally worn by women from South Asia.

Sema: A 700-year-old ritual or a rite of communal recitation; represents the human being's spiritual journey, an ascent by means of intelligence and love to Perfection.

Shiva lingam: An abstract or an iconic representation of the Hindu god Shiva.

Shoora: An ancient tribe in India.

Shravan: A month in Hinduism; Monsoon season.

Svaha: 'So be it'; chanted to offer oblation to the gods.

Swayamvar: A practice in ancient India in which a girl of marriageable age from a royal family chose a husband from a group of suitors; Sanskrit in origin.

Thali: Plate.

Tilak: A mark worn on the forehead.

Tirobhava: Disappearance in Sanskrit.

Upanishads: Philosophical-religious texts of Hinduism; translates to 'sitting down near' referring to the student sitting down near the teacher while receiving spiritual knowledge.

Upri: Bribe under the table.

Vada: A fried snack.

Vairagya: Detachment or renunciation from the pains and pleasures of the material world.

Vanamala: A garland made from leaves and forest flowers that reaches down to God's feet.

Vatsalya Bhava: A form of devotional love where the devotee regards God as his/her child; Yashoda and Nanda toward Krishna.

Viraha: The realization of love through separation.

Viveka: Sanskrit for right understanding or discrimination knowledge; ability to differentiate between the real and unreal.

Yadavas: A clan in Mahabharata; descendent of King Yadu.

Yajnaseni: Draupadi; translates to a woman born out of fire.

Yogi: One who practices yoga.

Bibliography

Vaidya, K. (2011). *Krishna-The God who lived as Man*. (B. Somaaya, Trans.) New Delhi: Pustak Mahal.

Osho (2006). Krishna: *The Man and His Philosophy*. Mumbai: Jaico Publishing House.

Varma, P. (2001). *The Book of Krishna*. New Delhi: Penguin Books.

Prabhupada, A.C.B.S. (1977). *The science of Self realization*. The Bhaktivedanta Book Trust

Acharya, K., Pavan, M. C., Parker, W., Sawarkar, H., & Upasani, P. (2008). *Fullness of life*. Mumbai: Somaiya Publications.

Chinmayananda. (1990). *Glory of Krishna*. Bombay: Central Chinmaya Mission Trust.

Feuerstein, G. (1998). *Tantra the path of ecstasy*. Boston: Shambhala Publications Inc.

Lal, M., & Gokhale, N. (Eds.). (2018). *Finding Radha: The quest for love*. Penguin Books India.

Camhi, B., & Isenberg, E. (1990). *Sunyata: The life & sayings of a rare-born mystic*. Berkeley, CA: North Atlantic Books.

Vanamali. (2012). *The complete life of Krishna: Based on the earliest oral traditions and the sacred scriptures*. Rochester, VT: Inner Traditions.

Barks. 2004 Jalāl al-Dīn Rūmī, from Mathnawi, excerpted from a translation by Coleman Barks and John Moyne in *The Essential Rumi* page 146). This poem can also be found in [Khan-HI 1993].